U0063338

幫助記憶統整的
背誦表

只需20天，背起
600句**道地英語**
表達用法

每天15分鐘，
英語思維訓練

背誦與訓練同時
進行，**強力有效的**
mp3音檔

「聽·說」英語
速成班！

實戰命中率100%，
實用性滿分的
英語會話句型

可個人化訓練
閱讀技巧的
聽力題

問題→應用→複習，
系統性的
3階段學習法

貼近生活的對話內容，
訓練完美語感！

客觀式問題，
圈圈點點就OK！

警告！

本書不是只用眼睛就可以學習的書。
請大家將眼、耳、嘴通通動起來。

Preface 前言

用每天15分鐘的英語思維訓練，
達到顯著學習效果

　　我們的大腦需要刺激。現有的英語書大多按照「學習→做題」的順序進行編排，學習的第一步便是要熟記各種英語句型。但是，這種記憶方式只是一種單純的刺激，即使一天背誦幾十個句子，幾天以後還是會忘得一乾二淨。當然，這樣的過程反覆多次，短期記憶也會轉化成長期記憶，但這需要大量的努力和時間，使學習者很容易選擇放棄。

　　本書採用「做題（10分鐘）→學習（5分鐘）」的順序，對大腦先進行刺激。思考「這句話用英語怎麼說？」之後，解決問題的過程就能夠幫助學習者加深記憶。因此，這種學習方法比單純的背誦學習法更有效率和效果。189名普通人（包括已經進入社會的職場人和大學生）使用本書進行了為期2周的測試，根據每天學習15分鐘的結果顯示，使用本書比單純的背誦學習在學習效率和堅持時間上都至少提高了3倍。

做題（10分鐘）

聽 + 跟讀
（5分鐘）

解決英語口語難題

在關鍵時刻，
讓急需使用的英文脫口而出

英語會話就是在最需要的那個時刻，腦子裡馬上浮現出對應的英文句子並能脫口而出，如果不是這樣，英語會話就失去了它本該有的意義。「你被逮住了」、「我腦子裡一片空白。」、「這是千載難逢的好機會。」、「我很感興趣。」、「是我沒考慮周全。」等句子都是經常說的話，可是想要用英語表達，又會表達不出來。

在我12年教授英語的過程中，我總結了很多最想要表達又總是說錯的句子，經過嚴格的篩選，將它們收錄在這本書中。在學習語言的過程中，最重要的就是情境，即脈絡。僅僅是背誦英語句子，到了要用英語表達的時候，就搞不清楚應該在哪種情境下、用什麼樣的語氣說出來。因此本書採用客觀題的方式讓讀者熟悉英語句子，在對話中使用這些句子，以達到在實戰中應用的效果。聽著母語人士錄製的類比現實的對話，進行口語練習，能夠準確地使用學過的句子，訓練英語思維方式。

「嗯……英語怎麼說？」　　　閃電突擊　　　啊，就是這麼說！

從基礎、考證照，到商務會話！

　　此系列由「日常會話」、「生活表達」，以及「商務英文」3本書組成。每本書都包括20天600句英文【客觀式問題→對話練習→複習】三個階段性的訓練。因此，僅僅2個月的時間就可以學會1,800句英文，從基礎會話到商務英文，甚至透過考試認證。

　　用1天的1%來學習這本書。感受隨心所欲說英語的快樂。

I hope you enjoy this book.

Good luck!

金在憲

김재헌

Features 本書的特點

⚡ 即時

即時檢查自己的實力，立刻彌補自己的不足！

任何學習都應該在明確了解自己實力的基礎上開始。本書按照《解題→學習》的順序編排，在做題的過程中，您能夠馬上瞭解自己能不能用英語表達相應的句子。因此能夠更加有效地彌補自己的不足之處，提高學習效率。

⚡ 快

說明性文字簡潔明瞭，便於記憶！

在對話中，閱讀冗長的說明性文字，感到壓力山大？本書只收錄了讀者理解英文語句必不可少的簡練說明。時間有限的讀者，或是容易靜不下心來的讀者都可以毫無壓力地學習這本書。

⚡ 長效

解答問題有利於長期記憶！

死記硬背的英文句子2～3天之後就會忘掉。但是，在做題過程中記住的英文語句，記憶時間更長久。就像堅持運動能夠鍛煉全身肌肉一樣，堅持進行思維訓練能夠更有效地提高英語實力。

⚡ 擴張風暴

在對話中進行應用，英語口語實力快速提高！

英語只有在現實中得到應用才算真正的實力。本書能夠將在解題環節學會的句子應用到實際對話訓練中，幫助讀者將學會的英文句子在合適的情況下說出來，提高應用能力；透過類似的表達方法及對方的回答，提高英語的表現力。

Usage 使用本書的正確方法

STEP 1　**透過解答問題，檢查自己的水準！**

在進行 Quick Test 的客觀式問題的同時，檢查自己現在的英語水準。做完問題後，背誦英語句子。使用螢光筆等標示正確答案對背誦英文句子有很大的幫助。

STEP 2　**挑戰實戰對話！**

將 Quick Test 中學到的英語句子填到合適的空格裡，並在完成 Quick Practice 對話的過程中，提高實際應用能力。為了最大限度地調動讀者的潛能，本書規定了時間限制。沒能在規定時間內做完所有問題也沒有關係，請逐一完成所有問題。

STEP 3　**邊聽邊整理！**

結束了每個 Day 學習後，透過 Review 來確認自己是不是完全掌握了之前學過的英語句子。這時，請不要只用眼睛來學習，要聽著mp3進行跟讀，這樣才能真正提高英語實力。

此系列可以與 mp3 搭配使用，獲得更強大的學習效果。書中作者提供由母語人士錄製的 mp3 檔案，相信可以幫助讀者將學習效果最大化，完整翻轉英語聽說即戰力！

★ 一掃 QR Code

便能透過連結讀取每個題目的 mp3 音檔。

200% 活用mp3

做完英文練習題後，聽著mp3進行跟讀，將學過的英語句子完全消化吸收。

STEP 1 複習英語表達方式：

mp3 順序：英語句子（Quick Test）→對話（Quick Practice）→複習（Review），做完問題後，聽著mp3大聲跟讀英語句子和對話。每個英語句子反覆兩遍，認真聽英語母語者的發音，反覆練習直到能夠自然正確地說出句子。

STEP 2 會話練習：

利用同樣的音檔，透過【英語句子（Quick Test）→對話（Quick Practice）】的順序，聽到英文立即回想中文意思，亦可以直接利用 Review 的音檔，一句一句練習聽力和口說，達到最強的聽說複習效果！

Structures 本書的結構

 Quick Test 客觀題

透過客觀題檢查自己的英語會話實力。根據提示的情境選擇與中文意思一致的英文表達方法。做完問題後，練習背誦之前不清楚或不知道的英語句子。

Quick Practice客觀題

將前面學過的句子填寫在相應情境的空格中，複習 Quick Test 中學過的英文句子，回憶這些句子應在什麼樣的情境下使用，之後完成對話，這是鞏固學習成果的環節。本書收錄像電視劇情節一樣生動的對話，能夠有效提高讀者的實戰語感。

── **5分鐘**（1分鐘*5遍）── 🎧 01_1.mp3

── **5分鐘**（1分鐘*5遍）──

Day Review 複習學過的英文句子

此為加強記憶當天學過的英語句子的複習環節。先聽mp3進行跟讀，之後用書籤擋住英語部分，試著看中文自信滿滿地說出英語句子，反覆練習直到能夠在1秒之內流利地說出英語句子為止。

─── 5分鐘 ───

英語母語者
錄製mp3

眼睛一耳朵一嘴巴，全部動起來

本書中出現的600個英語句子和對話全部由英語母語者進行錄音。不要只用眼睛看，請聽著mp3進行跟讀，眼睛、耳朵、嘴巴全部動起來進行學習。

Table of Content 目錄

Table of Content 目錄

Lightening!

Learn to Boost Your
English Skills
Everyday Expression **600**

Day 1

Day 5

DAY **1**

談論手機

學習日期 月 日

 學習時間

聽例句

手機沒電的時候、請別人將手機調成震動模式的時候，
或是手機螢幕碎了的時候，
你會用英語説這些有關手機的句子嗎？來檢測一下吧。

01_1.mp3

這些句子用英語怎麼說？

規定時間 1 min

001 手機快沒電的時候

手機快沒電了。

ⓐ The battery is slim.

ⓑ I'm low on battery.

ⓒ I have only a few batteries.

002 手機沒電後自動關機了

我手機沒電了。

ⓐ My phone battery is dead.

ⓑ My phone battery is passed out.

ⓒ My phone battery is closed.

003 手機充電的時候

我的手機需要充電。

ⓐ I need to reboot my battery.

ⓑ I need to remake my battery.

ⓒ I need to recharge my battery.

004 找不到充電器的時候

充電器在哪裡？

ⓐ Where's my sneezer?

ⓑ Where's my energizer?

ⓒ Where's my charger?

005 電池沒用多久就沒電了時

電池耗電太快。

ⓐ The battery is done so soon.

ⓑ The battery goes out too quickly.

ⓒ The battery gets down too fast.

006 找插座的時候

插座在哪裡？

ⓐ Where's the power outlet?

ⓑ Where's the electric hole?

ⓒ Where's the power switch?

Answer **001** ⓑ ……不多了，快沒有了 ▶ be low on：電池 ▶ battery **002** ⓐ（電池等）沒電了 ▶ be dead **003** ⓒ（電池等）充電 ▶ recharge **004** ⓒ 充電器 ▶ charger **005** ⓑ（電池等）沒電了 ▶ go out **006** ⓐ 插座 ▶ power outlet

現在可以自信地說出來了嗎？

規定時間 1 min

001

😊 怎麼了？
What's the matter?

😮 天哪。手機快沒電了。
Oh, no.

002

🎩 我手機沒電了。你能借我手機嗎？
Can I borrow your phone?

😊 好，不過別用太久。
Okay, but make it short.

003

😎 能等我一下嗎？我的手機要充電一下。
Could you wait a while?

😊 當然。慢慢來。
Sure. Take your time.

004

😊 充電器在哪裡？在你那嗎？ Do you have it?

😊 嗯。在我書包裡。
Oh, yes. It's inside my bag.

005

😎 你對你的智慧型手機哪裡不滿意？
What don't you like about your smartphone?

😊 外觀設計等等的都算滿意，就是電池耗電太快。
I like the design and all, but

006

🎩 我的手機要充電。插座在哪裡？
I need to recharge my phone.

😊 窗簾後面。
It's behind that curtain.

Answer **001** I'm low on battery. 手機快沒電了。 **002** My phone battery is dead. 我手機沒電了。
003 I need to recharge my battery. 我的手機需要充電。 **004** Where's my charger? 充電器在哪裡？
005 the battery goes out too quickly. 電池耗電太快。 **006** Where's the power outlet? 插座在哪裡？

18

Quick Test 02　這些句子用英語怎麼說？

規定時間 1 min

DAY 1　▼ 談論手機

---

007 電話鈴響起的時候。

接電話。

ⓐ Dial the phone.
ⓑ Grab the phone.
ⓒ Answer the phone.

---

008 打電話時，有禮貌地詢問對方能否接電話時

現在方便接電話嗎？

ⓐ Are you busy calling people?
ⓑ Did I make a telephone?
ⓒ Is this a good time for you?

---

009 因為有事情要掛斷電話時

我等等再回撥給你。

ⓐ I'll take you back.
ⓑ I'll call you back.
ⓒ I'll answer back.

---

010 要到了自己傾慕的人的電話號碼時

我要到她的電話號碼了。

ⓐ I got her number.
ⓑ She gave me a number.
ⓒ I have her smartphone.

---

011 打電話時，對方突然掛斷了電話

為什麼掛斷我的電話？

ⓐ Why did you hang up on me?
ⓑ Why did you break my phone?
ⓒ Why did you click the phone?

---

012 一直打電話，但是他一直不接電話時

為什麼一直不接我電話？

ⓐ Why are you chewing up my phone?
ⓑ Why are you ignoring my calls?
ⓒ Why are you not touching the phone?

Answer **007** ⓒ 接（電話）▶ answer　**008** ⓒ方便的時間 ▶ good time　**009** ⓑ（之後）再打（電話）給…… ▶ call ...back　**010** ⓐ 電話號碼 ▶ (phone) number；得到，要到了 ▶ get　**011** ⓐ 掛斷……的電話 ▶ hang up on　**012** ⓑ（不接電話）不理 ▶ ignore

---

007

👧 麥克，你電話響了！
Michael, your phone is ringing!

👦 我在廁所裡。幫我接電話吧。
I'm in the bathroom.
_____ for me.

008

👩 你好，維克托。現在方便接電話嗎？
Hi, Victor. _____

👨 其實，現在不太方便。我正在忙。
Actually, no. I was in the middle of something.

009

👨 剛才是你家門鈴響了吧？
Was that your doorbell ringing just now?

👩 嗯，應該是來送披薩的。我等等再回撥給你。
Oh, yes. That must be the pizza delivery. _____

010

👩 你怎麼一直咧著嘴笑。有什麼好事嗎？
You're grinning from ear to ear. What's the good news?

👨 你知道凱特吧？我要到她的電話號碼了。
You know Kate, right? _____

011

🎩 為什麼掛斷我的電話？
_____

👩 不是，你誤會了。剛才停電了。
No, you've got it wrong. I had a blackout.

012

👨 為什麼一直不接我電話？
_____

👩 對不起。我的手機被偷了。
Sorry. Someone stole my smartphone.

---

blackout 停電

Answer **007** Answer the phone 接電話 **008** Is this a good time for you? 現在方便接電話嗎？ **009** I'll call you back. 我等等再回撥給你。 **010** I got her number. 我要到她的電話號碼了。 **011** Why did you hang up on me? 為什麼掛斷我的電話？ **012** Why are you ignoring my calls? 為什麼一直不接我電話？

 01_3.mp3

Quick Test 03 — 這些句子用英語怎麼說？

規定時間 1 min

---

013 不想因為手機鈴聲響而尷尬

把手機調成震動模式吧。

ⓐ Put your phone on vibrate.
ⓑ Make your phone deaf.
ⓒ Switch your phone to dummy mode.

---

014 把手機調到靜音模式時

我把手機調成靜音模式了。

ⓐ I put mine to deaf.
ⓑ I put mine to sleep.
ⓒ I put mine on silent.

---

015 請別人把手機關掉時

將手機關機。

ⓐ Take it off.
ⓑ Turn it off.
ⓒ Turn it down.

---

016 很喜歡對方的手機鈴聲時

你的手機鈴聲真好聽。

ⓐ I like your ringtone.
ⓑ I like your cowbell.
ⓒ I like your jingle bell.

---

017 在不知道的情況下，撥打了對方的電話時

對不起，我不知道我打了電話給你。

ⓐ Sorry, I finger-dialed.
ⓑ Sorry, I face-dialed.
ⓒ Sorry, I butt-dialed.

---

018 想要知道對方手機的電信時

你用哪家電信？

ⓐ What's your mobile carrier?
ⓑ What's your electric carrier?
ⓒ What's your air carrier?

Answer 013 ⓐ 震動模式 ▶ vibrate (mode) 014 ⓒ 靜音模式 ▶ silent (mode) 015 ⓑ 關掉…… ▶ turn...off 016 ⓐ （手機）鈴聲 ▶ ringtone 017 ⓒ 不小心撥打了電話 ▶ butt-dial（由來：把手機放在屁股後面的口袋裡，屁股（butt）壓到螢幕，撥了（dial電話） 018 ⓐ 手機電信行 ▶ mobile carrier

現在可以自信地說出來了嗎？ 規定時間 1 min

013

👩 我們在劇場裡。把手機調成震動模式吧。

We're inside the theater.

😎 別擔心。我已經關機了。

Don't worry. I've already turned it off.

014

😀 你的手機怎麼都不響啊？

Why isn't your phone ringing?

😮 啊，我忘了。我把手機調成靜音模式了。

Oh, I forgot.

015

😃 那是誰的手機？請將手機關機。

Whose phone is that?

🎩 呃……按這個就行了嗎？

Umm... Do I press this?

016

👩 嘿！你的手機鈴聲真好聽。

Hey!

😊 謝謝。這是我自己作的曲。

Thanks. I wrote it myself.

017

😮 你為什麼打給我又不說話？

Why didn't you say anything after calling me?

😅 啊，那個？我不知道我打了電話給你。

Oh, that?

018

🎩 我用XK電信。你用哪家電信？

I use XK Telecom.

😃 有什麼差嗎？

Does it matter?

Answer **013** Put your phone on vibrate. 把手機調成震動模式吧。 **014** I put mine on silent. 我把手機調成靜音模式了。 **015** Turn it off. 將手機關機。 **016** I like your ringtone. 你的手機鈴聲真好聽。 **017** Sorry, I butt-dialed. 我不知道我打了電話給你。 **018** What's your mobile carrier? 你用哪家電信？

Test 04 這些句子用英語怎麼說？ 規定時間 1 min

DAY 1 ▼ 談論手機

---

019 因為訊號問題，電話撥不通的時候

手機沒有訊號。

ⓐ The phone is quiet.
ⓑ The phone makes no noise.
ⓒ I'm getting no service.

---

020 電話裡對方的聲音總是斷斷續續時

你的聲音總是斷斷續續的。

ⓐ You're breaking off.
ⓑ You're breaking down.
ⓒ You're breaking up.

---

021 聽到手機裡發出雜音時

有雜音。

ⓐ I'm getting rumours.
ⓑ I'm getting static.
ⓒ I'm getting ghosts.

---

022 聽不清楚對方聲音時

聽不清楚。

ⓐ I'm losing you.
ⓑ I'm missing you.
ⓒ I'm breaking you.

---

023 通話的音質很好時

訊號很好。

ⓐ I'm getting good waves.
ⓑ I'm getting in good condition.
ⓒ I'm getting good reception.

---

024 通話時，電話突然斷掉了時

電話突然斷了。

ⓐ The line went dead.
ⓑ The line has been chewed.
ⓒ The phone is damaged.

Answer 019 ⓒ 電信服務 ▶ service 020 ⓒ （電話裡的聲音）斷了 ▶ break up 021 ⓑ （收訊設備）雜音 ▶ static 022 ⓐ 聽不懂，聽不見（對方的話）▶ lose 023 ⓒ （電視、電話等）收訊狀態，連接狀態 ▶ reception 024 ⓐ 電話線 ▶ line；電話沒有訊號了 ▶ go dead

019

😮 哦，不。手機沒有訊號。

Oh, no.

👧 因為我們在樹林裡。我的手機也沒有訊號。

It's because we're in the woods. Mine's not working, either.

020

🎩 你的聲音總是斷斷續續的。我再給你打一次看看。

Let me call you again.

⛄ 什麼？你說什麼？

Huh? What did you say?

021

👦 你能再說一遍嗎？有雜音。

Can you repeat that?

😊 這樣啊。那我用座機打給你。

I see. Let me call you on the landline.

landline 座機

022

🤓 什麼？親愛的，我聽不清楚。先掛斷吧，好嗎？

What? Darling, Just hang up, okay?

👩 但是我有重要的事情要問你。

But I have something important to ask you.

023

👩 呼！現在訊號很好。你那邊呢？

Phew! Finally How about you?

😊 聽得很清楚。

Loud and clear!

024

🎩 真奇怪。電話突然斷了。

That's strange.

⛄ 可能是天氣的原因。我過去幫你把窗戶打開。

Maybe it's the weather. Let me go and open the window.

Answer **019** I'm getting no service. 手機沒有訊號。 **020** You're breaking up. 你的聲音總是斷斷續續的。 **021** I'm getting static. 有雜音。 **022** I'm losing you. 我聽不清楚。 **023** I'm getting good reception. 訊號很好。 **024** The line went dead. 電話突然斷了。

DAY 1

▼ 談論手機

---

025 手機不能正常運作時

我的手機壞了。

ⓐ My cell phone's shot down.

ⓑ My cell phone isn't working.

ⓒ My cell phone is gone.

---

026 手機螢幕有裂痕時

螢幕碎了。

ⓐ The mirror is cracked.

ⓑ The screen has a crack.

ⓒ The monitor is cracked up.

---

027 想要免費修理時

可以免費修理嗎？

ⓐ Is free repair possible?

ⓑ Is a free check-up possible?

ⓒ Is free fixation possible?

---

028 計畫購買新手機時

我要換智慧型手機了。

ⓐ I'm going to trade my smartphone.

ⓑ I will transform my smartphone.

ⓒ I'm going to get a new smartphone.

---

029 購買手機時，想要把自己的舊手機給商家以得到一定的優惠時

可以折價換新嗎？

ⓐ Can I call out my old phone?

ⓑ Can I buy out my old phone?

ⓒ Can I trade-in my old phone?

---

030 電信合約期限快要到了時

2年的合約快要到期了。

ⓐ My two-year contract is almost over.

ⓑ My two-year term paper is almost over.

ⓒ My two-year condition is almost over.

Answer **025** ⓑ 運作 ▶ work **026** ⓑ （手機）螢幕 ▶ screen：裂痕 ▶ crack **027** ⓐ 免費修理 ▶ free repair
028 ⓒ 買，購買 ▶ get：智慧型手機 ▶ smartphone **029** ⓒ 折舊換新 ▶ trade-in **030** ⓐ 合約，協議 ▶
contract

025

有什麼可以幫您的，先生？
How can I help you, sir?

您好，我的手機壞了。
Hello.

026

怎麼又把手機拿回來了？
Why did you bring back your phone?

這裡！螢幕裂了。
Look over here!

027

我在這裡買了這部手機。可以免費修理嗎？
I bought this smartphone at your store.

有帶保固卡來嗎？
Did you bring your warranty card?

028

你今天看起來很激動。怎麼了？
You seem giddy today. What's the matter?

我終於要換智慧型手機了。

at last.

giddy （因為太高興）激動

029

我想知道，可以折價換新嗎？
I don't know if it's possible, but

我看看。哦，不好意思。這個型號太舊了。
Let's see. Oh, sorry. This model is too outdated.

outdated 舊式的

030

2年的合約快要到期了。不過我還是要繼續用這個手機。

But I'm going to keep using this smartphone.

好主意！這個手機狀態還很好。
Good thinking! It's still in good condition.

Answer 025 My cell phone isn't working. 我的手機壞了。 026 The screen has a crack. 螢幕裂了。 027 Is free repair possible? 可以免費修理嗎？ 028 I'm going to get a new smartphone 我要換智慧型手機了。 029 Can I trade-in my old phone? 可以折價換新嗎？ 030 My two-year contract is almost over. 2年的合約快要到期了。

Day 1 **Review**	**在忘記以前複習一遍，怎麼樣？**	規定時間 **5** **min**

聽著MP3跟讀	看著中文說英語
手機快沒電的時候 **I'm low on battery.**	手機快沒電了。
手機沒電後自動關機了 **My phone battery is dead.**	我的手機沒電了。
要把手機充電的時候 **I need to recharge my battery.**	我的手機需要充電。
電池沒用多久就沒電了時 **The battery goes out too quickly.**	電池耗電太快。
來電了，電話鈴響起的時候 **Answer the phone.**	接電話。
打電話時，有禮貌地詢問對方能否接電話時 **Is this a good time for you?**	現在方便接電話嗎？
因為有事情要掛斷電話時 **I'll call you back.**	我等等再回撥給你。
一直打電話，但是他一直不接電話時 **Why are you ignoring my calls?**	為什麼一直不接我電話？
不想因為手機鈴聲響起而尷尬的話 **Put your phone on vibrate.**	把手機調成震動模式吧。
把手機調到靜音模式時 **I put mine on silent.**	我把手機調成靜音模式了。

DAY 1 ▼ 談論手機

看著中文說英文時，用書籤擋住這個部分。

很喜歡對方的手機鈴聲時 **I like your ringtone.**	你的手機鈴聲真好聽。
在不知道的情況下,撥打了對方的電話時 **Sorry, I butt-dialed.**	對不起,我不知道我打了電話給你。
因為訊號問題,電話撥不通時 **I'm getting no service.**	手機沒有訊號。
電話裡對方的聲音總是斷斷續續時 **You're breaking up.**	你的聲音總是斷斷續續的。
聽到手機裡發出雜音時 **I'm getting static.**	有雜音。
聽不清楚對方聲音時 **I'm losing you.**	我聽不清楚。
手機不能正常運作時 **My cell phone isn't working.**	我的手機壞了。
手機螢幕有裂痕時 **The screen has a crack.**	螢幕裂了。
想要免費修理時 **Is free repair possible?**	可以免費修理嗎?
計畫購買新手機時 **I'm going to get a new smartphone.**	我要換智慧型手機了。

已經學會的句型
30個/600個

看著中文說英文時,用書籤擋住這個部分。

DAY 2

談論智慧型手機和照片

聽例句

訊號不好的時候、沒有收到對方簡訊回覆的時候,或是自拍的時候,
你會用英語說這些有關智慧型手機和照片的句子嗎?來檢測一下吧。

Quick Test 01

這些句子用英語怎麼說？

規定時間 1 min

DAY 2 ▼ 談論智慧型手機和照片

---

031 充分考慮到使用便利性的智慧型手機

用起來很方便。

ⓐ It's comfortable.
ⓑ It's user-friendly.
ⓒ The grip is great.

---

032 炫耀最新款的手機時

這是最新款的手機。

ⓐ This is the first model.
ⓑ This is the latest model.
ⓒ This is the top model.

---

033 炫耀新增加的功能或特點時

有很多新功能。

ⓐ It's equipped with new parts.
ⓑ It's got many new shows.
ⓒ It has many new features.

---

034 不讓別人用自己的手機

我設了密碼。

ⓐ It's password protected.
ⓑ It's password hanged.
ⓒ It's password hidden.

---

035 手機玩上癮的時候

他一直在滑手機。

ⓐ His eyes are stuck.
ⓑ He lives with his smartphone.
ⓒ He's glued to his smartphone.

---

036 沒有無線網路的時候

沒有無線網路。

ⓐ There's no WiFi explosion.
ⓑ There's no WiFi connection.
ⓒ There's no WiFi highway.

Answer **031** ⓑ（使用的人）用起來方便 ▶ user-friendly **032** ⓑ 最新的型號 ▶ latest model **033** ⓒ 功能，特點 ▶ feature **034** ⓐ 有密碼保護 ▶ password protected **035** ⓒ（好像被膠水黏上了一樣）特別集中精神做…… ▶ be glued to（glue 黏合劑，用膠水黏上） **036** ⓑ 連接 ▶ connection

---

031

😎 你為什麼選這款智慧型手機？
Why did you pick this smartphone?

👩 用起來很方便。

032

👦 看！這是最新款的手機。
Look!

😊 哇，真薄。
Wow, it's very slim.

033

🎩 這款手機哪裡好？
What's so great about this smartphone?

👩 你不知道嗎？有很多新功能。
You don't know?

034

😎 聽說你弄丟了智慧型手機。
I heard you lost your smartphone.

👩 短時間內還沒關係。我設了密碼。
It's okay for now.

for now 短時間內，暫時

035

👩 約翰自己待在房間裡幹什麼呢？
What's John doing alone in his room?

😊 他在玩手機遊戲。他一直在滑手機。
He's playing mobile games.

036

🎩 這裡沒有無線網路。

here.

👩 我們去附近的其他咖啡店吧？
Should we move to another cafe nearby?

Answer **031** It's user-friendly. 用起來很方便。 **032** This is the latest model. 這是最新款的手機。 **033** It has many new features. 有很多新功能。 **034** It's password protected. 我設了密碼。 **035** He's glued to his smartphone. 他一直在滑手機。 **036** There's no Wi-Fi connection. 沒有無線網路。

Quick
Test 02
這些句子用英語怎麼說？

規定時間 1 min

DAY 2 ▼ 談論智慧型手機和照片

---

037 想要用kakao talk聊天的時候

你有用kakao talk嗎？

ⓐ Do you use Kakao Talk?

ⓑ Is it you on Kakao Talk?

ⓒ Are you with Kakao Talk?

---

038 要傳訊息或者kakao talk時

我等等傳訊息給你。

ⓐ I'll massage you later.

ⓑ I'll mini-letter you later.

ⓒ I'll text you later.

---

039 傳了訊息對方也沒有回覆時

她一直不回我訊息。

ⓐ She's closing my text messages.

ⓑ She's biting my text messages.

ⓒ She's ignoring my text messages.

---

040 傳訊息打了錯字時

我打錯字了。

ⓐ That was a hippo.

ⓑ That was a typo.

ⓒ That was a lipo.

---

041 好幾個人在群裡聊天時

把我拉進群組裡吧。

ⓐ Invite me to your group chat.

ⓑ Bring me to your meeting room.

ⓒ Call me to your group chatting room.

---

042 請對方用手機傳照片的時候

把照片傳給我。

ⓐ Send me that photo with a messenger.

ⓑ Send me that photo for the messenger.

ⓒ Send me that photo via messenger.

Answer **037** ⓐ cf)（line等）行動通訊軟體 ▶ mobile messenger **038** ⓒ 傳訊息 ▶ text **039** ⓒ 不理會 ▶ ignore ：訊息 ▶ text message **040** ⓑ 打錯了字 ▶ typo **041** ⓐ A邀請到B ▶ invite A to B ：群組 ▶ group chat **042** ⓒ 透過訊息 ▶ via messenger（via透過……）

現在可以自信地說出來了嗎？ 規定時間 1 min

037

😎 你用kakao talk嗎？

🙂 沒用，我撤銷帳號了。
No, I got rid of my account.

account 帳號

038

🙂 我們什麼時候見面？
When should we meet?

😊 我要確定一下我的行程，我等等傳訊息給你。
I need to check my schedule.
So

039

😊 你怎麼這麼生氣？
What are you so angry about?

🙂 你認識我的前女友海倫吧？她一直不回我訊息。
You know my ex-girlfriend
Helen?

040

🎩 剛才我打錯字了。別管它。
just
now. Ignore it.

👩 哦，難怪。
Oh, no wonder.

041

😊 我想認識你的朋友。把我拉進群組裡吧。
I want to get to know your
buddies. So

😎 嗯……這好像不是一個好主意。
Umm... I don't think that's a
good idea.

042

👩 你會喜歡你的照片的。
You'll like your picture.

🙂 真的？把照片傳給我。
Really?

Answer **037** Do you use Kakao Talk? 你用kakao talk嗎？ **038** I'll text you later. 我等等傳訊息給你。 **039** She's ignoring my text messages. 她一直不回我訊息。 **040** That was a typo 我打錯字了。 **041** invite me to your group chat. 把我拉進群組裡吧。 **042** Send me that photo via messenger. 把照片傳給我。

Quick
Test 03   這些句子用英語怎麼說？   規定時間 1 min

043 為了聚會留念，建議拍照時

拍張合照吧。

ⓐ Let's make a picture together.

ⓑ Let's shoot a picture together.

ⓒ Let's take a picture together.

044 因為要拍照片，請對方不要動時

別動。

ⓐ Keep still.

ⓑ Stop kneeling.

ⓒ Maintain motion.

045 拍照片時，為了讓對方笑

說起司！

ⓐ Say Christmas!

ⓑ Say cheese!

ⓒ Say boo!

046 拍照片的時候，建議再拍一張時

再拍一次。

ⓐ Take one more dip.

ⓑ Take one more shot.

ⓒ Take one more clip.

047 炫耀自己的留念照片時

這是我的留念照。

ⓐ Here's my best shot.

ⓑ Here's my mug shot.

ⓒ Here's my proof shot.

048 別人拍照片時，自己擠進鏡頭裡，可是影響了別人的照片時

不好意思，我把你的照片毀了。

ⓐ Sorry I barged in.

ⓑ Sorry I photobombed you.

ⓒ Sorry I missed it.

Answer **043** ⓒ 拍照片 ▶ take a picture **044** ⓐ 保持靜止 ▶ still **045** ⓑ 發cheese音的時候，嘴角會自然上揚 **046** ⓑ 照片 ▶ shot **047** ⓒ 留念照 ▶ proof shot **048** ⓑ（像炸彈一樣）破壞了別人的照片 ▶ photobomb

前面的句子都記熟了嗎？試著對比有標底色的空格，完成對話吧！

現在可以自信地說出來了嗎？

043

😊 今天的聚會玩得真開心。
I really enjoyed today's gathering.

😄 差點忘了！拍張合照吧。
I almost forgot!

gathering 聚會

045

😊 你們太嚴肅了。說起司！
You guys are too serious.

😄 快點拍！
Just take it, already!

047

😎 我終於去了巴黎。這是我的留念照。
I've finally been to Paris.

😄 哈哈，在艾菲爾鐵塔前面照的啊。
Oh, you took it in front of the Eiffel Tower.

044

😎 快點拍。
Hurry up with the photograph.

😊 別動，行不行？
_____, will you?

046

🎩 滿意了？我現在可以走了吧？
Are you satisfied? Can I go now?

😄 不行，等一下，再拍一次。
No, wait!

048

😊 來看看。什麼！這是誰的頭，這麼大啊？
Let's see. What! Whose giant head is this?

😄 啊，是我。不好意思，我把你的照片毀了。
Oh, it's me.

Answer **043** Let's take a picture together. 拍張合照吧。 **044** Keep still. 別動。 **045** Say cheese! 說起司！ **046** Take one more shot. 再拍一次。 **047** Here's my proof shot. 這是我的留念照。 **048** Sorry I photobombed you. 不好意思，我把你的照片毀了。

36

049 在自拍的時候

我在自拍。

ⓐ I was shooting a lonely photo.

ⓑ I was taking a selfie.

ⓒ I was clicking at a solo camera.

050 想要拍好自拍

我們用自拍棒吧。

ⓐ Let's use the selfie rod.

ⓑ Let's use the selfie stick.

ⓒ Let's use the selfie wand.

DAY 2

▼ 談論智慧型手機和照片

051 拍照的時候手抖了

拍得不清楚。

ⓐ It came out spooky.

ⓑ It came out gloomy.

ⓒ It came out blurry.

052 照片拍得不清楚的原因

焦距沒對好。

ⓐ It was out of focus.

ⓑ I was beyond the range.

ⓒ The focus was shaken.

053 迎著陽光拍照時

照片是逆光的。

ⓐ The photo was taken reversely.

ⓑ The picture has a backdraft.

ⓒ The photo was backlit.

054 照片上人的眼睛像兔子的眼睛一樣是紅的

這是紅眼現象。

ⓐ There's a red-eye effect.

ⓑ There's a bloody-eye effect.

ⓒ There's a rabbit's-eye effect.

Answer **049** ⓑ 自拍 ▶ selfie（是由self（自己）衍生而來的新造詞） **050** ⓑ 自拍棒 ▶ selfie stick **051** ⓒ 不清楚的 ▶ blurry **052** ⓐ 沒對好焦距 ▶ out of focus（focus焦距） **053** ⓒ（照片、畫等）逆光 ▶ backlit **054** ⓐ 紅眼現象 ▶ red-eye effect

---

049

😊 我在自拍。要和我一起拍嗎？

Do you want to join me?

😎 不用了，謝謝。你還是自己自拍吧。

No, thanks. You just keep taking them by yourself.

050

😊 我覺得拍不到我們兩個。

I don't think we can both fit in the frame.

😊 別擔心。我們用自拍棒吧。

Don't worry.

051

🎩 什麼？拍得不清楚。

Huh?

👧 對阿。我在幫你拍照的時候，正好打了個噴嚏。

Yeah. I sneezed while taking your picture.

052

🎩 照片又沒拍好！

The photograph is ruined again!

👧 真的。這次焦距沒對好。

Yeah.
this time.

053

😊 哎呦。我弄錯了。照片是逆光的。

Oops. I was wrong.

😊 我看看。哦，我喜歡這張！

Let's see. Hey, I like it!

054

🎩 哎呦，我的眼睛像兔子的眼睛一樣。

Oh, my. My eyes look like a rabbit's.

😊 這是紅眼現象。我重新幫你拍。

I'll take it again.

Answer **049** I was taking a selfie. 我在自拍。 **050** Let's use the selfie stick. 我們用自拍棒吧。 **051** It came out blurry. 拍得不清楚。 **052** It was out of focus 焦距沒對好。 **053** The photo was backlit. 照片是逆光的。 **054** There's a red-eye effect. 這是紅眼現象。

Quick Test 05

這些句子用英語怎麼說？

規定時間 1 min

---

055 想看看照片拍得好不好時

我們來看看拍得怎麼樣。

ⓐ Let's see how it came out.
ⓑ Let's see how it went out.
ⓒ Let's see how it got out.

---

056 比起本人，照片中的人更漂亮時

你蠻上相的。

ⓐ You're photo-shining!
ⓑ You're photogenic!
ⓒ You're a photomon!

---

057 比起照片，本人更漂亮的時候

你不上相。

ⓐ I prefer the real you.
ⓑ I like the original photo.
ⓒ You look better in person.

---

058 照片拍得很奇怪時

這張照片太丟臉了。

ⓐ This photo is so humiliating!
ⓑ This photo is so mind-bending!
ⓒ This photo is so eye-closing!

---

059 也想要一張洗出來的照片時

也幫我洗一張。

ⓐ I'd like a duplex.
ⓑ I'd like a copy.
ⓒ I'd like an autograph.

---

060 提議把照片放進相框裡時

放進相框裡吧。

ⓐ Let's keep it in a glass jar.
ⓑ Let's put it inside some wood.
ⓒ Let's frame it.

Answer **055** ⓐ 出來 ▶ come out　**056** ⓑ 上相 ▶ photogenic　**057** ⓒ 真人，親自 ▶ in person　**058** ⓐ 丟臉的 ▶ humiliating　**059** ⓑ 影本 ▶　**060** ⓒ 放進相框 ▶ frame

055

你還沒刪掉吧？我們來看看拍得怎麼樣。

You didn't erase it, right?

哎呦，對不起！剛才刪掉了。

Oops, sorry! I just deleted it.

056

我才知道，你蠻上相的！

I didn't know until now, but

可能是因為我的頭比較小吧。

Maybe it's because I have a small head.

057

說實話，你不上相。

To be honest,

我經常聽人這麼說，所以我才不喜歡拍照。

I get that a lot. That's why I hate taking photos.

058

快刪掉！這張照片太丟臉了。

Erase it right now!

不會啊，蠻自然的。

No, it's not. It looks natural.

059

你這張照片拍得真好。也幫我洗一張吧。

You look gorgeous in this picture!

我也想幫你洗一張，可是照片印表機壞了。

I would, but the photo printer is broken.

060

我們把照片洗出來吧。我喜歡這張。

I printed our picture. I love this photo.

好。放進相框裡吧。

Great.

Answer **055** Let's see how it came out. 我們來看看拍得怎麼樣。 **056** you're photogenic! 你蠻上相的！ **057** you look better in person. 你不上相。 **058** This photo is so humiliating! 這張照片太丟臉了。 **059** I'd like a copy. 也幫我洗一張吧。 **060** Let's frame it. 放進相框裡吧。

Day 2 **Review**	在忘記以前複習一遍，怎麼樣？	規定時間 5 min

聽著MP3跟讀	看著中文說英語
充分考慮到使用便利性的智慧型手機 **It's user-friendly.**	用起來很方便。
炫耀最新款的手機時 **This is the latest model.**	這是最新款的手機。
不讓別人用自己的手機 **It's password protected.**	我設了密碼。
沒有無線網路的時候 **There's no WiFi connection.**	沒有無線網路。
要傳訊息時 **I'll text you later.**	我等等傳訊息給你。
傳了訊息對方也沒有回覆時 **She's ignoring my text messages.**	她一直不回我訊息。
發簡訊打了錯字時 **That was a typo.**	我打錯字了。
請對方用手機傳照片的時候 **Send me that photo via messenger.**	把照片傳給我。
為了聚會留念，建議拍照時 **Let's take a picture together.**	拍張合照吧。
因為要拍照片，請對方不要動時 **Keep still.**	別動。

DAY 2

▼ 談論智慧型手機和照片

看著中文說英文時，用書籤擋住這個部分。

聽著MP3跟讀	看著中文說英語
拍照片的時候，建議再拍一張時 **Take one more shot.**	再拍一次。
炫耀自己的留念照片時 **Here's my proof shot.**	這是我的留念照。
在自拍的時候 **I was taking a selfie.**	我在自拍。
想要拍好自拍 **Let's use the selfie stick.**	我們用自拍棒吧。
拍照片的時候手抖了 **It came out blurry.**	拍得不清楚。
照片拍得不清楚的原因 **It was out of focus.**	焦距沒對好。
想看看照片拍得好不好時 **Let's see how it came out.**	我們來看看拍得怎麼樣。
比起本人，照片上的人更漂亮時 **You're photogenic!**	你蠻上相的。
比起照片，本人更漂亮的時候 **You look better in person.**	你不上相。
照片拍得很奇怪時 **This photo is so humiliating!**	這張照片太丟臉了。
	已經學會的句型 60個/600個

看著中文說英文時，用書籤擋住這個部分。

DAY 3

品嘗食物及評價味道

聽例句

食物不合口味的時候、覺得湯很新鮮的時候，或是麵條糊成一團的時候，
你會用英語說這些有關食物和味道的句子嗎？來檢測一下吧。

這些句子用英語怎麼說？

規定時間 1 min

---

061 想知道食物合不合對方口味時

那道菜合你的口味嗎？

ⓐ Is the food to your mouth?

ⓑ Is the food to your tongue?

ⓒ Is the food to your taste?

---

062 吃了辣的東西，嘴裡很辣的時候

太辣了。

ⓐ It's red hot.

ⓑ It's very chilly.

ⓒ It's a very hot pepper.

DAY 3

▼ 品嘗食物及評價味道

---

063 食物的味道太淡時

太淡了。

ⓐ It's too bland.

ⓑ It's too bold.

ⓒ It's too minimal.

---

064 因為我不太喜歡吃甜的

我覺得太甜了。

ⓐ It's too sweet for my taste.

ⓑ My mouth is only tasting sugar.

ⓒ The taste is too much like candy.

---

065 同時感到甜味和酸味的時候

是酸甜的味道。

ⓐ It's sweet and slimy.

ⓑ It's sweet and sour.

ⓒ It's sugary and flavored.

---

066 食物的味道很特別的時候

味道很特別。

ⓐ It's a tongue twister.

ⓑ It has a unique taste.

ⓒ The taste is one and only.

Answer **061** ⓒ 合……的口味 ▶ be to one's taste（taste味道，口味） **062** ⓐ 辣 ▶ red hot **063** ⓐ 味道很淡，不鹹 ▶ bland **064** ⓐ **065** ⓑ 酸的 ▶ sour **066** ⓑ 特別的 ▶ unique

061

那道菜合你的口味嗎？

其實，味道有點太重了。
Actually, it's a bit pungent.

pungent （味道、氣味）濃烈

062

你為什麼不嚐嚐這道韓國菜呢？
Why don't you try this Korean dish?

好。啊！太辣了。
Sure. Yikes!

063

我做的菜怎麼樣？
How do you like my cooking?

嗯，把鹽遞給我，好嗎？太淡了。
Umm, could you pass me the salt?

064

再吃點吧？
Why don't you have some more?

不了，謝謝。我覺得太甜了。
No, thank you.

065

你會怎麼描述這種味道呢？
How would you describe the flavor?

嗯。是酸甜的味道。
Hmm.

066

你嚐嚐這個拉麵。味道很特別。
Try this ramen.

真的？啊，裡面放了薑！
Really? Oh, it's got ginger in it!

ginger 薑

Answer **061** Is the food to your taste? 那道菜合你的口味嗎？　**062** It's red hot. 太辣了。　**063** It's too bland. 太淡了。　**064** It's too sweet for my taste. 我覺得太甜了。　**065** It's sweet and sour. 是酸甜的。
066 It has a unique taste. 味道很特別

Quick Test 02 這些句子用英語怎麼說？ 規定時間 1 min

---

067 因為太油，覺得膩時

太油膩了。

ⓐ It's too oily.

ⓑ It's too lumpy.

ⓒ It's too feeble.

---

068 吃完食物後，口留餘香的時候

它留下很好的餘味。

ⓐ It has a good lasting taste.

ⓑ It has a good smiling taste.

ⓒ It has a good aftertaste.

---

069 嚐到很濃烈豐富的味道時

味道又濃又豐富。

ⓐ It's deep and foamy.

ⓑ It's dark and profuse.

ⓒ It's rich and flavorful.

---

070 同時嚐到甜味和苦味的時候

是甜中帶苦的味道。

ⓐ The taste is sour and sweet.

ⓑ It has a bittersweet taste.

ⓒ The mouth sweats and dribbles.

---

071 食物在嘴裡，滿口生香的時候

好香。

ⓐ It has a tingling taste.

ⓑ It has a savory taste.

ⓒ The taste is numbing.

---

072 不喜歡食物味道時

我不喜歡這種味道。

ⓐ I don't like the aroma.

ⓑ I don't like the stink.

ⓒ I don't like the stench.

DAY 3 ▶ 品嘗食物及評價味道

Answer **067** ⓐ 油膩的 ▶ oily **068** ⓒ 餘味 ▶ aftertaste **069** ⓒ（味道）濃的 ▶ rich；（味道）豐富的 ▶ flavorful **070** ⓑ 甜中帶苦的 ▶ bittersweet **071** ⓑ 很香的 savory taste **072** ⓐ 香味，味道 ▶ aroma

067

😃 日本拉麵合你的口味嗎？

How do you find Japanese ramen?

👧 我覺得太膩了。

＿＿＿＿＿ for my taste.

068

😃 真好吃！用了什麼調料？它留下很棒的餘味。

Yummy! What kind of condiments did you use?

👧 我婆婆不告訴我。

My mother-in-law won't tell me.

condiment 調料，作料

069

😃 你是不是覺得醬料太淡了？

Is the sauce a bit bland for you?

😃 沒有，完全不會。味道又濃又豐富。

No, not at all.

070

😃 是甜中帶苦的味道。

👧 你猜猜這道菜的名字。

Try to guess the name of the dish.

071

🎩 哇！好香。再給我一盤。

Wow!
I would like another helping.

😃 可是再一盤就是第四盤了！

But that would be your fourth helping!

helping （一人份的）量，盤

072

😃 你為什麼搗著鼻子？

Why are you covering your nose?

😃 因為這道外國菜。我不喜歡這種味道。

It's that exotic food.

Quick Test 03

這些句子用英語怎麼說？

規定時間 1 min

---

073 做飯的時候放了太多水時

飯太軟了。

ⓐ The rice is slushy.

ⓑ The rice is mushy.

ⓒ The rice is wobbly.

---

074 碳酸飲料的瓶子打開後，放了太久時

都沒氣了。

ⓐ It's gone flat.

ⓑ The carbon is off.

ⓒ It has vanished.

---

075 覺得湯很鮮甜時

湯很鮮甜。

ⓐ The broth is devastatingly hot!

ⓑ The broth is burning up my chest!

ⓒ The broth is refreshing!

---

076 麵條放了太久，都糊了的時候

我的麵條都糊了。

ⓐ My noodles have gone chubby.

ⓑ My noodles have gone soggy.

ⓒ My noddles have gone barmy.

---

077 一起搭配著吃，味道更好的食物

米飯配海苔很好吃。

ⓐ Rice goes along with seaweed.

ⓑ Rice goes well with laver.

ⓒ Rice goes around with sea mustard.

---

078 別分很多口吃

一口吃下去。

ⓐ One bite at a time.

ⓑ Swallow it at once.

ⓒ Eat it in one bite.

Answer **073** ⓑ 軟軟的，像粥一樣的 ▸ mushy　**074** ⓐ（碳酸飲料的）沒有氣 ▸ go flat　**075** ⓒ 湯，粥 ▸ broth：鮮美 ▸ refreshing　**076** ⓑ 麵條 ▸ noodles；（麵條等）糊了 ▸ go soggy　**077** ⓑ 與……很配 ▸ go well with；海苔 ▸ laver　**078** ⓒ 一口 ▸ bite

DAY 3 ▸ 品嘗食物及評價味道

073

😀 媽！飯太軟了。

Mom!

👩 噢，真的嗎？可能是我放太多水了。

Oh, really? Maybe I put in too much water.

074

😎 嘿，別喝這瓶可樂了。都沒氣了。

Hey, don't drink this coke.

😊 我不介意。其實我比較喜歡這樣的可樂。

I don't mind. In fact, I prefer it.

075

😊 湯很鮮甜。

👦 在韓國，人們宿醉後都會喝這種湯來緩解胃部的不適。

In Korea, people drink this as a hangover remedy.

hangover remedy 緩解宿醉後胃部的不適

076

🎩 我的麵條都糊了。

👩 所以你少說話，快點吃。

That's why you should talk less and eat.

077

😊 米飯配海苔很好吃。我最喜歡這麼吃了。

They're my favorite combination.

🎩 你也得吃點肉。

You should eat some meat, too.

078

😎 這種海鮮怎麼吃？

How do you eat this seafood?

😊 一口吃下去。這樣。

Like this.

Answer **073** The rice is mushy. 飯太軟了。 **074** It's gone flat. 都沒氣了。 **075** The broth is refreshing! 湯很鮮甜！ **076** My noodles have gone soggy. 我的麵條都糊了。 **077** Rice goes well with laver. 米飯配海苔很好吃。 **078** Eat it in one bite. 一口吃下去。

Quick Test 04

這些句子用英語怎麼說？

規定時間 1 min

---

079 挑食的人

我比較挑食。

ⓐ I'm a narrow eater.
ⓑ I'm a shallow eater.
ⓒ I'm a picky eater.

---

080 能吃2-3人份飯菜的人

我的胃口很大。

ⓐ I have a big mouth.
ⓑ I have a big plate.
ⓒ I have a big appetite.

---

081 愛吃零食的人

他太喜歡吃零食。

ⓐ He is crazy about jamborees.
ⓑ He loves snacking.
ⓒ He is a cookie monster.

---

082 喜歡吃甜食的人

我喜歡吃甜食。

ⓐ I have a sugary tooth.
ⓑ I have a sweet tooth.
ⓒ I have a candy tooth.

---

083 對特定的食物過敏的人

我不能吃生魚片。

ⓐ Raw fish doesn't agree with me.
ⓑ Sushi is poison to me.
ⓒ Sashimi is allergic to me.

---

084 不吃肉，只吃蔬菜的人

我是素食主義者。

ⓐ I'm a green person.
ⓑ I have vegetable fingers.
ⓒ I'm a vegetarian.

DAY 3

▼ 品嘗食物及評價味道

Answer **079** ⓒ 挑剔的 ▶ picky **080** ⓒ 食慾 ▶ appetite **081** ⓑ 吃零食 ▶ snack **082** ⓑ 這是很有趣的表達方式，因為有甜的牙齒（tooth）所以喜歡吃甜食 **083** ⓐ 生魚片 ▶ raw fish；適合…… ▶ agree with **084** ⓒ 素食主義者 ▶ vegetarian cf（不僅不吃肉，就連牛奶、雞蛋都不吃的）全素食主義者 ▶ vegan

Quick Practice 現在可以自信地說出來了嗎？ 規定時間 1 min

079

我放棄了。我們別吃飯了。

I give up. Let's just not eat.

煩了吧？我比較挑食。

Frustrating, huh?

080

你點了漢堡套餐？我們剛吃完披薩！

You're ordering a hamburger set? We just had pizza!

你不知道嗎？我的胃口很大。

You didn't know?

081

他在廚房裡幹什麼？還沒到吃午餐的時間。

What's he doing in the kitchen? It's not lunch time yet.

別管他。他太喜歡吃零食了。

Leave him be.

082

你書包裡怎麼有這麼多糖？

What are all these candies in your handbag?

我喜歡吃甜食。要吃一點嗎？

Do you want some?

083

我想請你去吃日本菜。

I'd like to treat you at a Japanese restaurant.

不好意思。我不能吃生魚片。

Sorry.

084

這是我幫你做的沙朗牛排。

Here's a sirloin steak I made for you.

不好意思。我是素食主義者。

I'm sorry, but

Answer **079** I'm a picky eater. 我比較挑食。 **080** I have a big appetite. 我的胃口很大。 **081** He loves snacking. 他太喜歡吃零食。 **082** I have a sweet tooth. 我喜歡吃甜食。 **083** Raw fish doesn't agree with me. 我不能吃生魚片。 **084** I'm a vegetarian. 我是素食主義者。

Quick Test 05 這些句子用英語怎麼說？

規定時間 1 min

---

085 談論自己對於咖啡濃度的喜好時

我喜歡濃咖啡。

ⓐ I like strong coffee.

ⓑ I like deep coffee.

ⓒ I like dark coffee.

---

086 不加糖和奶的咖啡

我要黑咖啡。

ⓐ I'll take mine black.

ⓑ I'll have mine naturally.

ⓒ I want mine without any white.

---

087 咖啡涼了的時候

咖啡不熱了。

ⓐ The taste of coffee is dead.

ⓑ The coffee is vague.

ⓒ The coffee is lukewarm.

---

088 比起咖啡，更喜歡茶

我通常都是喝綠茶。

ⓐ I usually drink green tea.

ⓑ I seldom drink green tea.

ⓒ I rarely drink green tea.

---

089 說自己比較喜歡的飲料時

比起咖啡，我更喜歡紅茶。

ⓐ I bet black tea over coffee.

ⓑ I prefer black tea to coffee.

ⓒ I taste black tea with coffee.

---

090 我喜歡茶的原因

茶能讓我放鬆緊張的情緒。

ⓐ Tea arrests my nerves.

ⓑ Tea presses down my nerves.

ⓒ Tea calms down my nerves.

DAY 3

▼ 品嘗食物及評價味道

Answer 085 ⓐ 濃咖啡 ▶ strong coffee cf）淡咖啡 ▶ weak coffee 086 ⓐ 我要…… ▶ take mine... 087 ⓒ 溫的 ▶ lukewarm 088 ⓐ 通常，一般 ▶ usually ：綠茶 green tea 089 ⓑ 比起A，更喜歡B ▶ prefer B to A ：紅茶 ▶ black tea 090 ⓒ 使放鬆 ▶ calm down：神經，緊張 ▶ nerve

085

😊 我喜歡濃咖啡。因為我喜歡咖啡的香味。

_____ For the aroma.

😎 對，而且疲憊的時候，喝了更有效。

Yeah, and it also helps you to stay awake better.

086

😀 你要什麼樣的咖啡？

How do you like your coffee?

😃 我要黑咖啡。

087

🎩 不好意思。咖啡不熱了。

Excuse me.

😊 對不起，先生。我幫您換一杯。

Sorry, sir. I'll get you another one.

088

😄 你喜歡喝咖啡嗎？

Do you like to drink coffee?

😊 不喜歡。我通常都是喝綠茶。

Not really.

089

😊 喝杯咖啡，怎麼樣？

How about a cup of coffee?

😄 比起咖啡，我更喜歡紅茶。希望這裡有紅茶。

Hope they have it here.

090

🎩 你為什麼總是喝茶？

Why do you drink tea all the time?

😊 啊，因為茶能讓我放鬆緊張的情緒。

Oh, it's because

Answer **085** I like strong coffee. 我喜歡濃咖啡。 **086** I'll take mine black. 我要黑咖啡。 **087** The coffee is lukewarm. 咖啡不熱了。 **088** I usually drink green tea. 我通常都是喝綠茶。 **089** I prefer black tea to coffee. 比起咖啡，我更喜歡紅茶。 **090** Tea calms down my nerves. 茶能讓我放鬆緊張的情緒。

Day 3 Review 在忘記以前複習一遍，怎麼樣？	規定時間 5 min

聽著MP3跟讀	看著中文說英語
想知道食物合不合對方口味時 **Is the food to your taste?**	那道菜合你的口味嗎？
吃了辣的東西，嘴裡火辣辣的時候 **It's red hot.**	太辣了。
食物的味道太淡時 **It's too bland.**	太淡了。
我不太喜歡吃甜的 **It's too sweet for my taste.**	我覺得太甜了。
因為太油，覺得膩時 **It's too oily.**	太膩了。
嚐到很濃烈豐富的味道時 **It's rich and flavorful.**	味道又濃又豐富。
同時嚐到甜味和苦味的時候 **It has a bittersweet taste.**	是甜中帶苦的味道。
食物在嘴裡，滿口生香的時候。 **It has a savory taste.**	好香。
做飯的時候放了太多水 **The rice is mushy.**	飯太軟了。
碳酸飲料的瓶子打開後，放了太久 **It's gone flat.**	都沒氣了。

DAY 3 ▼ 品嘗食物及評價味道

看著中文說英文時，用書籤擋住這個部分。

覺得湯很鮮甜時
The broth is refreshing!

湯很鮮甜。

麵條放了太久，都糊了的時候
My noodles have gone soggy.

我的麵條都糊了。

挑食的人
I'm a picky eater.

我比較挑食。

能吃2-3人份飯菜的人
I have a big appetite.

我的胃口很大。

喜歡吃甜食的人
I have a sweet tooth.

我喜歡吃甜食。

對特定的食物過敏的人
Raw fish doesn't agree with me.

我不能吃生魚片。

談論自己對咖啡濃度的喜好時
I like strong coffee.

我喜歡濃咖啡。

要不加糖和奶的咖啡
I'll take mine black.

我要黑咖啡。

咖啡涼了的時候
The coffee is lukewarm.

咖啡不熱了。

說自己更喜歡的飲料時
I prefer black tea to coffee.

比起咖啡，我更喜歡紅茶。

已經學會的句型
90個/600個

📖 看著中文說英文時，用書籤擋住這個部分。

DAY 4

找飯店及點餐

聽例句

找飯店的時候、選擇想吃的食物時，或是使用打折優惠　的時候，
你會用英語說有關飯店和點餐的句子嗎？來檢測一下吧。

Quick Test 01

這些句子用英語怎麼說？

規定時間 1 min

091 要餓死了的時候

我快餓死了。

ⓐ I'm starving.
ⓑ I'm howling.
ⓒ I'm growling.

092 肚子在傳遞餓的訊號時

我的肚子餓得咕嚕咕嚕叫。

ⓐ My bowl is moving.
ⓑ My belly is crying.
ⓒ My stomach is growling.

093 特別想吃特定的一種食物時

我好想吃披薩。

ⓐ I taste pizza.
ⓑ I pull pizza.
ⓒ I crave pizza.

094 因為疾病、壓力等沒有食慾的時候

我沒胃口。

ⓐ I've lost my oral sense.
ⓑ I've lost my appetite.
ⓒ I've lost my taste buds.

095 簡單吃一頓的時候

我們簡單吃點什麼吧。

ⓐ How about a tip?
ⓑ Let's grab a bite.
ⓒ Let's get some small food.

096 建議到餐廳吃飯的時候

我們到外面吃吧。

ⓐ Let's eat out.
ⓑ Let's eat away.
ⓒ Let's eat off.

DAY 4 ▼ 找飯店及點餐

Answer **091** ⓐ 極度飢餓 ▶ starve **092** ⓒ 咕嚕咕嚕叫 ▶ growl **093** ⓒ 非常想要，渴望 ▶ crave **094** ⓑ 〔直譯〕我沒食慾。（appetite食慾） **095** ⓑ 簡單地吃 ▶ grab a bite **096** ⓐ 到外面吃飯 ▶ eat out

091

😊 我快餓死了。晚餐吃什麼？
What's for dinner?

🧑 不好意思。我忘了買菜了。
Sorry. I forgot to pick up the groceries.

092

👦 我的肚子餓得咕嚕咕嚕叫。

👩 再等一會。拉麵馬上就好了。
Just a little longer. The ramen is almost ready.

093

😊 我好想吃披薩。我們叫外賣吧。
Let's order some.

🧑 現在都晚上11點半了。你確定不會後悔嗎？
It's 11:30 p.m. Sure you won't regret it?

094

😊 怎麼了？你什麼都沒吃。
What's wrong? You haven't touched your food.

😟 沒胃口。可能因為壓力太大了吧。
Maybe it's the stress.

095

🎩 我有點餓了。我們簡單吃點什麼吧。
I'm feeling peckish.

🧑 這好像不是個好主意。馬上就到午餐時間了。
I don't think that's wise. It'll be lunch time soon.

096

👧 我不想做晚餐了。我們去外面吃吧。
I don't feel like making dinner.

🧑 好。不過我以為你在減肥？
Okay. But I thought you were on a diet?

peckish 肚子有點餓

Answer **091** I'm starving. 快餓死了。 **092** My stomach is growling. 我的肚子餓得咕嚕咕嚕叫。 **093** I crave pizza. 我好想吃披薩。 **094** I've lost my appetite. 我沒胃口。 **095** Let's grab a bite. 我們簡單吃點什麼吧。 **096** Let's eat out. 我們去外面吃吧。

097 建議吃什麼的時候

吃中國菜，怎麼樣？

ⓐ Does the Chinese palate suit you?
ⓑ How about Chinese?
ⓒ How's the Chinese cuisine?

098 不在餐廳裡吃，打包帶走的時候

打包壽司帶走吧。

ⓐ Let's get some sushi to go.
ⓑ We should take out sashimi.
ⓒ Bring out the raw fish.

099 指著新開業的飯店

這家是新開的店。

ⓐ It just opened.
ⓑ It just sprang up.
ⓒ It's just a new brand.

100 提議去沒有去過的餐廳時

我們去嚐嚐看吧。

ⓐ Let's eat it up.
ⓑ Let's check it out.
ⓒ Let's make it ours.

101 想要吃好吃的飯菜時

幫我找個好吃的餐廳。

ⓐ Get me a tasty restaurant.
ⓑ Find me a great restaurant.
ⓒ Search a delicious dinner for me.

102 飯店裡坐滿了客人的時候

客人爆滿啊。

ⓐ The guests are bursting up.
ⓑ The patrons are suffocating.
ⓒ It's bustling with customers.

DAY 4 ▼ 找飯店及點餐

Answer **097** ⓑ（提出建議）……怎麼樣？▶ How about...?：中國菜 ▶ Chinese (food) **098** ⓐ 壽司 ▶ sushi：（不在餐廳裡吃）打包帶走 ▶ to go **099** ⓐ 開業，開門 ▶ open **100** ⓑ 確認…… ▶ check...out **101** ⓑ 好吃的飯 ▶ great restaurant **102** ⓒ 散佈著……，熙熙攘攘的 ▶ be bustling with：（飯店的）客人 ▶ customer

現在可以自信地說出來了嗎？ 規定時間

097

😈 該死，每天都要決定吃什麼，真煩人！
Darn, choosing what to eat every day is so cumbersome!

😊 中國菜，怎麼樣？

cumbersome 煩人，麻煩

098

😊 餓了吧？打包壽司帶走吧。
Hungry?

🎩 啊，這樣可以嗎？太好了。
Oh, can you do that? Great.

099

😈 這家餐廳看起來開了很久。
This restaurant looks very old.

😊 不是，這家是新開的店。
No, no.

100

😊 哦？這家餐廳以前沒看過。
Huh? I've never seen this restaurant before.

😎 真的？我們去嚐嚐看吧。
Really?

101

😎 嘿！幫我找個好吃的餐廳。
Hey!

🎩 好。我幫你查查。不過你請客。
Okay. I'll look it up for you. But you're buying.

102

😊 哇！客人爆滿啊。
Wow!

😊 聽說連總統都來這裡吃飯呢。
They say even the president comes here.

Answer **097** How about Chinese? 中國菜，怎麼樣？ **098** Let's get some sushi to go. 打包壽司帶走吧。 **099** It just opened. 這家是新開的店。 **100** Let's check it out. 我們去嚐嚐看吧。 **101** Find me a great restaurant. 幫我找個好吃的餐廳。 **102** It's bustling with customers. 客人爆滿啊。

Quick Test 03

這些句子用英語怎麼說？

規定時間 1 min

---

103 排隊等候的人很多時

還要等多久？

ⓐ What is the line?

ⓑ How much is the time?

ⓒ How long is the wait?

---

104 詢問飯店的招牌料理時

這裡的招牌料理是什麼？

ⓐ What's today's menu?

ⓑ What's the house specialty?

ⓒ What's your bestseller?

---

105 點菜的時候，告訴服務員要幾人份時

五花肉兩人份。

ⓐ Two servings of pork belly.

ⓑ Two persons with pork belly.

ⓒ Two mouthfuls of pork belly.

---

106 要和旁邊的人一樣的菜時

我也要那個。

ⓐ I'll equal that.

ⓑ I'll have the same.

ⓒ Makes no difference to me.

---

107 想要吃2倍的量時

我要雙份的。

ⓐ Multiply it by two.

ⓑ Give me that twice.

ⓒ Make it a double.

---

108 要求不放特定的材料時

別放洋蔥。

ⓐ Take the onions.

ⓑ Hold the onions.

ⓒ Cut away the onions.

Answer **103** ⓒ 等，排隊等 ▶ wait **104** ⓑ（這個餐廳裡）做得最好的菜 ▶ house specialty **105** ⓐ 食物的
1人份 ▶ serving ：五花肉 ▶ pork belly **106** ⓑ **107** ⓒ〔直譯〕給我那個的2倍。 **108** ⓑ 別放…… ▶ Hold...

Quick Practice 現在可以自信地說出來了嗎？ 規定時間 1 min

103

😊 還要等多久？

😊 現在不需要等太久了，先生。
It won't take long now, sir.

104

🎩 我第一次來這裡。嗯，這裡的招牌料理是什麼？
It's our first visit here. Umm,

😊 每道菜都好吃，先生。
Everything, sir.

105

😊 您要點菜嗎，先生？
Are you ready to order, sir?

🎩 先來個五花肉兩人份，謝謝。

to start with, please.

106

😎 我要乳酪披薩。
I'll have the Gorgonzola pizza.

😊 我也要一樣的。

107

😊 您的菜都點完了嗎，先生？
Would that be all, sir?

😊 啊，等一下，我要雙份的。
Oh, wait.

108

😊 您的三明治裡要放什麼？
What would you like in your sandwich?

😊 什麼都行。不過別放洋蔥，謝謝。
Anything. But   , please.

Answer **103** How long is the wait? 還要等多久？ **104** what's the house specialty? 這裡的招牌料理是什麼？ **105** Two servings of pork belly. 五花肉兩人份。 **106** I'll have the same. 我也要一樣的。 **107** Make it a double. 我要雙份的。 **108** hold the onions 別放洋蔥。

Quick Test 04 這些句子用英語怎麼說？ 規定時間 1 min

109 點自己想要的飲料時

我要檸檬水。

ⓐ I'll probably get lemonade.

ⓑ I'll just have lemonade.

ⓒ I must take the lemonade.

110 想要可樂、雪碧這樣的飲料時

有碳酸飲料嗎？

ⓐ Do you have non-dairy drinks?

ⓑ Do you have soda?

ⓒ Do you have fuzzy drinks?

111 需要親自去倒水喝時

水是自助的。

ⓐ Water is self-served.

ⓑ Water is not served.

ⓒ Water is selfish.

112 餐廳贈送食物的時候

這是免費贈送的。

ⓐ It's on the table.

ⓑ It's on my lap.

ⓒ It's on the house.

113 確認優惠券是否過期時

這張優惠券過期了嗎？

ⓐ Is this coupon valid?

ⓑ Do I still have a date?

ⓒ Would you check the guarantee?

114 飯前分別結算的時候

各付各的。

ⓐ Let's go our separate ways.

ⓑ We'll split the wallet.

ⓒ Let's go Dutch.

DAY 4 ▼ 找飯店及點餐

Answer **109** ⓑ（看著菜單）我要…… ▶ I'll have... **110** ⓑ 碳酸飲料 ▶ soda **111** ⓐ〔直譯〕水是自取的。（be self-served自助服務） **112** ⓒ（在酒館或者餐廳，酒、食物）免費贈送 ▶ on the house **113** ⓐ（法定的，規定的）有效期 ▶ valid **114** ⓒ 各付各的，AA制 ▶ go Dutch（源自荷蘭人（Dutch）的習慣）

109

😀 你想喝什麼？啤酒怎麼樣？
What would you like to drink?
How about a beer?

😊 我要檸檬水。

110

😊 有碳酸飲料嗎？

😀 對不起，先生。碳酸飲料剛好都賣完了。
I'm sorry, sir. We're out of soda at the moment.

111

😊 你好，可以幫我們拿些水來嗎？
Excuse me. Can you get me some water?

😎 嗯。水是自助的。
Umm.

112

😊 什麼？嗯，我沒點這杯雞尾酒。
What? Umm, I didn't order this cocktail.

😊 這是免費贈送的。

113

😊 你好，這張優惠券過期了嗎？
Excuse me.

😀 我看看。哦，這不是我們店的優惠券。
Let's see. Oh, this is not our coupon.

114

😎 是不是該你請客吃午餐了？
Isn't it your turn to buy lunch?

😀 不是吧。各付各的。
No, I don't think so.

Answer 109 I'll just have lemonade. 我只要檸檬汽水。 110 Do you have soda? 有碳酸飲料嗎？ 111 Water is self-served. 水是自助的。 112 It's on the house. 這是免費贈送給您的。 113 Is this coupon valid? 這張優惠券過期了嗎？ 114 Let's go Dutch. 各付各的吧。

Quick
Test 05

這些句子用英語怎麼說？

規定時間 1 min

---

115 提議盡情大吃的時候

快吃吧。

ⓐ Let's dig out.
ⓑ Let's dig under.
ⓒ Let's dig in.

116 主人招待客人吃菜時

多吃一點。

ⓐ Please dig yourself.
ⓑ Please open yourself.
ⓒ Please help yourself.

DAY 4 ▶ 找飯店及點餐

---

117 看著食物吞口水的時候

我都流口水了。

ⓐ My spit is flowing.
ⓑ My mouth is watering.
ⓒ My tongue is rolling up.

118 想要嚐嚐旁人的食物時

我可以吃一口嗎？

ⓐ I'd like a mouthful.
ⓑ Can I have a bite?
ⓒ Can you lend me your food?

---

119 要求喝一口飲料的時候

我喝一口就好。

ⓐ Just a sip.
ⓑ Only one round.
ⓒ Limited drinking only.

120 想要再吃一些的時候

再給我一碗。

ⓐ One more disc, please.
ⓑ Another helping, please.
ⓒ An extra dish, please.

Answer **115** ⓒ（祈使句的形態）吃吧，開始吃吧 ▶ dig in **116** ⓒ 意思是想吃什麼就盡情地吃吧 **117** ⓑ 流口水 ▶ water **118** ⓑ 吃一口 ▶ have a bite **119** ⓐ（非常少的量）一口 ▶ sip **120** ⓑ（用餐時，一個人吃的）量，一碗 ▶ helping

現在可以自信地說出來了嗎？ 規定時間

115

🤓 這是披薩、漢堡、馬鈴薯沙拉。快吃吧。

Here's pizza, hamburgers, and potato salad.

🎩 好，快吃。祝你生日快樂！

Yeah, let's. Happy birthday, man!

116

🎩 歡迎你們來我的喬遷派對。多吃一點。

Welcome to my housewarming party.

🙂 謝謝。天哪，看這道菜！

Thank you. Oh, look at all this food!

117

🤓 我都流口水了。我們點電視上的那個吧。

Let's order what's on TV.

🙂 現在都半夜11點了。

But it's half past eleven at night.

118

😃 我可以吃一口嗎？我的都吃完了。

I've finished mine.

🙂 我感冒了也沒關係嗎？好，那你吃吧。

Even though I have a cold? Okay, here you go.

119

🙂 不行，別碰那瓶威士忌！

No, get away from that whisky bottle!

🎩 該死，被你抓到了。哦，親愛的，我喝一口就好。

Darn, you caught me. Oh, come on, dear.

120

🙂 還有很多呢。你還想吃的話⋯⋯

There's plenty of food. So if you want...

🤓 真的？再給我來一碗。

Really?

Answer **115** Let's dig in. 快吃吧。 **116** Please help yourself. 多吃一點。 **117** My mouth is watering. 我都流口水了。 **118** Can I have a bite? 我可以吃一口嗎？ **119** Just a sip. 我喝一口就好。 **120** Another helping, please. 再給我來一碗。

Day 4 Review	在忘記以前複習一遍，怎麼樣？	規定時間 5 min

聽著MP3跟讀 🔊	看著中文說英語 👄
要餓死了的時候 **I'm starving.**	我快餓死了。
肚子在傳遞餓的訊號時 **My stomach is growling.**	我的肚子餓得咕嚕咕嚕叫。
特別想吃特定的一種食物時 **I crave pizza.**	好想吃披薩。
因為疾病、壓力等沒有食慾的時候 **I've lost my appetite.**	我沒胃口。
建議吃什麼的時候 **How about Chinese?**	吃中國菜，怎麼樣？
不在餐廳裡吃，打包帶走的時候 **Let's get some sushi to go.**	打包壽司帶走吧。
提議去沒有去過的飯店時 **Let's check it out.**	我們去嚐嚐看吧。
飯店裡坐滿了客人的時候 **It's bustling with customers.**	客人爆滿啊。
排隊等候的人很多時 **How long is the wait?**	還要等多久？
詢問飯店的特色菜時 **What's the house specialty?**	這裡的招牌料理是什麼？

DAY 4 ▼ 找飯店及點餐

📖 看著中文說英文時，用書籤擋住這個部分。

要和旁邊的人一樣的菜時 **I'll have the same.**	我也要一樣的。
想要吃2倍的量時 **Make it a double.**	我要雙份的。
點自己想要的飲料時 **I'll just have lemonade.**	我要檸檬水。
需要親自去倒水喝時 **Water is self-served.**	水是自助的。
確認優惠券是否過期時 **Is this coupon valid?**	這張優惠券過期了嗎？
飯錢分別結算的時候 **Let's go Dutch.**	各付各的。
提議盡情大吃的時候 **Let's dig in.**	快吃吧。
看著食物吞口水的時候 **My mouth is watering.**	我都流口水了。
想要嚐嚐旁邊人的食物時 **Can I have a bite?**	我可以吃一口嗎？
想要再吃一些的時候 **Another helping, please.**	再給我一碗。

已經學會的句型
120個/600個

📖 看著中文說英文時，用書籤擋住這個部分。

DAY **5**

談論外貌年齡

 **05** **學習日期** 月 日

 學習時間

聽例句

說個子矮的時候、說要亮出腹肌的時候,或是擔心眼角皺紋的時候,
你會用英語說這些有關外貌或者年齡的句子嗎?來檢測一下吧。

Quick Test 01 這些句子用英語怎麼說？

規定時間 1 min

---

121 說別人其實個子不高時

他連一百七都不到。

ⓐ He's just 170 cm tall.

ⓑ He's not even 170 cm tall.

ⓒ He's barely 170 cm tall.

---

122 談論一年長高了多少時

她一年長高了10公分。

ⓐ She grew 10 cm in a year.

ⓑ She inched 10 cm forward this year.

ⓒ She went up 10 cm per year.

---

123 見到好久沒見的孩子，發現孩子一下子長大了時

都這麼大了。

ⓐ Look how you've been!

ⓑ Look how you've expanded!

ⓒ Look how you've grown!

---

124 有點胖的體型

他有點胖。

ⓐ He's a bit quirky.

ⓑ He's a bit chubby.

ⓒ He's a bit unstable.

DAY 5

▼ 談論外貌年齡

---

125 體型健壯結實

他體型很好。

ⓐ He's well-built.

ⓑ He's well-bred.

ⓒ He's well-born.

---

126 平均身高，身材很瘦

她身高中等，很苗條。

ⓐ She's normal and skinny.

ⓑ She's of medium height and slim.

ⓒ Her weight is medium, and height is light.

Answer **121** ⓑ 還不到⋯⋯ ▶ be not even **122** ⓐ 長大 ▶ grow **123** ⓒ 〔直譯〕看你長多大了！ **124** ⓑ 胖嘟嘟的 ▶ chubby **125** ⓐ 體型好的 ▶ well-built **126** ⓑ 中等身高 ▶ of medium height ；苗條的 ▶ slim

現在可以自信地說出來了嗎？ 規定時間

121

😊 你男朋友多高？

How tall is your boyfriend?

😊 他連一百七都不到。比我還矮。

He's shorter than me.

122

🎩 你認識蘇菲吧？哇！她一年長高了10公分。

You know Sophia, right? Man!

😊 真羨慕她。她有什麼秘訣嗎？

I envy her. What's her secret?

123

😊 您好，克萊拉阿姨。我們5年沒見了吧？

Hello, Aunt Clara. It's been five years, huh?

😊 泰德！都長這麼大了。

Ted!

124

😊 你以前說你男朋友是練健美的？

Did you say your boyfriend was a bodybuilder?

😊 嗯，他和我交往以後就不練了。現在他有點胖。

No, he quit after he met me. Now

125

🎩 你幫我描述一下嫌疑人的外貌。

Describe the suspect's appearance for me.

😊 嗯，他體型很好，個子很高，長得很帥。

Well, _____, tall, and handsome.

126

🤓 幫我介紹一下貝琳達。我好期待和她見面。

Tell me about Belinda. I'm so excited to meet her.

😊 嗯，她中等身高，很苗條。

Well,

suspect 嫌疑人

127 有雙眼皮的人

她有雙眼皮。

ⓐ She has double eyebrows.

ⓑ She has double eyelashes.

ⓒ She has double eyelids.

128 笑起來時有酒窩的人

他有酒窩。

ⓐ He has add-ons.

ⓑ He has pimples.

ⓒ He has dimples.

129 用左手寫字的人

她是左撇子。

ⓐ She's left-handed.

ⓑ She left hand-in-hand.

ⓒ Her hand is left-sided.

130 給人感覺很好的人

他讓人很有好感。

ⓐ He has a likable body.

ⓑ He has a likable appearance.

ⓒ He has likable special features.

131 腹部脂肪很多，肚子鼓出來的人

他有肚子。

ⓐ He's got a pot belly.

ⓑ He's got a mountain belly.

ⓒ He's got a piggy belly.

132 為六塊腹肌而感歎時

他的腹肌太棒了。

ⓐ He owns the abdomen.

ⓑ He's got killer abs.

ⓒ He has a belly made of chocolate.

DAY 5　▼ 談論外貌年齡

Answer **127** ⓒ 雙眼皮 ▶ double eyelid **128** ⓒ 酒窩 ▶ dimple **129** ⓐ 左撇子 ▶ left-handed **130** ⓑ 產生好感的 ▶ likable：外貌 appearance **131** ⓐ 因腹部脂肪堆積而鼓起的肚子 ▶ pot belly cf）因為喝啤酒而鼓起的肚子 ▶ beer belly **132** ⓑ 非常棒的 ▶ killer：腹肌 ▶ abs（abdominal muscles的縮寫）cf）六塊腹肌 ▶ six pack abs

127

😊 媽媽，我真羨慕莎倫。她有雙眼皮。

Mom, I really envy Sharon. _____

😊 別擔心，孩子。媽媽正在存錢。

Don't worry, dear. I've been saving up some money.

128

😊 你到底喜歡他哪裡？

What do you see in him?

😊 他有我喜歡的酒窩。

_____ that I love.

129

😎 我為什麼要跟她換座位？

Why should I trade places with her?

🎩 她是左撇子，謝謝你啦。

_____ Thanks.

130

😊 你會喜歡他的。他讓人很有好感。

You'll like him. _____

😊 你上次也是這麼說的！

That's what you said last time, too!

131

😊 這條褲子你爸爸穿適合嗎？

Would these trousers fit your Dad?

😊 要再更大一點。他有肚子。

They need to be bigger. _____

132

😊 聽說你和保羅一起去游泳？他游得好嗎？

So you went swimming with Paul? Is he a good swimmer?

😊 他的腹肌太棒了。

_____

Answer **127** She has double eyelids. 她有雙眼皮。 **128** He has dimples. 他有酒窩。 **129** She's left-handed. 她是左撇子。 **130** He has a likable appearance. 他讓人很有好感。 **131** He's got a pot belly. 他有肚子。 **132** He's got killer abs. 他的腹肌太棒了。

Quick
Test 03

這些句子用英語怎麼說？

規定時間 1 min

---

133 經常穿的衣服不再合適時

我胖了。

ⓐ I've gained weight.
ⓑ I've made weight.
ⓒ I've put in weight.

---

134 經常掉頭髮時

我開始掉頭髮了。

ⓐ I'm losing my hair.
ⓑ My hair is falling down.
ⓒ The headline is losing.

---

135 額頭的頭髮一直掉，額頭越來越高時

我的頭頂開始禿了。

ⓐ My hair is going bald.
ⓑ My hairline is receding.
ⓒ My forehead is peeling off.

---

136 發現白頭髮時

我長白頭髮了。

ⓐ I'm getting snowy.
ⓑ I'm going gray.
ⓒ I'm going white.

DAY 5

▼ 談論外貌年齡

---

137 眼睛周圍長細小的皺紋時

我長魚尾紋了。

ⓐ I have pigeon's feet.
ⓑ I have magpie's feet.
ⓒ I have crow's feet.

---

138 發現臉上有斑時

我臉上長斑了。

ⓐ I'm getting manicures.
ⓑ I'm getting polka dots.
ⓒ I'm getting liver spots.

Answer **133** ⓐ 胖了 ▶ gain weight **134** ⓐ 掉頭髮 ▶ lose hair **135** ⓑ 髮際線 ▶ hairline：頭髮脫落 ▶ recede **136** ⓑ 長白頭髮 ▶ go gray cf）白頭髮 ▶ gray hair（注意不是white hair） **137** ⓒ 由來：眼睛周圍細小的皺紋就像烏鴉的爪子（crow's feet）一樣 **138** ⓒ 斑，老年斑 ▶ liver spot cf）雀斑 ▶ freckle

---

133

😎 你的襯衫破了。你該不會……？

Your shirt is ripped. Have you maybe...?

😊 嗯，我知道。我胖了。

Yeah, I know.

134

😊 你怎麼戴著帽子？現在是晚上啊。

Why are you wearing a hat? It's nighttime.

😎 跟你說實話，我開始掉頭髮了。

To tell you the truth,

135

😎 我可能該戴假髮了。我的頭頂開始禿了。

I'm thinking of wearing a wig.

😊 看不出來啊。別擔心。

You look fine. Don't worry.

136

😎 哦，你看。我長白頭髮了。

Oh, look.

😊 你難道不知道嗎？

You mean you didn't know?

137

😊 不會吧。我長魚尾紋了。

I don't believe it.

😊 那又怎樣？其實蠻適合你的。

So what? Actually, it suits you.

138

😊 最近我臉上長斑了。怎麼才能去斑呢？

nowadays.
How do I get rid of them?

😎 哦，你怎麼不試試這種藥呢？

Oh, why don't you try these pills?

Answer **133** I've gained weight. 我胖了。 **134** I'm losing my hair. 我開始掉頭髮了。 **135** My hairline is receding. 我的頭頂開始禿了。 **136** I'm going gray. 我長白頭髮了。 **137** I have crow's feet. 我長魚尾紋了。 **138** I'm getting liver spots 我臉上長斑了

Quick Test 04　這些句子用英語怎麼說？

規定時間 1 min

---

139 含糊其辭地說年齡時

我二十好幾了。

ⓐ My age is over twenties.

ⓑ My twenties is bent.

ⓒ I'm in my late twenties.

---

140 說馬上就到的年齡時

我快要三十了。

ⓐ I'm pushing thirty.

ⓑ I'm pulling thirty.

ⓒ I'm making thirty.

---

141 過生日長了一歲時

我三十歲了。

ⓐ I've turned thirty.

ⓑ I've equaled thirty.

ⓒ I've timed thirty.

---

142 見到好久不見的朋友，發現他沒有變老的時候

你一點都沒變老。

ⓐ You don't look any age!

ⓑ Age has stolen you!

ⓒ You haven't aged a bit!

DAY 5

▼ 談論外貌年齡

---

143 說比自己大幾歲時

他比我大四歲。

ⓐ He's four years over me.

ⓑ He's four years my senior.

ⓒ He's four years better than me.

---

144 說生肖的時候

我屬牛。

ⓐ I'm a cow belt.

ⓑ I was born inside the cow.

ⓒ I was born in the year of the cow.

Answer **139** ⓒ 二十好幾歲 ▶ late twenties *cf*）開始的階段 ▶ early，中間階段 ▶ mid **140** ⓐ 向……接近 ▶ push **141** ⓐ 到了……（年齡）▶ turn **142** ⓒ 一點也不 ▶ a bit **143** ⓑ 年長者，比自己年齡大的人 ▶ senior **144** ⓒ（生肖中）屬……▶ the year of the...

139

我能問一下你的年齡嗎？

May I ask how old you are?

我二十好幾了。

140

看起來你很鬱悶。怎麼了？

You look down. What's up?

我快要三十了。可是連個男朋友都沒有。

　　　　　　　　　　　　But I
don't even have a boyfriend.

141

你怎麼收到這麼多禮物？

What are all these presents?

今天是我的生日。我三十歲了。

It's my birthday today.

142

你一點都沒變老！有什麼秘訣嗎？

What's your secret?

你能保守秘密嗎？

Can you keep a secret?

143

你未婚夫幾歲了？

How old is your fiance?

他比我大四歲。34歲了。

　　　　　　　　So,
he's 34 years old.

144

我屬牛。你屬什麼呢，安？

What about you, Anne?

哦，我對生肖不太瞭解。

Oh, I'm not familiar with these
Chinese zodiac signs.

Chinese zodiac signs 生肖

Answer **139** I'm in my late twenties. 我二十好幾了。 **140** I'm pushing thirty. 我快要三十了。 **141** I've turned thirty. 我三十歲了。 **142** You haven't aged a bit! 你一點都沒變老！ **143** He's four years my senior. 他比我大四歲。 **144** I was born in the year of the cow. 我屬牛。

145 比起實際年齡，長得很年輕

你有娃娃臉。

ⓐ You have a round face.

ⓑ You have a baby face.

ⓒ You have a puppy face.

146 比起實際年齡，看起來很年輕

你看起來很年輕。

ⓐ You have no age.

ⓑ You look young for your age.

ⓒ The age has forgiven you.

147 比起實際年齡，顯得年輕時

說你二十歲都有人相信。

ⓐ You could pass for twenty.

ⓑ Twenty can be your friend.

ⓒ You can fool a twenty-year-old.

148 年齡一樣的時候

你和我同歲。

ⓐ You're my lifetime.

ⓑ You're my age.

ⓒ You're my number.

149 不認為年齡很重要時

年齡只是個數字。

ⓐ Age is just a calendar.

ⓑ Age is just a calculation.

ⓒ Age is just a number.

150 感覺上了年紀，身體不如以前了時

不服老不行啊。

ⓐ I can't play a trick on time.

ⓑ Age can't be a fool.

ⓒ I'm feeling my age.

DAY 5

▼ 談論外貌年齡

Answer **145** ⓑ 童顏 ▶ baby face **146** ⓑ 根據你的年齡，比起你的年齡 ▶ for your age **147** ⓐ ……能通過 ▶ pass for **148** ⓑ **149** ⓒ just（只）可替換成 only **150** ⓒ〔直譯〕我感受著我的年齡。

Quick Practice 現在可以自信地說出來了嗎？ 規定時間 1 min

145

😎 你運氣真好。有娃娃臉。正是現在女孩們喜歡的類型。

You're lucky.
Girls dig that nowadays.

😎 嗯，我知道。

Yeah, I know.

dig 非常喜歡

146

😊 你看起來很年輕。有什麼秘訣嗎？

What's your secret?

😊 一天睡十個小時，喝兩公升的水。

I sleep ten hours and drink two liters of water a day.

147

😊 說你二十歲都有人信。

😊 其實我都說我是高中生。

Actually, I tell people I'm in high school.

148

😊 我的年齡？我二十九了。

My age? I'm 29 years old.

😎 哦！你和我同歲。

Oh!

149

😎 什麼？你這麼大年紀了還學跳傘？

Huh? You're learning to skydive at your age?

😎 年齡只是個數字。

150

😊 哎呦，我全身都痛。不服老不行啊。

Oh, I'm aching all over.

😊 沒有這回事！你還年輕，蘇菲阿姨。

Nonsense! You're still young, Aunt Sophie.

Answer **145** You have a baby face. 你真是童顏啊。 **146** You look young for your age. 你看起來很年輕。 **147** You could pass for twenty. 說你二十歲都有人信。 **148** You're my age. 你和我同歲。 **149** Age is just a number. 年齡只是個數字。 **150** I'm feeling my age. 不服老不行啊。

| **Day 5** **Review** | **在忘記以前複習一遍，怎麼樣？** 規定時間 ⏱ 5 min |

聽著MP3跟讀 👂	看著中文說英語 👄
說別人其實個子不高時 **He's not even 170 cm tall.**	他連一百七都不到。
見到好久沒見的孩子，發現孩子一下子長大了時 **Look how you've grown!**	都這麼大了。
有點胖的體型 **He's a bit chubby.**	他有點胖。
體型健壯結實 **He's well-built.**	他體型很好。
有雙眼皮的人 **She has double eyelids.**	她有雙眼皮。
用左手寫字的人 **She's left-handed.**	她是左撇子。
給人感覺很好的人 **He has a likable appearance.**	他讓人很有好感。
腹部脂肪很多，肚子鼓出來的人 **He's got a pot belly.**	他有肚子。
經常穿的衣服不再合適時 **I've gained weight.**	我胖了。
經常掉頭髮時 **I'm losing my hair.**	我開始掉頭髮了。

DAY 5 ▼ 談論外貌年齡

📖 看著中文說英文時，用書籤擋住這個部分。

發現白頭髮時
I'm going gray.

我長白頭髮了。

眼睛周圍長細小的皺紋時
I have crow's feet.

我長魚尾紋了。

含糊其辭地說年齡時
I'm in my late twenties.

我二十好幾了。

說馬上就到的年齡時
I'm pushing thirty.

我快要三十了。

過生日長了一歲時
I've turned thirty.

我三十歲了。

見到好久不見的朋友，發現他沒有變老的時候
You haven't aged a bit!

你一點都沒變老。

比起實際年齡來，長得很顯小
You have a baby face.

你有娃娃臉。

比起實際年齡來，看起來很年輕
You look young for your age.

你看起來很年輕。

不認為年齡很重要時
Age is just a number.

年齡只是個數字。

感覺上了年紀，身體不如以前了時
I'm feeling my age.

不服老不行啊。

已經學會的句型
150個/600個

📖 看著中文說英文時，用書籤擋住這個部分。

NOTE

Lightening!

Learn to Boost Your
English Skills
Everyday Expression **600**

Day 6

Day 10

DAY 6

談論衣服髮型

聽例句

告訴對方領帶顏色太鮮豔了時，或是抱怨髮質不好時，
你會用英語談論有關衣服和髮型的話題嗎？來檢測一下吧。

Quick Test 01 這些句子用英語怎麼說？ 規定時間 1 min

---

151 沒有合適的衣服穿時

我都沒有能穿的衣服了。

ⓐ I have only a body.

ⓑ Nothing fits my clothes.

ⓒ I have nothing to wear.

---

152 對精心打扮的人

你今天穿得真帥氣！

ⓐ You're all dressed up!

ⓑ You're all dressed down!

ⓒ You're all dressed out!

---

153 對穿衣打扮讓人關注的人

你穿得真漂亮。

ⓐ My mouth opens up for you.

ⓑ You're finishing the dress.

ⓒ You're dressed to kill.

---

154 覺得對方的領帶和衣服不相配時

你的領帶太突兀了。

ⓐ Your tie is too sticking out.

ⓑ Your tie is too loud.

ⓒ Your tie is too strong.

---

155 緊追流行風向的人

我喜歡時髦的衣服。

ⓐ I'm wearing fashion.

ⓑ I wear what's in fashion.

ⓒ Fashion wears me.

---

156 說自己平時最常穿的衣服

我通常穿西裝。

ⓐ I usually wear apparel.

ⓑ I usually wear a garment.

ⓒ I usually wear a suit.

DAY 6 ▼ 談論衣服髮型

Answer **151** ⓒ 完全沒有……▶ I have nothing to... ：穿▶ wear **152** ⓐ 穿衣服▶ dressed up **153** ⓒ 穿得很帥氣▶ dressed to kill **154** ⓑ（顏色・花紋）搶眼，豔麗▶ loud **155** ⓑ 時髦的▶ in fashion **156** ⓒ 西裝 ▶ suit

Quick Practice

現在可以自信地說出來了嗎？

規定時間 1 min

151

😊 親愛的，我都沒有能穿的衣服了。
Dear,

😄 我們上週才去買了衣服！
We went shopping last week!

152

😊 你今天穿得真帥氣！有什麼事嗎？

What's the occasion?

😎 今天我要去見戴安娜的父母。
I'm going to visit Diana's parents today.

153

😄 哇！今晚你穿得真漂亮。
Wow!
tonight.

😊 不會太暴露吧？
It's not too revealing, is it?

154

😊 你的領帶太突兀了。

🎩 你怎麼現在才告訴我？我們都從家裡出來了。
You're telling me this now? We've left home already!

revealing 太暴露的

155

😄 你喜歡什麼類型的衣服？
What kind of clothing do you prefer?

😊 我喜歡時髦的衣服。

156

😊 你上班時穿什麼樣的衣服？
What do you wear on the weekdays?

😎 我通常穿西裝。我是會計師嘛。

I'm an accountant, you see.

Answer **151** I have nothing to wear. 我都沒有能穿的衣服了。 **152** You're all dressed up! 你今天穿得真帥氣！ **153** You're dressed to kill. 你穿得真漂亮。 **154** Your tie is too loud. 你的領帶太突兀了。 **155** I wear what's in fashion. 我喜歡時髦的衣服。 **156** I usually wear a suit. 我通常穿西裝。

---

157 穿上那件衣服，看起來很漂亮時

那件衣服很適合你。

ⓐ That dress looks good on you.

ⓑ You're wearing a fitting dress.

ⓒ Your dress and you are the same.

---

158 很適合某種顏色時

你適合粉紅色。

ⓐ Pink is a good color.

ⓑ You look good in pink.

ⓒ Pink is good in you.

---

159 認為對方有眼光，會挑衣服時

你很有眼光。

ⓐ You have a good eyeball in clothes.

ⓑ You have an eye on clothes.

ⓒ You have good taste in clothes.

---

160 總是穿得很漂亮的人

她很會穿衣服。

ⓐ She's a clothes meister.

ⓑ She's a fashion stylist.

ⓒ She's a sharp dresser.

---

161 認為對方身材很好，穿衣服很漂亮

你真是個衣架子。

ⓐ You have the balance.

ⓑ You make the clothes look good.

ⓒ It emphasizes your body.

---

162 能把很特別的衣服穿得很好看的人

只有你才能這樣穿。

ⓐ Only you can pull that off.

ⓑ Only you can put that off.

ⓒ Only you can pull that on.

DAY 6

▼ 談論衣服髮型

Answer **157** ⓐ 適合……▶ look good on **158** ⓑ 適合……顏色 ▶ look good in ＋顏色 **159** ⓒ 品味很好，有眼光 ▶ good taste **160** ⓒ 很會穿衣服的人 ▶ sharp dresser **161** ⓑ〔直譯〕因為是你穿，那件衣服顯得很好看。 **162** ⓐ 做到……▶ pull...off

現在可以自信地說出來了嗎？

157

嗯！那件衣服很適合你。
Yeah!

真的？好，就買這件吧。
You think so? Okay, I'll take this one.

158

你適合粉紅色。

謝謝。我常聽人這麼說。
Thanks. I get that a lot.

159

你很有眼光。

您的意思是要錄取我了？
Does this mean you're hiring me?

160

她很會穿衣服。真羨慕她。

I envy her.

就是啊。她看起來就像明星一樣。
I know. She looks like a celebrity.

161

你是個衣架子。真不愧是模特兒。

No wonder you're a model.

謝謝。為了保持身材，我超級努力。
Thanks. I work really hard to stay in shape.

162

天哪，你穿的這是什麼？老天！只有你才能這樣穿。
Oh my, what's that you're wearing? Man!

我知道。
I know.

Answer **157** That dress looks good on you. 那件衣服很適合你。 **158** You look good in pink. 你適合粉紅色。 **159** You have good taste in clothes. 你很有眼光。 **160** She's a sharp dresser. 她很會穿衣服。 **161** You make the clothes look good. 你是個衣架子。 **162** Only you can pull that off. 只有你才能這樣穿。

Quick Test 03

這些句子用英語怎麼說？

規定時間 1 min

---

163 剛從理髮店回來時

我去做頭髮了。

ⓐ I had my hair done.

ⓑ I made my hair.

ⓒ My head is new.

---

164 適合某種頭型時

你適合短髮。

ⓐ The bob cut suits you.

ⓑ The mini hair suits you.

ⓒ The short bang suits you.

---

165 對毛躁粗硬的頭髮不滿時

我的髮質不好。

ⓐ The hair is too weak.

ⓑ My hair is so rough.

ⓒ My hair is too drippy.

---

166 頭髮細軟時

我頭髮太細了。

ⓐ I have fine hair.

ⓑ I have small hair.

ⓒ I have tiny hair.

DAY 6

▼ 談論衣服髮型

---

167 髮量很多時

你頭髮真多。

ⓐ You have large hair.

ⓑ You have big hair.

ⓒ You have thick hair.

---

168 染頭髮了時

你把頭髮染紅了！

ⓐ You're a red person now!

ⓑ You dyed your hair red!

ⓒ You twitched your red hair!

Answer **163** ⓐ〔直譯〕我去做了頭髮。：（在理髮店）做頭髮 ▶ have one's hair done **164** ⓐ 短髮 ▶
bob cut：適合 ▶ suit **165** ⓑ 毛躁 ▶ rough **166** ⓐ 纖細的 ▶ fine **167** ⓒ 髮量多 ▶ thick hair cf）髮量少 ▶
thin hair **168** ⓑ 染色 ▶ dye

現在可以自信地說出來了嗎？ 規定時間 1 min

163

我去做頭髮了。你看的出來哪裡不一樣嗎？

＿＿＿＿＿＿＿＿＿ Can't you tell the difference?

哦，當然。很適合你。
Oh, of course. It suits you.

164

我的新髮型怎麼樣？
How do you like my new hairstyle?

不好意思，不過你還是適合短髮。
I'm sorry, but ＿＿＿＿＿

165

我的髮質不好。怎麼辦呢？

What should I do?

那麼你試試這款洗髮精怎麼樣？
In that case, how about trying this shampoo?

166

你能描述一下自己的頭髮嗎？
Could you describe your hair for me?

我頭髮太細了。還經常掉頭髮。
＿＿＿＿＿＿ And it keeps falling out.

167

哇！你頭髮真多。
Wow! ＿＿＿＿＿＿＿＿

其實，我告訴你個秘密吧。
Actually, I'll let you in on a secret of mine.

168

天哪！你把頭髮染紅了！
What's this? ＿＿＿＿＿＿

嗯，我男朋友把我甩了。
Yeah, my boyfriend dumped me.

Answer **163** I had my hair done. 我去做頭髮了。 **164** The bob cut suits you. 你適合短髮。 **165** My hair is so rough. 我的髮質不好。 **166** I have fine hair. 我頭髮太細了。 **167** You have thick hair. 你頭髮真多。 **168** You dyed your hair red! 你把頭髮染紅了。

169 告訴美髮師只剪頭髮時

幫我剪一下就可以了。

ⓐ Just a wage cut.
ⓑ Just a haircut.
ⓒ Just a hairdo.

170 按照原來的髮型，只剪短一點就可以時

修一修就可以了。

ⓐ Mower it all over.
ⓑ Trim it all over.
ⓒ Brush it all over.

171 留著瀏海，不要剪的時候

別剪瀏海。

ⓐ Leave my bangs.
ⓑ Don't cut my sideburns.
ⓒ Don't touch my toupee.

172 想要燙頭髮時

我想燙頭髮。

ⓐ Give me a permanent burn.
ⓑ I want a permanent job.
ⓒ I'd like to get a perm.

173 髮量太多，需要打薄時

幫我打薄一點。

ⓐ Slash my hair.
ⓑ Thin out my hair.
ⓒ Tweak my hair.

174 想做頭皮護理時

幫我做個頭皮按摩。

ⓐ I'd like a scalp massage.
ⓑ Give me a hair scrub.
ⓒ Could you skin my head?

DAY 6 ▼ 談論衣服髮型

Answer **169** ⓑ 剪頭髮 ▶ haircut **170** ⓑ 修剪 ▶ trim；整體上 ▶ all over **171** ⓐ 不要剪瀏海（bang），留著不動（leave）的意思 **172** ⓒ 燙髮 ▶ get a perm **173** ⓑ 打薄 ▶ thin out **174** ⓐ 頭皮按摩 ▶ scalp massage

---

169

🧑 要幫您染頭髮嗎？

Do you want me to dye your hair?

🎩 不用，幫我剪一下就可以了。

No. _____, please.

170

👦 幫您像上次那樣剪就可以嗎？

Do you want it done like last time?

👩 對，修一修就可以了。

Yes. _____, please.

171

🧑 請別剪瀏海。我要把它留長。

_____, please. I'm growing them.

🧑 好。放心。

Of course. Don't worry.

172

🧑 您好，我想燙頭髮。

Excuse me. _____

👦 哦，要等一個小時，可以嗎？

Oh, you have to wait an hour. Is it okay with you?

173

👦 要怎麼幫您剪？

How would you like your hair done?

🧑 天氣太熱了。幫我打薄一點。

It's so hot. _____, please.

174

🧑 嗯，弄好了！希望你滿意。

There, all done! I hope you like it.

👩 哦，很滿意。請幫我做個頭皮按摩。

Oh, yeah. _____, please.

Answer **169** Just a haircut. 幫我剪一下就可以了。 **170** Trim it all over. 修一修就可以了。 **171** Leave my bangs. 別剪瀏海。 **172** I'd like to get a perm. 我想燙頭髮。 **173** Thin out my hair. 幫我打薄一些。 **174** I'd like a scalp massage. 幫我做個頭皮按摩。

175 為了出門，特意打扮了時

我化妝了。

ⓐ I've put on some makeup.

ⓑ I turned on my cosmetics.

ⓒ I applied my aesthetics.

176 妝化得太濃，不好看時

你妝化得太濃了。

ⓐ Your makeup is too dark.

ⓑ Your makeup is too deep.

ⓒ Your makeup is too strong.

177 每天都在用的化妝品見底了時

化妝水都用完了。

ⓐ I don't have skin.

ⓑ I'm short of cosmetic alcohol.

ⓒ I ran out of skin toner.

178 在臉頰上拍腮紅時

在這裡上點腮紅。

ⓐ Plaster some blush here.

ⓑ Apply blush here.

ⓒ Paint your blush here.

179 彩妝不貼合皮膚時

我的彩妝不服貼。

ⓐ My makeup is not sticking.

ⓑ My makeup is not glued on.

ⓒ My makeup is not rooted down.

180 建議使用美容技術修飾外貌時

你得改造一下。

ⓐ You need a makeover.

ⓑ A cosmetic turnover is necessary.

ⓒ Aesthetics should be applied.

DAY 6 ▼ 談論衣服髮型

Answer **175** ⓐ 化妝 ▶ put on makeup *cf* 卸妝 ▶ take off makeup **176** ⓒ 太濃 ▶ too strong **177** ⓒ 用完了 ▶ run out of：化妝水 ▶ skin toner **178** ⓑ 抹、上 ▶ apply：腮紅 ▶ blush(er) **179** ⓐ 服貼 ▶ stick **180** ⓐ（為了讓人的外貌變漂亮）改造 ▶ makeover

Quick Practice 現在可以自信地說出來了嗎？ 規定時間 1 min

175

😊 你是誰？艾麗西亞在哪裡？
Who are you? Where's Alicia?

😊 是我呀，笨蛋！我化妝了。
It's me, you fool!

176

😠 哎呦！你妝化得太濃了。
What's this?

😊 別管我。你跟我爸一樣。
Just leave me alone. You sound like my Dad.

177

😊 化妝水都用完了。我現在要去買。
That's why I'm going out to buy some.

😊 等一等！你生日的時候我送給你。
Oh, wait! I'll get it for your birthday.

178

😊 在這裡上點腮紅，我臉頰上。
, on my cheek.

😊 會不會太亮了？
Don't you think it'll be too bright?

179

🎩 快一點。電影都要開始了。
Let's hurry. We're going to miss the movie.

😊 再等我5分鐘。今天我的彩妝不服貼。
Could you give me five more minutes?
today.

180

😊 我一週以後要去相親。
I have a blind date in a week.

😊 這樣的話，你得改造一下。
In that case,

Answer **175** I've put on some makeup. 我化妝了。 **176** Your makeup is too strong. 你妝化得太濃了。 **177** I ran out of skin toner. 化妝水都用完了。 **178** Apply blush here. 在這裡上點腮紅。 **179** My makeup is not sticking. 我的彩妝不服貼。 **180** You need a makeover. 你得改造一下。

Day 6
Review 在忘記以前複習一遍，怎麼樣？ 規定時間 5 min

聽著MP3跟讀	看著中文說英語
沒有合適的衣服穿時 **I have nothing to wear.**	我都沒有能穿的衣服了。
對精心打扮的人 **You're all dressed up!**	你今天穿得真帥氣！
覺得對方的領帶和衣服不相配時 **Your tie is too loud.**	你的領帶太突兀了。
緊追流行風向的人 **I wear what's in fashion.**	我喜歡時髦的衣服。
穿上那件衣服，看起來很漂亮時 **That dress looks good on you.**	那件衣服很適合你。
很適合某種顏色時 **You look good in pink.**	你適合粉紅色。
認為對方很有眼光，會挑衣服時 **You have good taste in clothes.**	你很有眼光。
總是穿得很漂亮的人 **She's a sharp dresser.**	她很會穿衣服。
剛從理髮店回來時 **I had my hair done.**	我去做頭髮了。
適合某種頭型時 **The bob cut suits you.**	你適合短髮。

DAY 6 ▼ 談論衣服髮型

看著中文說英文時，用書籤擋住這個部分。

對毛躁粗硬的頭髮不滿時 **My hair is so rough.**	我的髮質不好。
頭髮染色了時 **You dyed your hair red!**	你把頭髮染紅了！
告訴美髮師只剪頭髮時 **Just a haircut.**	幫我剪一下就可以了。
按照原來的髮型，只剪短一些就可以時 **Trim it all over.**	修一修就可以了。
留著瀏海，不要剪的時候 **Leave my bangs.**	別剪瀏海。
想要燙頭髮時 **I'd like to get a perm.**	我想燙頭髮。
為了出門，特意打扮了時 **I've put on some makeup.**	我化妝了。
妝化得太濃，不好看時 **Your makeup is too strong.**	你妝化得太濃了。
每天都在用的化妝品見底時 **I ran out of skin toner.**	化妝水都用完了。
彩妝不貼合皮膚時 **My makeup is not sticking.**	我的彩妝不服貼。

已經學會的句型
180個/600個

📖 看著中文說英文時，用書籤擋住這個部分。

DAY **7**

/

購物及買菜

07 學習日期　　　月　　　日

 學習時間

聽例句

談論自己衣服的尺寸時、品嘗食物時，或是買啤酒時，
你會用英語購物或者買菜嗎？來檢測一下吧。

---

181 想要知道這件商品運作的方式時

能讓我看一下它怎麼開嗎？

ⓐ Can you show me how it works?

ⓑ Can you show me how it rolls?

ⓒ Can you show me how it turns?

---

182 告訴店員只是隨便看看時

我隨便看看。

ⓐ I'm just eye-hopping.

ⓑ I'm just surrounding.

ⓒ I'm just browsing.

---

183 詢問是否是最高檔的商品時

這是最高級的產品嗎？

ⓐ Would this be the top carrier?

ⓑ Is this the top of the line?

ⓒ Does this mean grade A?

---

184 詢問是否有自己要買的商品時

這裡有賣玩具嗎？

ⓐ Are toys made here?

ⓑ Do you carry toys?

ⓒ Why don't you sell toys?

---

185 在挑選衣服的時候，問有沒有其他顏色的

這件有白色的嗎？

ⓐ Do you have this in white as well?

ⓑ Does it make up white, too?

ⓒ Do you display it in white?

---

186 在一個店裡逛了一下要出去時

我再去別的地方看看。

ⓐ I think I'll look it up a bit more.

ⓑ I think I'll look into it a bit more.

ⓒ I think I'll look around a bit more.

DAY 7

▼ 購物及買菜

Answer **181** ⓐ 運作 ▶ work **182** ⓒ 流覽（商店裡的）商品 ▶ browse **183** ⓑ 同類商品中最好的 ▶ top of the line **184** ⓑ （商店裡）經營（的商品品目）▶ carry **185** ⓐ 白色的 ▶ in white；也，還 ▶ as well **186** ⓒ （為了進行比較）去不同的商店逛逛 ▶ look around

181

😃 噢，我喜歡這個。能讓我看一下它怎麼打開嗎？

Wow, I like it.

👩 只要按一下側面的紅色按鈕就行了。

Just press this red button on the side.

182

😎 您在找什麼嗎？

Are you looking for anything in particular?

😃 沒有，我隨便看看。

No,

183

😃 我喜歡這個設計！請問一下，這是最高級的產品嗎？

I like the design! Excuse me,

👩 啊，我們還有一款更高級的。

Oh, we also have one that's more high-end.

high-end 高級的

184

😃 嗯，這裡有賣玩具嗎？

Umm,

👩 沒有，現在不賣了。現在我們只賣書。

No, we don't any more. We only have books now.

185

👩 這就是我想要的。嗯，這件有白色的嗎？

This is what I wanted. Hmm.

😎 當然有。稍等。

Of course. Just a moment, please.

186

😃 您決定好了嗎？

So, have you made up your mind?

👩 沒有，還沒決定好。我再去別處看看。

No, not yet.

Answer **181** Can you show me how it works? 能讓我看一下它怎麼打開嗎？ **182** I'm just browsing. 我隨便看看。 **183** Is this the top of the line? 這是最高級的產品嗎？ **184** Do you carry toys? 這裡有賣玩具嗎？ **185** Do you have this in white as well? 這件有白色的嗎？ **186** I think I'll look around a bit more. 我再去別處看看。

Quick
Test 02
這些句子用英語怎麼說？

規定時間 1 min

---

187 想要試穿衣服時

能試穿嗎？

ⓐ May I put it up?

ⓑ Where can I wear it?

ⓒ Can I try it on?

---

188 在商店裡換衣服時

試衣間在哪裡？

ⓐ Where's the fitting room?

ⓑ Where's the sitting room?

ⓒ Where's the change?

---

189 說自己衣服的尺寸時

幫我拿這件66號的。

ⓐ I'd like this in size 66.

ⓑ I'd like size 66 in this shape.

ⓒ I'd like size 66 with this.

---

190 衣服太大或者太小時

不合適。

ⓐ It's not my taste.

ⓑ It doesn't fit.

ⓒ I'm not inside it.

---

191 衣服特定的部位太小，穿上覺得很緊時

大腿這裡太緊了。

ⓐ It's too tight on the knees.

ⓑ It's too tight in the ankle.

ⓒ It's too tight in the thigh.

---

192 衣服太小了，要大一號的時

幫我拿大一號的。

ⓐ Show me a larger one.

ⓑ Show me this in the next size up.

ⓒ Give me a push up.

DAY 7

▼ 購物及買菜

Answer **187** ⓒ 試穿…… ▶ try...on **188** ⓐ 試衣間 ▶ fitting room **189** ⓐ 尺寸 ▶ size **190** ⓑ（樣子、大小）適合（什麼人・東西）▶ fit **191** ⓒ 大腿 ▶ thigh **192** ⓑ 大一號的 ▶ next size up cf)小一號的 ▶ next size down

187

😀 能試穿嗎？

😊 當然。您穿什麼尺寸的？
Sure. What size are you?

188

🎩 你好，試衣間在哪裡？
Excuse me.

😊 那面鏡子後面。
It's just behind that mirror.

189

😀 我終於決定好了。請幫我拿這件66號的。
I've finally made up my mind.
, please.

🤓 不好意思。那個尺寸的都賣完了。
I'm sorry. We are all out of that size.

190

😀 哦，不行。不適合。我都不能呼吸了。
Oh, no.
I can't breathe.

😊 這樣的話，您試試大一號的吧。
In that case, let's try a bigger size.

191

😊 你覺得哪裡不舒服？
Where is it particularly uncomfortable?

🎩 這裡。大腿這裡太緊了。
Right here.

192

🤓 哦，天啊，我胖了。請幫我拿大一號的。
Oh, no. I've gained weight.
,
please.

😊 哦，大一號的都賣完了。
Oh, it's not in stock at the moment.

not in stock 沒有庫存

Answer **187** Can I try it on? 能試穿嗎？ **188** Where's the fitting room? 試衣間在哪裡？ **189** I'd like this in size 66 幫我拿這件66號的。 **190** It doesn't fit. 不合適。 **191** It's too tight in the thigh. 大腿這裡太緊了。 **192** Show me this in the next size up 幫我拿大一號的吧。

Quick Test 03

這些句子用英語怎麼說？

規定時間 1 min

---

193 試穿衣服後，詢問是否適合時

適合我嗎？

ⓐ Does it suit me?

ⓑ Does it choke me?

ⓒ Does it shake me?

---

194 穿上衣服後，詢問看起來怎麼樣時

我看起來怎麼樣？

ⓐ How do I look?

ⓑ How does it feel?

ⓒ Will it pass?

---

195 詢問是否可以用洗衣機清洗時

可以放在洗衣機裡洗嗎？

ⓐ Can I do the washing?

ⓑ Is it a washing machine?

ⓒ Is it machine washable?

---

196 詢問能否防水時

防水嗎？

ⓐ Is it waterlocked?

ⓑ Is it watercorked?

ⓒ Is it waterproof?

---

197 不再是流行的款式

好像過時了。

ⓐ The fashion is in the past.

ⓑ It seems outdated.

ⓒ It's not an edgy fashion.

---

198 身上穿的衣服顏色不搭時

顏色不搭。

ⓐ The colors are too loud.

ⓑ The colors don't like each other.

ⓒ The colors don't go together.

Answer **193** ⓐ 適合我 ▶ suit me **194** ⓐ〔直譯〕我看起來怎麼樣？ **195** ⓒ 可以用洗衣機清洗 ▶ machine washable **196** ⓒ 防水 ▶ waterproof *cf*）有隔音裝置的 ▶ soundproof **197** ⓑ 過時的，舊式的 ▶ outdated **198** ⓒ 互相搭配 ▶ go together

193

怎麼樣，適合我嗎？

How's this?

哦，好極了！那您就買這件了？

Oh, you look fabulous! So, are you going with this one?

fabulous 極好的，（美貌）驚人的

194

怎麼樣？袖子好像有點長。

The sleeves look a bit long.

哦，袖子可以改短。這個不用擔心。

Oh, we can shorten the sleeves. Don't worry.

195

哦，還有一件事。可以放在洗衣機裡洗嗎？

Oh, one more thing.

不行，絕對不可以。必須要乾洗。

No, absolutely not. It must be dry-cleaned.

196

這件外套防水嗎？

About this coat,

在一定程度上可以的。

To some degree, yes.

197

這件襯衫好像過時了。

This shirt.

當然了，先生。這是二手服裝店啊。

Of course, sir. This is a second-hand clothing shop.

second-hand 二手的

198

我選好派對要穿的衣服了。你覺得怎麼樣？

I picked out this outfit for the party. What do you think?

嗯，顏色不搭。

Hmm.

Answer **193** Does it suit me? 適合我嗎？ **194** How do I look? 我看起來怎麼樣？ **195** Is it machine washable? 可以放在洗衣機裡洗嗎？ **196** Is it waterproof? 防水嗎？ **197** It seems outdated. 好像過時了。 **198** The colors don't go together. 顏色不搭。

Test 04 這些句子用英語怎麼說？ 規定時間 1 min

---

199 去買食材時

我去買菜。

ⓐ I'm going to shoplift.

ⓑ I'm going to the grocery store.

ⓒ I'm going to the discount store.

---

200 看到用完了的生活用品時

牙膏都用完了。

ⓐ We ran over some toothpaste.

ⓑ We're out of toothpaste.

ⓒ We squeezed out the toothpaste.

---

201 寫購物清單時

有需要什麼嗎？

ⓐ Is there anything you care about?

ⓑ Are you a needy person?

ⓒ Do you need anything?

---

202 去超市的路上，說起相關的話題時

我正好要去超市。

ⓐ I was just going down the store.

ⓑ I was just on my way to the store.

ⓒ I was just on a road trip to the store.

---

203 希望商店裡有要買的商品

希望買得到。

ⓐ I hope they're in stock.

ⓑ I hope they're taken down.

ⓒ I hope they're ready.

---

204 商店裡沒有要買的商品，要去別處看看

我去便利商店看看。

ⓐ I'll try the tiny supermarket.

ⓑ I'll try for twenty-four hours.

ⓒ I'll try the convenience store.

DAY 7
▼ 購物及買菜

Answer **199** ⓑ 去買菜 ▶ go to the grocery store（grocery store 食品店，超市） **200** ⓑ ……用完了 ▶ out of **201** ⓒ 任何東西 ▶ anything **202** ⓑ 去……的路上 ▶ on my way to **203** ⓐ 有庫存 ▶ in stock **204** ⓒ 便利商店 ▶ convenience store

---

199

😊 我去買菜。車鑰匙在哪裡？

Where are the car keys?

🎩 在我這裡。等一下，我也一起去。

I have them. Wait, let me go with you.

200

😊 為什麼打電話來？媽媽在開車呢。

Why did you call? Mommy is driving right now.

😊 媽媽！家裡的牙膏都用完了。

Mom!

201

🤓 是我，老婆。我在超市。有什麼需要的嗎？

It's me, dear. I'm at the supermarket.

😊 什麼？我也在超市呢。啊，我看見你了！

What? I'm at the supermarket, too. Oh, I see you!

202

😊 我有點餓了。有什麼能吃的嗎？

I'm peckish. Do we have anything to eat?

🎩 我正好要去超市。你可以去那裡免費試吃。

You can taste test things over there.

taste test 免費試吃

203

🎩 艾迪有說要買新出的機器狗玩具嗎？

Did Eddie ask for the new RoboDog toy?

😊 嗯，希望買得到。

Yes.

204

😊 牙線都用完了。我去便利商店看看。

We're out of dental floss.

😊 現在？親愛的，等明天再去吧。

At this hour? Honey, just wait until tomorrow.

dental floss 牙線

Answer **199** I'm going to the grocery store. 我去買菜。 **200** We're out of toothpaste. 家裡的牙膏都用完了。 **201** Do you need anything? 有什麼需要的嗎？ **202** I was just on my way to the store. 正好要去超市。 **203** I hope they're in stock. 希望買得到。 **204** I'll try the convenience store. 我去便利商店看看。

Quick Test 05

這些句子用英語怎麼說？

規定時間 1 min

---

205 買食品之前試吃

我嚐嚐看。

ⓐ I'll try a demo.
ⓑ I'll try some.
ⓒ I'll try a model.

---

206 買食品之前看保存期限

看看保存期限。

ⓐ Open the label calendar.
ⓑ Look at the selling date.
ⓒ Check the sell-by date.

---

207 買一組更便宜時

買一組吧。

ⓐ Let's buy a bundle.
ⓑ Let's go for the group therapy.
ⓒ Let's choose the tied one.

---

208 買6個一組的東西時

給我六個一組的啤酒。

ⓐ Get me a 6-group of beer.
ⓑ Get me a 6-pack of beer.
ⓒ Get me a 6-basket of beer.

---

209 詢問是否有機食品時

這是有機的嗎？

ⓐ Is this an organism?
ⓑ Is this a vegetable?
ⓒ Is this organic?

---

210 在超市裡說明商品的位置時

肉在6號走道。

ⓐ You'll find meat in runway six.
ⓑ The meat is in aisle six.
ⓒ The meat is on the sixth shelf.

DAY 7

▼ 購物及買菜

Answer **205** ⓑ 試吃 ▶ try (a sample)　**206** ⓒ 保鮮期 ▶ sell-by date　**207** ⓐ 一捆，一組 ▶ bundle　**208** ⓑ 6
個一組的啤酒 ▶ a 6-pack of beer　**209** ⓒ 有機的 ▶ organic　**210** ⓑ 走道 ▶ aisle cf) 貨架 ▶ shelf

205

😎 啊，是餃子！我嚐嚐看。

Oh, dumplings!

😊 等一下，這裡有熱的。

Just a moment. Here are some that are hot.

206

🎩 要買哪個牌子的牛奶？

Which brand of milk should we buy?

😊 都差不多。啊，對了！看看保存期限。

They're all the same. Oh, yeah!

207

😊 像上次那樣買一組吧。

like last time.

😄 不要，還沒吃完就都壞了。

No, they'll go bad before we can eat them all.

208

🎩 啊，差一點忘了。幫我拿6個一組的啤酒。

Oh, I almost forgot.

😊 可是爸爸！你不是跟我說好要減啤酒肚嗎？

But Dad! You promised to get rid of your pot belly.

209

😊 這是有機的嗎？

210

😎 你好，火雞在哪裡？

Excuse me, where's the turkey?

😊 不是。要是有機的，可就貴多了。

No. If it was, it would be a lot more expensive.

😊 肉在6號走道。

Answer **205** I'll try some. 我嚐嚐看。 **206** Check the sell-by date. 看看保存期限。 **207** Let's buy a bundle 買一組吧。 **208** Get me a 6-pack of beer. 給我拿6個一組的啤酒。 **209** Is this organic? 這是有機的嗎？ **210** The meat is in aisle six. 肉在6號走道。

Day 7
Review

在忘記以前複習一遍，怎麼樣？

規定時間 5 min

聽著MP3跟讀	看著中文說英語
想要知道這件商品運作的方式時 **Can you show me how it works?**	能讓我看一下它怎麼運作的嗎？
告訴店員只是隨便看看時 **I'm just browsing.**	我隨便看看。
詢問是否有自己要買的商品時 **Do you carry toys?**	這裡有賣玩具嗎？
在挑選衣服的時候，問有沒有其他顏色的 **Do you have this in white as well?**	這件有白色的嗎？
想要試穿衣服時 **Can I try it on?**	能試穿嗎？
說自己衣服的尺寸時 **I'd like this in size 66.**	幫我拿這件66號的。
衣服大或者小時 **It doesn't fit.**	不合適。
衣服特定的部位太小，穿上覺得很緊時 **It's too tight in the thigh.**	大腿這裡太緊了。
試穿衣服後，詢問是否適合時 **Does it suit me?**	適合我嗎？
穿上衣服後，詢問看起來怎麼樣時 **How do I look?**	我看起來怎麼樣？

DAY 7

▼ 購物及買菜

📖 看著中文說英文時，用書籤擋住這個部分。

詢問是否可以用洗衣機清洗時 **Is it machine washable?**	可以放在洗衣機裡洗嗎？
不再時流行的款式 **It seems outdated.**	好像過時了。
去買食材時 **I'm going to the grocery store.**	我去買菜。
看到用完了的生活用品時 **We're out of toothpaste.**	牙膏都用完了。
寫購物清單時 **Do you need anything?**	有什麼需要的嗎？
商店裡沒有要買的商品，要去別處看看 **I'll try the convenience store.**	我去便利商店看看。
買食品之前試吃 **I'll try some.**	我嚐嚐看。
買食品之前看保鮮期 **Check the sell-by date.**	看看保存期限。
買一組更便宜時 **Let's buy a bundle.**	買一組吧。
在超市里說明商品的位置時 **The meat is in aisle six.**	肉在6號走道。

已經學會的句型
210個/600個

📖 看著中文說英文時，用書籤擋住這個部分。

DAY **8**

詢問價格及算帳

聽例句

詢問打折價格的時候、參加買一送一活動的時候，或是結帳的時候等，
你會用英語詢問價格並結帳嗎？來檢測一下吧。

211 同時為好幾件商品結帳時

一共多少錢？

ⓐ How can I pay?

ⓑ What's the whole thing?

ⓒ How much in total?

212 想要知道打折以前的價格時

定價是多少錢？

ⓐ What's the fixed cost?

ⓑ What's the final price?

ⓒ What's the regular price?

213 很多人一起大量購買時

團購價是多少？

ⓐ How much is the group-buy price?

ⓑ What's the together price?

ⓒ Do you take the package price?

214 想知道產品的原價時

原價多少錢？

ⓐ What's the inside price?

ⓑ What's the under cost?

ⓒ What's the manufacturing cost?

215 覺得一次付清壓力比較大時

我要分期付款。

ⓐ I'm going to pay a dear price.

ⓑ I'm going to pay in installments.

ⓒ I'm going to pay in slashed amounts.

216 相對於商品的品質，價格特別貴時

這不是坑人嗎？

ⓐ This is back-stabbing!

ⓑ This is a rip-off!

ⓒ This is an insult!

DAY 8

▼ 詢問價格及算帳

Answer **211** ⓒ（價格）是多少？▶ How much...?：一共，總共 ▶ in total **212** ⓒ 定價 ▶ regular price **213** ⓐ 團購價格 ▶ group-buy price **214** ⓒ 原價 ▶ manufacturing cost, production cost **215** ⓑ 分期付款 ▶ in installments **216** ⓑ 坑人 ▶ rip-off

211

😎 一共多少錢？

👩 哇，你買了好多啤酒。一共148美元。
Wow, you've bought a lot of beer. That will be $148.

212

😎 定價是多少錢？

😊 500美元。也就說打了八折。
$500. So this means you're getting a 20% discount.

213

😊 團購價是多少？

😎 參團的人數不同，價格也會不同。
It depends on the number of participants.

214

😊 原價是多少錢？

😎 您為什麼想要知道？我已經幫您打折了。
Why would you want to know? I've already given you a discount.

215

😎 哦，帳單來了。我看看。啊！
Oh, the statement is here. Let's see. Arrgh!

😊 沒關係。我要分期付款。
Don't worry.

216

😎 一共980美元。
That will be 980 dollars.

😎 什麼？這不是坑人嗎？別把我當傻瓜。
What?
Don't take me for a fool.

statement 帳單，明細

Answer　**211** How much in total? 一共多少錢？　**212** What's the regular price? 定價是多少錢？
213 How much is the group-buy price? 團購價是多少？　**214** What's the manufacturing cost? 原價是多少錢？　**215** I'm going to pay in installments. 我要分期付款。　**216** This is a rip-off! 這不是坑人嗎？

Quick
Test 02
這些句子用英語怎麼說？

規定時間 1 min

---

217 確認商品是否打折時

肉今天打折。

ⓐ Meat is in sale today.

ⓑ Meat is at sale today.

ⓒ Meat is on sale today.

218 告訴對方打折的幅度時

可以打七折。

ⓐ You can get 30% off.

ⓑ You can get 30% down.

ⓒ You can get 30% lighter.

---

219 以比定價便宜的價格購買商品時

我是用打折價買的。

ⓐ The discount price was cheap.

ⓑ I got it for a bargain.

ⓒ It was bought at a price.

220 一時衝動買下商品時

我一衝動就買了。

ⓐ I bought it on impulse.

ⓑ I bought it with pleasure.

ⓒ I bought it on my own.

---

221 買一送一活動

買一送一。

ⓐ It's one for all, and all for one.

ⓑ It's buy one, get one free.

ⓒ The price is one for two.

222 先到的人有優惠時

先到先得。

ⓐ As much as you want.

ⓑ Get in line quickly.

ⓒ First-come, first-served.

DAY 8 ▼ 詢問價格及算帳

Answer **217** ⓒ 正在打折 ▶ on sale **218** ⓐ 打……折 ▶ get ...% off **219** ⓑ 按打折價格 ▶ for a bargain **220** ⓐ 一時衝動 ▶ on impulse **221** ⓑ 〔直譯〕買一個，免費送一個。（free免費的） **222** ⓒ 〔直譯〕先到的人先接受服務。

217

哇！隊排得真長。怎麼回事？

Wow! Such a long line. What's going on?

啊，那個？肉今天打折。我們也排隊吧。

Oh, that?
Let's get in line.

218

我為什麼要現在買這輛汽車呢？

Why should I buy this car now?

因為可以打七折。

It's because

219

哦，我好喜歡你的包包！看這設計。

Oh, I love your bag! Look at the design.

你知道嗎？我是打折價買的。

Guess what?

220

什麼！這個手提包要2000美元？

What! This handbag costs $2,000?

親愛的，對不起。我一衝動就買了。我也沒辦法啊。

I'm sorry, darling.
I couldn't help it.

221

我們不需要兩個啊。放回去一個吧。

We don't need two. Take one back.

買一送一。我們沒得選。

We have no choice.

222

你說它們早都賣完了？可是我有優惠券啊。

You mean they're already gone? But I have a coupon.

真抱歉。先到先得。

I'm so sorry.

Answer **217** Meat is on sale today. 肉今天打折。 **218** You can get 30% off. 可以打七折。 **219** I got it for a bargain. 我是打折價買的。 **220** I bought it on impulse. 我一衝動就買了。 **221** It's buy one, get one free. 買一送一。 **222** First-come, first-served. 先到先得。

Test 03 這些句子用英語怎麼說？ 規定時間 1 min

---

223 想要買，但是價格太貴時

可以便宜一點嗎？

ⓐ Can you cut me the price?

ⓑ Can you give me a discount?

ⓒ Can you deal me a card?

---

224 詢問最多能便宜多少時

最多能便宜多少？

ⓐ What are you charging me with?

ⓑ What's your maximum cutting price?

ⓒ What's your best price?

---

225 說出自己希望的價格時

50美元我就買。

ⓐ I'll bring it for $50.

ⓑ I'll take it for $50.

ⓒ I'll make it for $50.

---

226 想要免費的贈品時

再送我幾個。

ⓐ Throw in a few more.

ⓑ Give me an additional bonus.

ⓒ I want to be more dumb.

---

227 討價還價的時候

再便宜3美元吧。

ⓐ Can I just get three dollars off?

ⓑ Can you cut out just three dollars?

ⓒ Please put off only three dollars.

---

228 討價還價後，提出最後價格時

就200美元吧。

ⓐ Let's run for 200 dollars.

ⓑ Let's join for 200 dollars.

ⓒ Let's settle for 200 dollars.

DAY 8

▼ 詢問價格及算帳

Answer **223** ⓑ 給予打折 ▶ give a discount **224** ⓒ 最好的（便宜的）價格 ▶ best price **225** ⓑ 買這個 ▶ take it **226** ⓐ 免費送 ▶ throw in *cf*) 贈品 ▶ freebie **227** ⓐ 減去……，拿掉 ▶ get...off **228** ⓒ 定為…… ▶ settle for

現在可以自信地說出來了嗎？

223

我真的很想買這款智慧型手機。可以便宜一點嗎？

I really want to buy this smartphone.

不行啊，真不好意思。我也得養家糊口啊。

No, I'm sorry. I have to make a living, you know.

224

最多能便宜多少？我是這裡的老顧客了。

I'm your regular, remember?

好。75美元。不能再便宜了。

Okay. 75 dollars. Nothing lower.

225

您想要多少錢？

How much do you have in mind?

50美元我就買。

226

您的芒果。

Here are your mangos.

等一下，才十個？哎呀，再送我幾個吧。

Wait, only ten? Come on.

227

這就是最低價格了。真不好意思。

This is as low as I can go. I'm sorry.

再便宜一點！再便宜3美元吧。

Just a little more!

228

給您240美元吧。這是我能給的最低價格了。

I can give it to you for 240 dollars. This is my best offer.

不是吧。就200美元吧。

I don't think so.

Answer **223** Can you give me a discount? 可以便宜一點嗎？ **224** What's your best price? 最多能便宜多少？ **225** I'll take it for $50. 50美元我就買。 **226** Throw in a few more. 再送我幾個吧。 **227** Can I just get three dollars off? 再便宜3美元吧。 **228** Let's settle for 200 dollars. 就200美元吧。

Quick
Test 04

這些句子用英語怎麼說？

規定時間 1 min

---

229 選擇要買的東西時

就買這個吧。

ⓐ I'll take it.
ⓑ I'll loan it.
ⓒ I'll toss it.

---

230 詢問自己要支付的價格時

要給您多少錢？

ⓐ How much do I lend you?
ⓑ How much do I owe you?
ⓒ How much do I charge you?

---

231 用信用卡結算時

我用信用卡。

ⓐ I'll charge it.
ⓑ I'll push it.
ⓒ I'll lay it.

---

232 用現金結算時

我用現金。

ⓐ I'm laying down my coins.
ⓑ The payment is in bills.
ⓒ I'll pay in cash.

---

233 結帳後，要發票時

把發票給我。

ⓐ I'd like a document.
ⓑ I'd like a card.
ⓒ I'd like a receipt.

---

234 零錢不夠時

我零錢不夠。

ⓐ My money is small.
ⓑ I'm short on change.
ⓒ I'm broke.

DAY 8 ▼ 詢問價格及算帳

Answer **229** ⓐ 買（東西）▶ take **230** ⓑ〔直譯〕我欠你多少錢？（owe欠帳） **231** ⓐ 用信用卡結帳 ▶ charge **232** ⓒ 用現金結帳 ▶ pay in cash **233** ⓒ 發票 ▶ receipt **234** ⓑ 硬幣，零錢 ▶ change；……不夠 ▶ short on

229

😊 先生，還有其他種類的項鍊。

We have another line of necklaces, sir.

😊 不，不用，我喜歡這條。就買這個吧。

No, no. I like this one.

230

😊 先生，這就是了。

This is it, sir.

😊 啊，這麼快？要給您多少錢？

Oh, already?

231

😊 先生，您要怎麼付款？

How would you like to pay, sir?

😊 我看看，啊，我用信用卡。

Let's see. Ah,

232

😊 我用現金。我忘記帶信用卡了。

　　　　　　　　I forgot to bring my credit card.

😊 啊，這樣的話，我可以幫您打九五折。

Ah, in that case, I can give you a 5% discount.

233

😊 啊，請給我發票。

Wait.

😊 哎呦，我翻翻垃圾桶。

Oops, let me look for it in the trash can.

234

😊 我零錢不夠。能幫我把這1美元的紙幣換成硬幣嗎？

　　　　　　　　Can you break this one dollar bill for me?

😊 好，沒問題。

Sure, no problem.

Quick Test 05 — 這些句子用英語怎麼說？

235 要求進行禮品包裝時

幫我包成禮物包裝吧。

ⓐ I would like it presently.

ⓑ I would like it gift-wrapped.

ⓒ I would like it package-free.

236 在飯店裡，把剩下的飯菜打包帶走時

幫我把剩下的菜打包。

ⓐ Give me your leftover food.

ⓑ Put this food with the rest.

ⓒ I'd like a doggy bag.

237 購買了商品，需要換貨時

幫我換一下。

ⓐ I'd like to change this.

ⓑ I'd like to mail this.

ⓒ I'd like to exchange this.

238 購買了商品，需要退貨時

我要退貨。

ⓐ I'd like a refund.

ⓑ I'd like to be returned.

ⓒ I'd like my money refurbished.

239 想要換貨，但是包裝已經打開了時

盒子我已經打開了。

ⓐ I've already ripped the label.

ⓑ I've already opened the box.

ⓒ I've already crushed the casing.

240 不滿意可無理由退貨

無理由退貨保證。

ⓐ It comes with a money-back guarantee.

ⓑ There is an unlimited supply.

ⓒ The guarantee can be returned.

Answer **235** ⓑ 做禮物包裝 ▶ gift-wrap **236** ⓒ （在飯店裡）打包剩下食物的袋子 ▶ doggy bag *cf*）剩下的食物 ▶ leftover **237** ⓒ 換 ▶ exchange **238** ⓐ 退貨 ▶ refund **239** ⓑ **240** ⓐ 與……一起提供 ▶ come with ： 退貨保證 ▶ money-back guarantee

Quick Practice

現在可以自信地說出來了嗎？ 規定時間 1 min

235

🎩 幫我包成禮物包裝吧。

＿＿＿＿＿＿＿＿＿＿＿＿＿＿，
please.

👩 那您要多付3美元，可以嗎？
That will cost you 3 dollars more. Is that okay?

236

🧑 不好意思，服務生。幫我把剩下的菜打包，謝謝。
Excuse me, waiter?
＿＿＿＿＿＿＿＿＿＿＿＿, please.

😊 好的。嗯？您幾乎沒有吃啊。
Sure. Oh? You've hardly touched it.

237

🧑 幫我換一下。這個太小了。

＿＿＿＿＿＿＿＿＿＿＿
It's too small for me.

😊 好的。您有帶發票嗎？
Sure thing. Did you bring your receipt?

238

🧑 我要退貨。發票不見了。
＿＿＿＿＿＿＿＿＿＿＿ The receipt is lost.

👩 哦，這樣的話，就不太容易了。
Ooh, it's going to be tricky, then.

tricky 複雜的，不容易的

239

👩 都原封不動吧？
Is everything intact?

🎩 嗯，但盒子我已經打開了。
Yes, but ＿＿＿＿＿＿＿＿＿＿

intact （原封未動）完整的

240

😎 為什麼要推薦我這個牌子的手錶呢？
Why do you recommend buying this brand of watch?

🧑 有20年的無理由退貨保證。
＿＿＿＿＿＿＿＿＿＿＿
for 20 years.

Answer **235** I would like it gift-wrapped. 幫我包成禮物包裝吧。 **236** I'd like a doggy bag 幫我把剩下的菜打包。 **237** I'd like to exchange this. 幫我換一下。 **238** I'd like a refund. 我要退貨。 **239** I've already opened the box. 盒子我已經打開了。 **240** It comes with a money-back guarantee 無理由退貨保證。

Day 8 Review 在忘記以前複習一遍，怎麼樣？	規定時間 5 min
聽著MP3跟讀	看著中文說英語

同時為幾件商品結帳時 **How much in total?**	一共多少錢？
想要知道打折以前的價格時 **What's the regular price?**	定價是多少錢？
覺得一次付清壓力比較大時 **I'm going to pay in installments.**	我要分期付款。
相對於商品的品質，價格特別貴時 **This is a rip-off!**	這不是坑人嗎？
確認商品是否打折時 **Meat is on sale today.**	肉今天打折。
告訴對方打折的幅度時 **You can get 30% off.**	可以打七折。
以比定價便宜的價格購買商品時 **I got it for a bargain.**	我是打折價買的。
買一送一活動 **It's buy one, get one free.**	買一送一。
想要買，但是價格太貴時 **Can you give me a discount?**	可以便宜一點嗎？
詢問最多能便宜多少時 **What's your best price?**	最多能便宜多少？

DAY 8　▼ 詢問價格及算帳

📖 看著中文說英文時，用書籤擋住這個部分。

說出自己希望的價格時 **I'll take it for $50.**	50美元我就買。
想要免費的贈品時 **Throw in a few more.**	再送我幾個吧。
詢問自己要支付的價格時 **How much do I owe you?**	我要給您多少錢？
用信用卡結算時 **I'll charge it.**	我用信用卡。
用現金結算時 **I'll pay in cash.**	我用現金。
零錢不夠時 **I'm short on change.**	我零錢不夠。
要求進行禮品包裝時 **I would like it gift-wrapped.**	幫我包成禮物包裝吧。
在飯店裡，把剩下的飯菜打包帶走時 **I'd like a doggy bag.**	幫我把剩下的菜打包。
購買了商品，需要換貨時 **I'd like to exchange this.**	幫我換一下。
購買了商品，需要退貨時 **I'd like a refund.**	我要退貨。

已經學會的句型
240個/600個

看著中文說英文時，用書籤擋住這個部分。

DAY 9

談論天氣&時間

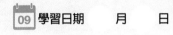

09 學習日期 ⃞ 月 ⃞ 日

學習時間

聽例句

空氣乾燥的時候、沙塵暴嚴重的時候,或是覺得時間過得很慢的時候,
你會用英語說有關天氣和時間的句子嗎?來檢測一下吧。

Quick Test 01

這些句子用英語怎麼說？

規定時間 1 min

241 天空沒有雲彩，非常晴朗的時候

今天天氣很晴朗。

ⓐ The weather is white today.
ⓑ It's clear today.
ⓒ Today is a great day.

242 天氣很暖和的時候

天氣真暖和。

ⓐ The weather is soft.
ⓑ The weather is mild.
ⓒ The weather is like cotton.

243 開始下雨的時候

開始下雨了。

ⓐ A dew drop is starting.
ⓑ I can see the sky tears dropping.
ⓒ It's beginning to sprinkle.

244 雨反覆下下停停的時候

雨下得斷斷續續的。

ⓐ It's raining on and off.
ⓑ It's raining in and out.
ⓒ It's raining here and there.

245 雨好像不會下很久時

這只是陣雨。

ⓐ It's only a passing shower.
ⓑ The rain is only short.
ⓒ There goes the visiting rain.

246 風越來越小時

風變小了。

ⓐ The wind has gone away.
ⓑ The wind has fallen asleep.
ⓒ The wind has died down.

DAY 9

▼ 談論天氣&時間

Answer **241** ⓑ 天氣晴朗 ▶ clear **242** ⓑ （天氣）溫暖，溫和 ▶ mild **243** ⓒ 下小雨 ▶ sprinkle **244** ⓐ 時斷時續，有時候 ▶ on and off **245** ⓐ 陣雨 ▶ passing shower **246** ⓒ 變小了，變弱了 ▶ die down

Quick Practice 現在可以自信地說出來了嗎？ 規定時間 1 min

241

😀 天氣怎麼樣？
What's the weather like?

😎 今天天氣很晴朗。去野餐，怎麼樣？
_____ How about a picnic?

242

😀 天氣真暖和，我真不應該穿這件毛衣。
_____ I shouldn't have worn this sweater.

😎 需要我幫你拿著嗎？
Do you want me to carry it for you?

243

😀 哎呦！開始下雨了。
Oh, no!

😎 那就待在車裡聽音樂吧。
Then, let's just stay in the car and listen to some music.

244

😀 雨下得斷斷續續的。我們還是回家吧？
Should we head home?

😎 好，等雨停了，我們就回家。
Yeah, let's go back while it has stopped raining.

245

😎 噢，不！我出來的時候沒關窗戶。
Oh, no! I left my window open at home.

😀 這只是陣雨。所以沒事的。
_____ So it should be okay.

246

😀 呼！風終於變小了。
Phew! finally.

😎 哈哈！看看你的頭髮。太好笑了！
Ha ha! Look at your hair. It's hilarious!

hilarious 非常可笑的

Answer **241** It's clear today. 今天天氣很晴朗。 **242** The weather is mild. 天氣真暖和。 **243** It's beginning to sprinkle. 開始下雨了。 **244** It's raining on and off. 雨下得斷斷續續的。 **245** It's only a passing shower. 這是陣雨。 **246** The wind has died down 風變小了。

Quick
Test 02

這些句子用英語怎麼說？

規定時間 1 min

---

247 在下傾盆大雨時

在下傾盆大雨。

ⓐ It's raining cats and dogs.

ⓑ The sky is falling down.

ⓒ The rain is like a waterfall.

---

248 起大霧時

霧太大了。

ⓐ The fog is scary.

ⓑ The fog is thick.

ⓒ The fog is crafty.

---

249 颱風就要來了時

颱風要來了。

ⓐ A typhoon is reserved.

ⓑ There's a typhoon coming.

ⓒ Get ready for a windy reception.

---

250 非常乾燥時

空氣太乾燥了。

ⓐ The air is humid.

ⓑ The air is dry.

ⓒ The air is thirsty.

---

251 冷風從縫隙裡鑽到室內時

冷風吹進來了。

ⓐ There's a draft.

ⓑ There's a breeze.

ⓒ There's a blizzard.

---

252 風、雨、雪等越來越大時

天氣越來越不好了。

ⓐ There's a hole in the weather.

ⓑ The climate is going strong.

ⓒ The weather is getting worse.

DAY 9

▼ 談論天氣&時間

Answer **247** ⓐ 將雨傾瀉下來的樣子比喻成狗和貓打作一團的樣子 **248** ⓑ （霧）很重 ▶ thick **249** ⓑ 颱風 ▶ typhoon **250** ⓑ 乾燥的 ▶ dry **251** ⓐ （吹進房間裡的一縷）冷風，外面的風 ▶ draft **252** ⓒ 更不好了 ▶ get worse

Quick Practice

現在可以自信地說出來了嗎？

規定時間 1 min

247

😄 哇！在下傾盆大雨。
Wow! _____

😊 而且我們在咖啡店裡。太浪漫了！
And we are inside a cafe. How romantic!

248

😃 霧太大了。開車的話，太危險了。
_____ Driving will be dangerous.

😊 哎呀，我們要趕不上婚禮了。
Oh, no. We'll be late for the wedding.

249

🎩 你有看到新聞嗎？颱風要來了。
Did you hear the news? _____

😊 我們還是像去年一樣，到地下室待著吧。
Let's stay inside the basement like last year.

250

😃 空氣太乾燥了。哎呀，我戴著隱形眼鏡呢。
_____ Uh-oh, I wear contact lenses.

😊 你為什麼不戴眼鏡呢？
Why don't you just wear your glasses instead?

251

😃 冷風吹進來了。怎麼回事呢？
_____ Why is that?

😊 這房子就是這麼蓋的。
It's the way this house was built.

252

😎 別打高爾夫球了。天氣越來越不好了。
Let's stop playing golf. _____

🎩 不，天氣反而好像在幫我呢。
No, no. I think the weather is rather helping me.

Answer **247** It's raining cats and dogs. 在下傾盆大雨。 **248** The fog is thick. 霧太大了。 **249** There's a typhoon coming. 颱風要來了。 **250** The air is dry. 空氣太乾燥了。 **251** There's a draft. 冷風吹進來了。 **252** The weather is getting worse. 天氣越來越不好了。

Quick
Test 03
這些句子用英語怎麼說？

規定時間 1 min

---

253 天氣正好適合既定的活動時

天氣正合適。

ⓐ The weather is perfect.

ⓑ The weather is clapping its hands.

ⓒ The weather is a hundred percent.

---

254 一天之內天氣變動很大時

天氣真是變化無常啊！

ⓐ What crazy weather!

ⓑ What mixed weather!

ⓒ What epic weather!

---

255 對冷特別敏感的體質

我特別怕冷。

ⓐ I get chilled easily.

ⓑ The weather scares me.

ⓒ I shiver with cold.

---

256 對熱特別敏感，容易出汗的體質

我特別會出汗。

ⓐ I tingle a lot.

ⓑ I puke a lot.

ⓒ I sweat a lot.

---

257 烏雲逐漸散去的時候

天氣要變好了。

ⓐ The climate will agree soon.

ⓑ The weather's going to improve.

ⓒ The other side of the weather is coming.

---

258 在空氣不流通的密閉空間裡時

這裡太悶了。

ⓐ It's bulky in here.

ⓑ It's dark in here.

ⓒ It's stuffy in here.

DAY 9

▼ 談論天氣&時間

Answer **253** ⓐ（天氣）正好 ▶ perfect　**254** ⓑ（最好的和最壞的）混合在一起 ▶ mixed　**255** ⓐ 變冷，怕冷 ▶ get chilled　**256** ⓒ 汗，出汗 ▶ sweat　**257** ⓑ（天氣）變好 ▶ improve　**258** ⓒ 不通氣的 ▶ stuffy

253

😊 去露營吧，天氣正適合。我們快去準備吧。

_____ for camping. Let's get our things ready.

😆 啊，可是我們的露營車壞了。

Oh, but our camping car is broken.

254

🎩 天氣真是變化無常啊！出去就是受罪。

_____ We'd be fools to go out.

😊 好，我們就待在家吧。來杯熱咖啡，怎麼樣？

Yeah, let's stay home. How about a cup of hot coffee?

255

😮 什麼？你穿了三件毛衣？

What? You're wearing three sweaters?

😊 我很怕冷。話說回來，我這樣看起來會很胖嗎？

_____ By the way, do I look fat?

256

🤓 我們進桑拿房才一分鐘！

We've only been inside the sauna for a minute!

🎩 嗯，我知道。我很會出汗。

Yeah, I know.

257

😮 天哪，我明天還要去現場實習呢。

Man, I have field trip tomorrow.

😊 好消息。明天天氣要變好了。

Good news. _____ tomorrow.

258

😊 這裡太悶了。我能把窗戶打開嗎？

_____ Can I open the window?

😊 不行吧。外面的人不喜歡煙味。

I'm sorry. The people outside don't like cigarette smoke.

Quick Test 04

這些句子用英語怎麼說？

規定時間 1 min

---

259 精神非常集中，連時間怎麼過的都不知道

都這時候了？

ⓐ What time is it?
ⓑ Is it my time?
ⓒ Is that the time?

260 因為太無聊，感覺時間過得非常慢時

時間過得太慢了。

ⓐ Time is heaving.
ⓑ Time is crawling.
ⓒ Time is shy.

---

261 手錶不快也不慢時

我的手錶很準。

ⓐ My watch keeps good time.
ⓑ My watch makes good time.
ⓒ My watch ties good time.

262 鐘錶快或者慢時

那個布穀鐘不準。

ⓐ That clock is a cuckoo.
ⓑ Don't believe that cuckoo clock.
ⓒ That cuckoo clock keeps bad time.

---

263 手錶快的時候

那支手錶快3分鐘。

ⓐ That clock is three minutes forward.
ⓑ That clock is three minutes fast.
ⓒ That clock is three minutes in a hurry.

264 看錯或是記錯了見面時間時

我弄錯時間了。

ⓐ I timed it wrong.
ⓑ I mistook the time.
ⓒ The time fooled me.

DAY 9
▼ 談論天氣&時間

Answer **259** ⓒ 〔直譯〕那是現在的時間嗎？ **260** ⓑ 〔直譯〕時間在爬著走。（crawl爬） **261** ⓐ （鐘錶）準 ▶ keep good time **262** ⓒ （鐘錶）不準 ▶ keep bad time **263** ⓑ （鐘錶）快……分鐘 ▶ be...minute fast **264** ⓑ 弄錯了，看錯了 ▶ mistake (mistake-mistook-mistaken)

259

😊 已經這時候了？

😎 嚇了一跳吧？打了撲克牌一下就到這時候了。
Surprised? It happens when you're playing poker.

260

😊 時間過得太慢了。我最討厭等轉接班機了。
_____ I hate waiting for connecting flights.

😊 用我的蘋果手機一起看電影吧。
Let's watch a movie together on my iPhone.

261

😊 我確定。我的手錶很準。
I'm positive.

😊 那麼這意味著我面試遲到了。
That means I'm late for my job interview.

262

😊 那個布穀鐘不準。

🎩 哦，今天布穀先生有點懶。
Oh, Mr. Cuckoo is a bit lazy today.

263

😊 好，我們進去吧。
Okay, let's go in.

🎩 等一下！時間還沒到。那支手錶快3分鐘。他說要4點準時進去。
Wait! Not yet. _____ He told us to enter exactly at four o'clock.

264

😎 你怎麼遲到了？
Why are you late?

😊 我弄錯時間了。

Answer **259** Is that the time? 已經這時候了？ **260** Time is crawling. 時間過得太慢了。 **261** My watch keeps good time. 我的手錶很準。 **262** That cuckoo clock keeps bad time. 那個布穀鐘不準。 **263** That clock is three minutes fast. 那支手錶快3分鐘。 **264** I mistook the time. 我弄錯時間了。

Quick
Test 05

這些句子用英語怎麼說？

規定時間 1 min

---

265 有禮貌地詢問時間時

請問現在幾點了？

ⓐ Can I know the watch?

ⓑ Do you have the time?

ⓒ May I have the clock?

---

266 正好是整點時

現在12點整。

ⓐ It's twelve o'clock sharp.

ⓑ It's twelve o'clock at the top.

ⓒ It's twelve o'clock largely.

---

267 整點過了30分鐘時

現在10點半了。

ⓐ It's half missed ten.

ⓑ It's half past ten.

ⓒ It's half-eaten ten.

---

268 整點過了1-2分鐘時

剛過6點。

ⓐ It's just past six.

ⓑ The time is hardly six.

ⓒ The watch passed six definitely.

---

269 更道地地說出7點50分

差十分鐘就八點了。

ⓐ It's ten on eight.

ⓑ It's ten for eight.

ⓒ It's ten to eight.

---

270 更道地地說出4點45分

差一刻5點。

ⓐ The time is before five fifteen.

ⓑ It's pointing at five before fifteen.

ⓒ It's quarter to five.

DAY 9

▼ 談論天氣&時間

Answer **265** ⓑ 是比What time is it now?更有禮貌地向不認識的人詢問時間的表達方式　**266** ⓐ 整點 ▶ sharp　**267** ⓑ 表達整點過了幾分鐘 ▶ past　**268** ⓐ 剛過了 ▶ just past　**269** ⓒ 表達差幾分鐘到整點 ▶ to　**270** ⓒ 15分鐘 ▶ quarter（60分的1/4（quarter）的意思）

現在可以自信地說出來了嗎？

265

😀 請問現在幾點了？

🎩 好，我掛了電話就告訴您。
Yes, let me just finish my phone call.

266

😀 現在12點整。太驚人了，它太準了。
Amazing, it keeps perfect time.

👧 就是啊，這是有200年歷史的錶。
Yeah, and it's two hundred years old.

267

😀 現在10點半了。他還不來。
He's not coming.

😀 別急，肯定是因為塞車。
Let's be patient. It must be the traffic.

268

😀 我肯定是打瞌睡了。現在幾點了？
I must have dozed off. What time is it now?

😀 剛過6點。你作業都寫完了？
Did you finish your homework?

269

😀 再十分鐘就8點了。你準備好了嗎？
Are you ready?

😀 你說現在7點50了？
You mean it's seven fifty?

270

👧 快起來！再一刻就5點了。
Wake up!

😀 再睡15分鐘。我5點起床。
15 more minutes. I'll wake up at 5 o'clock.

Answer **265** Do you have the time? 請問現在幾點了？ **266** It's twelve o'clock sharp. 現在12點整。 **267** It's half past ten. 現在10點半了。 **268** It's just past six. 剛過6點。 **269** It's ten to eight. 再十分鐘8點了。 **270** It's quarter to five. 再一刻5點了。

Day 9 Review	在忘記以前複習一遍，怎麼樣？	規定時間 5 min

聽著MP3跟讀	看著中文說英語
天氣暖和的時候 **The weather is mild.**	天氣真暖和。
開始下雨的時候 **It's beginning to sprinkle.**	開始下雨了。
雨反覆下下停停的時候 **It's raining on and off.**	雨下得斷斷續續的。
風越還越小時 **The wind has died down.**	風小了。
下傾盆大雨時 **It's raining cats and dogs.**	在下傾盆大雨。
起大霧時 **The fog is thick.**	霧太大了。
颱風就要來了時 **There's a typhoon coming.**	颱風要來了。
風、雨、雪等越來越大時 **The weather is getting worse.**	天氣越來越不好了。
天氣正好適合既定的活動時 **The weather is perfect.**	天氣正合適。
對冷特別敏感的體質 **I get chilled easily.**	我特別怕冷。

DAY 9 ▼ 談論天氣&時間

看著中文說英文時，用書籤擋住這個部分。

烏雲逐漸散去的時候 **The weather's going to improve.**	天氣要變好了。
在空氣不流通的密閉空間裡時 **It's stuffy in here.**	這裡太悶了。
精神非常集中，連時間怎麼過的都不知道 **Is that the time?**	都這時候了？
因為太無聊，感覺時間過得非常慢時 **Time is crawling.**	時間過得太慢了。
手錶不快也不慢時 **My watch keeps good time.**	我的手錶很準。
看錯了表或是記錯了見面時間時 **I mistook the time.**	我弄錯時間了。
有禮貌地詢問時間時 **Do you have the time?**	請問現在幾點了？
正好是整點時 **It's twelve o'clock sharp.**	現在12點整。
整點過了30分鐘時 **It's half past ten.**	現在10點半了。
整點過了1~2分鐘時 **It's just past six.**	剛過6點。

已經學會的句型
270個/600個

📖 看著中文說英文時，用書籤擋住這個部分。

142

DAY **10**

談論季節和日期

聽例句

經歷春寒時、踩著落葉感受秋天時，或是享受假期時，
你會用英語說有關季節和日期的句子嗎？來檢測一下吧。

這些句子用英語怎麼說？　規定時間 1 min

271 植物發芽，天氣變暖和時

春天來了。

ⓐ The spring has sprung.
ⓑ I can see the spring.
ⓒ It's a spring beginning.

272 一到春天就精神不佳的人

我得了春倦症。

ⓐ I have spring mind.
ⓑ I have spring heart.
ⓒ I have spring fever.

273 在春天馬上就要來臨時，天氣再次變冷

春寒冷得不得了啊。

ⓐ The flower winter is angry.
ⓑ We're in the middle of a cold snap.
ⓒ It's the full swing of a crazy spring cold.

274 天氣開始轉暖時

天氣轉暖了。

ⓐ The weather has thawed.
ⓑ The weather has cracked.
ⓒ The weather has a fireplace.

275 天氣轉暖，花都開了時

真是春意盎然啊。

ⓐ I can smell the spring air.
ⓑ Spring is in the air.
ⓒ There's a full spring coming.

276 在春天不受歡迎的客人

發布了沙塵暴預警。

ⓐ There's a yellow desert warning.
ⓑ There's a yellow dirt warning.
ⓒ There's a yellow dust warning.

DAY 10

▼ 談論季節和日期

Answer **271** ⓐ a sprung是spring（（嫩芽從土裡）鑽出來）的過去分詞，與spring（春天）押韻 **272** ⓒ 初春的疲乏，憂鬱症 ▶ spring fever **273** ⓑ 春寒 ▶ cold snap **274** ⓐ 天氣轉暖，天氣變暖和 ▶ thaw **275** ⓑ（某種）氣氛在空中彌漫 ▶ in the air **276** ⓒ 沙塵暴預警 ▶ yellow dust warning（dust灰塵）

271

哇！春天來了。
Yahoo!

嗯，我都能聞到春天的味道。
Yes, I can smell it!

272

我得了春倦症。所以我才打了電話給你。
That's why I called you.

我們去兜風吧。一個小時之內我去接你。
Let's go for a drive. I'll pick you up in an hour.

273

春寒冷得不得了了啊。小心點，別感冒了。

Be careful. You'll catch a cold.

我已經感冒了。
I already have.

274

太好了。天氣轉暖了。
Thank goodness.

呼，終於可以和這些笨重的衣服說再見了。
Phew, it's goodbye to these cumbersome clothes!

275

真是春意盎然啊。去散步吧？

Want to go for a walk?

好主意！
What a great idea!

276

今天發布了沙塵暴預警。

today.

不會吧！我戴了隱形眼鏡。
Oh, no! I'm wearing contact lenses.

go for a walk 去散步

Answer **271** The spring has sprung. 春天來了。 **272** I have spring fever. 我得了春倦症。 **273** We're in the middle of a cold snap. 春寒冷得不得了了啊。 **274** The weather has thawed. 天氣轉暖了。 **275** Spring is in the air. 真是春意盎然啊。 **276** There's a yellow dust warning 發布了沙塵暴預警。

10_2.mp3

Quick Test 02　這些句子用英語怎麼說？

規定時間 1 min

---

277 一直持續的酷熱天氣

簡直像蒸籠一樣熱。

ⓐ Summer is on fire.
ⓑ I'm boiling inside a stove.
ⓒ It's scorching hot.

---

278 熱得難以忍受時

熱得受不了了。

ⓐ The heat is underscored.
ⓑ The heat is unbearable.
ⓒ The heat is unthinkable.

---

279 熱得睡不著覺時

這是熱帶夜現象。

ⓐ There's a tropical night phenomenon.
ⓑ What a Hawaiian fever phenomenon.
ⓒ This is a hot phenomenon.

---

280 因為酷熱暴曬而口乾舌燥時

我要渴死了。

ⓐ I'm dying of thirst.
ⓑ My throat is burning.
ⓒ It's the lack of water.

---

281 因為濕氣重而身上汗水淋漓的時候

太悶熱了。

ⓐ It's drowsy.
ⓑ It's sluggish.
ⓒ It's muggy.

---

282 因為濕度太高而發霉時

有一股發霉的味道。

ⓐ It smells moldy.
ⓑ It smells spunky.
ⓒ It smells gory.

DAY 10　▼ 談論季節和日期

Answer **277** ⓒ 像所有東西都要著火般的熱 ▶ scorching hot **278** ⓑ 難以忍受，堅持不住 ▶ unbearable （bear 忍受） **279** ⓐ 熱帶夜 ▶ tropical night（tropical 熱帶的）；現象 ▶ phenomenon **280** ⓐ 口渴 ▶ thirst **281** ⓒ 悶熱 ▶ muggy cf）潮濕的 ▶ humid **282** ⓐ 發霉 ▶ moldy

147

277

天氣簡直像蒸籠一樣熱。我急需清涼的啤酒。

_____ I badly need a cold beer.

我們進去吧。我冰箱裡有幾瓶啤酒。

Let's go inside. I have some in the fridge.

278

我熱得受不了了。我好像要暈倒了。

_____ I feel like fainting.

天哪！你可能中暑了。

Oh, dear! You might have heatstroke.

faint 暈倒 heatstroke 中暑

279

這是熱帶夜現象。我睡不著。

_____ I can't sleep.

我們到小溪邊躺著吧？那裡應該很涼快。

Should we go and lie by the brook? It'll be cool.

brook 小溪

280

我快渴死了。你有零錢嗎？

_____ Do you have change?

我有好多零錢。可是自動販賣機在哪裡？

I have plenty. But where's the vending machine?

vending machine 自動販賣機

281

我討厭這樣的天氣。太悶熱了。

I hate this kind of weather.

那我們別打網球了。

Should we stop playing tennis, then?

282

你來聞聞。有一股發霉的味道。

Come here and smell this.

天哪！把那件皮外套送到洗衣店去吧。

Oh, no! Let's take that leather jacket to the dry cleaners.

Answer **277** It's scorching hot. 簡直像蒸籠一樣熱。 **278** The heat is unbearable. 熱得受不了了。 **279** There's a tropical night phenomenon. 這是熱帶夜現象啊。 **280** I'm dying of thirst. 我要渴死了。 **281** It's muggy. 太悶熱了。 **282** It smells moldy. 有一股發霉的味道。

Quick Test 03　這些句子用英語怎麼說？

規定時間 1 min

10_3.mp3

283 楓葉開始變紅時

秋天馬上就要來了。

ⓐ Fall is just around the corner.
ⓑ Autumn is in the horizon.
ⓒ You can see autumn hiding.

284 道路兩旁的樹開始變顏色時

樹葉開始變黃了。

ⓐ The leaves are sucking in color.
ⓑ The leaves are changing color.
ⓒ The leaves are jumping color.

285 提議去看落葉時

我們去看落葉吧。

ⓐ Let's go to a leaf show.
ⓑ Let's go on a leaf picnic.
ⓒ Let's go leaf peeping.

286 地上鋪著厚厚的落葉時

看那裡堆滿了落葉。

ⓐ Take a look at the raked leaves.
ⓑ There are the bodies of dead leaves.
ⓒ Look at the piles of fallen leaves.

287 到了秋天，開始傷感時

我到了秋天就變得容易感傷。

ⓐ I get weather-beaten in autumn.
ⓑ I get sentenced in autumn.
ⓒ I get sentimental in autumn.

288 適合讀書的季節

秋天是讀書的季節。

ⓐ Autumn should read a book.
ⓑ Autumn is the perfect season for reading.
ⓒ People love reading in fall.

DAY 10 ▼ 談論季節和日期

Answer **283** ⓐ 馬上就到了，臨近的 ▶ just around the corner **284** ⓑ 變顏色 ▶ change color **285** ⓒ 觀賞落葉 ▶ leaf peeping （peep偷看，窺視） **286** ⓒ 落葉 ▶ fallen leaves；（堆積的）堆 ▶ pile **287** ⓒ 感傷 ▶ get sentimental **288** ⓑ

Quick Practice

現在可以自信地說出來了嗎？

規定時間 1 min

283

😊 秋天馬上就要來了。我們要做些什麼嗎？

What should we do?

😀 搭火車去旅行，怎麼樣？

How about a train trip?

284

😊 看。樹葉開始變黃了。

Look at that.

🎩 大自然在施展魔法啊。

It's the magic of Mother Nature.

Mother Nature 大自然

285

😊 我們去看落葉吧。現在是最好的時候。

It's the perfect time.

😀 好。我來準備午餐，你開車。

Okay. I'll pack lunch, and you do the driving.

286

😎 那裡堆滿了落葉。我們跳進去，怎麼樣？

Should we jump into one?

😊 不要，你把落葉堆到一起吧。

No, I want you to rake the leaves.

rake 用耙子聚攏

287

😊 你怎麼還看著窗外！外面有什麼？

You're still looking out the window! What's out there?

🎩 啊，沒有……我到了秋天就變得容易感傷。

Oh, it's just...

288

😊 你為什麼要帶我去書店啊？

Why are you taking me to the bookstore?

😊 秋天是讀書的季節。

Answer **283** Fall is just around the corner. 秋天馬上就要來了。 **284** The leaves are changing color. 樹葉開始黃了。 **285** Let's go leaf peeping. 我們去看落葉吧。 **286** Look at the piles of fallen leaves. 那裡堆滿了落葉。 **287** I get sentimental in autumn. 我到了秋天就變得容易感傷。 **288** Autumn is the perfect season for reading. 秋天是讀書的季節。

Quick Test 04

這些句子用英語怎麼說？

規定時間 1 min

---

289 大雪紛紛揚揚地飄落時

鵝毛大雪紛紛飄落。

- ⓐ It's snowing snow cannons.
- ⓑ It's snowing cats and dogs.
- ⓒ It's snowing big, fat snowflakes.

---

290 白雪覆蓋的一片銀白的世界

整個世界都是銀白色的。

- ⓐ The world is snow.
- ⓑ It's a white world.
- ⓒ Everything is covered in snow.

---

291 早上一看，外面是一片銀白的世界

一定下了整夜的雪吧。

- ⓐ Snow fell twenty four hours.
- ⓑ It must have snowed all night long.
- ⓒ There must have been a snow owl.

---

292 在屋簷下發現冰柱時

有冰柱。

- ⓐ There are ice-sticks.
- ⓑ There are icicles.
- ⓒ There are ice-fangs.

---

293 走路的時候，在冰上滑倒時

我在冰上滑倒了。

- ⓐ I slipped on the ice.
- ⓑ The ice hit me.
- ⓒ I kissed the ice.

---

294 因為天氣寒冷，手腳都凍了時

他被凍傷了。

- ⓐ He's got snowman's foot.
- ⓑ He's got frostbite.
- ⓒ He's got the winter trap.

Answer **289** ⓒ 雪花 ▸ snowflake **290** ⓒ 被……覆蓋 ▸ be covered in *cf*）暴風雪 ▸ blizzard **291** ⓑ 一整夜 ▸ all night long：一定……了吧（對過去非常肯定的推測）▸ must have + p.p **292** ⓑ 冰柱 ▸ icicle **293** ⓐ 滑倒 ▸ slip **294** ⓑ 凍傷 ▸ frostbite

289

看！鵝毛大雪紛紛飄落。
Look!

我們帶你的狗出去吧。它肯定會很開心。
Let's take your dog outside.
She'll love it.

290

哇！整個世界都是銀白色的。咦？你為什麼跪著？
Wow!
Huh? Why are you on your knees?

你願意嫁給我嗎？
Will you marry me?

291

約翰，來窗戶這邊！你能看到那裡嗎？
John, come to the window! Do you see that?

哇！一定下了整夜的雪吧。
Wow!

292

有冰柱。我來嚐嚐吧？
                    Should I taste one?

不。你的舌頭可能會被黏住。
Don't. Your tongue could get stuck.

293

你怎麼打石膏了？
What's with the plaster cast?

昨天我在冰上滑倒了。

yesterday.

294

他被凍傷了。腳趾頭……
                    His toe...

要截肢？
Has to come off?

plaster cast 打石膏

Answer **289** It's snowing big, fat snowflakes. 鵝毛大雪紛紛飄落。 **290** Everything is covered in snow. 整個世界都是銀白色的。 **291** It must have snowed all night long. 一定是下了整夜的雪吧。 **292** There are icicles. 有冰柱。 **293** I slipped on the ice 我在冰上滑倒了。 **294** He's got frostbite. 他被凍傷了。

295 將星期幾和日期進行對照計算時

下週日是幾號？

ⓐ What day is next Sunday?

ⓑ What date is next Sunday?

ⓒ What weekday is next Sunday?

296 查看特定的節日是今年的幾月幾號時

今年的中秋節是9月27號。

ⓐ Chuseok stays on Sep 27 this year.

ⓑ Chuseok lies on Sep 27 this year.

ⓒ Chuseok falls on Sep 27 this year.

297 表達從今天開始的兩天之後

是後天。

ⓐ It's the day after tomorrow.

ⓑ It's tomorrow's tomorrow.

ⓒ It's the day next to tomorrow.

298 說明制憲節、國慶日等的時候

今天是韓國的國慶日。

ⓐ Today is a playing day in Korea.

ⓑ Today is a national holiday in Korea.

ⓒ Today is a resting day for Korea.

299 法定的公休日

光復節是法定公休日。

ⓐ National New Day is a legal holiday.

ⓑ National Freedom Day is a legal holiday.

ⓒ National Liberation Day is a legal holiday.

300 公休日趕上週末成為一個小長假時

是小長假。

ⓐ It's a rainbow weekend.

ⓑ It's a long weekend.

ⓒ It's a skybridge weekend.

Answer **295** ⓑ 日期 ▶ date *cf*）星期 ▶ day **296** ⓒ（某個日子）正好是…… ▶ fall on *cf*）感恩節 ▶ Thanksgiving Day **297** ⓐ 後天 ▶ the day after tomorrow *cf*）大後天 ▶ two days after tomorrow **298** ⓑ 國慶日 ▶ national holiday **299** ⓒ 光復節 ▶ National Liberation Day：法定公休日 ▶ legal holiday **300** ⓑ 週末 ▶ weekend

DAY 10 ▼ 談論季節和日期

295

😊 下週日是幾號？

🎩 25號。怎麼了？你不能來了？
It's the 25th. Why? You can't come?

296

😊 今年的中秋節是9月27號。

😎 真的嗎？可是那時候是我的生日！
Really? But that's my birthday!

297

😊 今天是你的生日吧？來，這是你的生日禮物。
Today's your birthday, right? Here, it's your birthday present.

😊 謝謝，可是，其實我生日是後天。
Thanks. But actually

298

😎 今天是韓國的國慶日。

😊 啊，這就是為什麼你今天不用去上班。
Oh, that's why you're not working today.

299

🎩 8月15號你也要上班嗎？
Do you go to work on August 15th?

😊 不用。光復節是法定公休日。
No.

300

😠 嘿，幹嘛大吼大叫的？
Hey, what's with the screaming?

😊 從明天開始是小長假。我剛剛才知道。
from tomorrow. I didn't know, you see.

Answer **295** What date is next Sunday? 下週日是幾號？ **296** Chuseok falls on Sep 27 this year. 今年的中秋節是9月27號。 **297** it's the day after tomorrow. 是後天。 **298** Today is a national holiday in Korea. 今天是韓國的國慶日。 **299** National Liberation Day is a legal holiday. 光復節是法定公休日。 **300** It's a long weekend 是小長假。

Day 10 Review	在忘記以前複習一遍，怎麼樣？	規定時間 5 min

聽著MP3跟讀	看著中文說英語
在春天馬上就要來臨時，天氣再次變冷 **We're in the middle of a cold snap.**	春寒冷得不得了。
天氣開始轉暖時 **The weather has thawed.**	天氣轉暖了。
天氣轉暖，花都開了時 **Spring is in the air.**	真是春意盎然啊。
春天不受歡迎的客人 **There's a yellow dust warning.**	發布了沙塵暴預警。
一直持續的酷熱天氣 **It's scorching hot.**	簡直像蒸籠一樣熱。
熱得難以忍受時 **The heat is unbearable.**	熱得受不了了。
熱得睡不著覺時 **There's a tropical night phenomenon.**	這是熱帶夜現象。
因為濕氣重而身上汗涔涔的時候 **It's muggy.**	天氣太悶熱了。
楓葉開始變紅時 **Fall is just around the corner.**	春天馬上就要來了。
道路兩旁的樹開始變顏色時 **The leaves are changing color.**	樹葉開始變黃了。

看著中文說英文時，用書籤擋住這個部分。

DAY 10　▼ 談論季節和日期

提議去看紅葉時 **Let's go leaf peeping.**	我們去看落葉吧。
地上鋪著厚厚的落葉時 **Look at the piles of fallen leaves.**	看那裡堆滿了落葉。
大雪紛紛揚揚地飄落時 **It's snowing big, fat snowflakes.**	鵝毛大雪紛紛飄落。
白雪覆蓋的一片銀白的世界 **Everything is covered in snow.**	整個世界都是銀白色的。
走路的時候，在冰上滑倒時 **I slipped on the ice.**	我在冰上滑倒了。
因為天氣寒冷，手腳都凍了時 **He's got frostbite.**	他被凍傷了。
將星期幾和日期進行對照計算時 **What date is next Sunday?**	下週日是幾號？
查看特定的節日是今年的幾月幾號時 **Chuseok falls on Sep 27 this year.**	今年的中秋節時9月27號。
表達從今天開始的兩天之後 **It's the day after tomorrow.**	是後天。
說明制憲節、國慶日等的時候 **Today is a national holiday in Korea.**	今天是韓國的國慶日。

已經學會的句型
300個/600個

📖 看著中文說英文時，用書籤擋住這個部分。

NOTE

Lightening!

Learn to Boost Your
English Skills
Everyday Expression **600**

Day 11

—

Day 15

談論電腦

聽例句

剛做的文件檔沒有保存的時候、中了病毒的時候，或是被駭客侵入的時候等，
你會用英語說有關電腦的句子嗎？來檢測一下吧。

Quick Test 01　這些句子用英語怎麼說？

規定時間 1 min

DAY 11
▼ 談論電腦

---

301 為了避免因沒儲存文件而導致文件遺失的狼狽

你儲存文件了嗎？

ⓐ Did you memorize your file?

ⓑ Did you cork your file?

ⓒ Did you save your file?

---

302 不小心刪除了文件時

我不小心把文件刪除了。

ⓐ I deliberately took the file.

ⓑ I accidentally deleted the file.

ⓒ I momentarily paused the file.

---

303 將刪除的文件復原時

我可以恢復文件。

ⓐ The file can be alive.

ⓑ I can sever the file.

ⓒ I can recover the file.

---

304 為了以防外一，備份文件時

你有備份文件嗎？

ⓐ Is it back yet?

ⓑ Did you backup this file?

ⓒ Did you bag this file?

---

305 想知道電腦記憶體大小時

記憶體是多大的？

ⓐ How big is the memory?

ⓑ How deep is the memory?

ⓒ How hard is the memory?

---

306 使用滑鼠移動文件時

把文件拖到這裡。

ⓐ Take the file and put it here.

ⓑ Drag and drop the file here.

ⓒ Allow the file to find the mark.

Answer **301** ⓒ 保存（文件）▶ save　**302** ⓑ 一不小心 ▶ accidentally；刪除 ▶ delete　**303** ⓒ 恢復 ▶ recover　**304** ⓑ（為了以防外一將文件等）備份 ▶ backup　**305** ⓐ 記憶體 ▶ memory *cf* 容量 ▶ capacity　**306** ⓑ 拖過來放在（一個地方）▶ drag and drop

Quick Practice 現在可以自信地說出來了嗎？ 規定時間 1 min

301

😎 太好了！我的論文完成了。我們去喝一杯吧。

Yes! My report is finished. Let's go out for a drink.

👩 你儲存文件了嗎？

302

👩 你幹嘛大叫？

Why did you scream?

😀 天啊。我不小心把文件刪除了。

Oh, my God.

303

🎩 別哭了。我可以恢復文件。

Stop crying.

👩 我一定是喝醉了。

I must have been drunk.

304

👦 你有備份文件了嗎？

😀 當然。我總是備三份文件。

Of course. I always make three of them.

305

😀 記憶體是多大的？

👩 才1G。

It's only 1 gigabyte.

306

😎 先把文件拖到這裡。

To begin with,

😀 沒問題。之後呢？

Sure thing. And then what?

Answer **301** Did you save your file? 你儲存文件了嗎？ **302** I accidentally deleted the file. 我不小心把文件刪除了。 **303** I can recover the file. 我可以恢復文件。 **304** Did you backup this file? 你備份文件了嗎？ **305** How big is the memory? 記憶體是多大的？ **306** Drag and drop the file here. 把文件拖到這裡。

Quick
Test 02
這些句子用英語怎麼說？

規定時間 1 min

---

307 請人列印自己的文件時

能幫我列印一下嗎？

ⓐ Can you print this out for me?

ⓑ Will you make a copier for me?

ⓒ Would you type it out to me?

---

308 請人彩色列印時

能幫我印成彩色的嗎？

ⓐ Can you print this on color?

ⓑ Can you print this in color?

ⓒ Can you print this with color?

---

309 將電腦與印表機連接時

連上印表機。

ⓐ Hook it up to the printer.

ⓑ Rope it to the printer.

ⓒ Grab the printer.

---

310 將隨身碟連到電腦上時

把隨身碟插上。

ⓐ Touch the USB flash drive.

ⓑ Plug in the USB flash drive.

ⓒ Pull in the USB flash drive.

---

311 影印機壞了時

影印機壞了。

ⓐ The copy machine is out of order.

ⓑ The copier is dead.

ⓒ The photocopier is taken.

---

312 影印機卡紙時

卡紙了。

ⓐ The paper is locked up.

ⓑ The paper is crammed

ⓒ The paper is jammed.

Answer **307** ⓐ 列印 ▶ print (out) **308** ⓑ 彩色列印 ▶ print in color **309** ⓐ 將A與B連接 ▶ hook A up to B **310** ⓑ 插上，連接（電子器件）▶ plug in **311** ⓐ 影印機 ▶ copy machine, photocopier；壞了 ▶ out of order **312** ⓒ （因為堵住了或是被夾住了）一點也不動 ▶ jammed

---

307

😊 能幫我列印一下嗎？

😀 當然可以。要幾份？
Sure. How many copies do you need?

308

😊 能幫我印成彩色的嗎？10份，謝謝。

10 copies, please.

😀 不好意思，你不能用彩色印表機。
Sorry. You can't use it.

309

😊 連上印表機。印表機可以用，對吧？

The printer is working, right?

😊 嗯，但是沒有接頭。
Yeah, but there's no connector cable.

310

😎 我看看，把隨身碟插上。
Let's see.

😀 等一下。我找不到U盤接口。
Wait. I can't find the USB port.

311

🎩 會議怎麼還不開始？
Why haven't you started the meeting?

😊 影印機壞了。

312

😀 你為什麼要朝影印機大叫啊？
Why are you shouting at the copier?

😊 卡紙了。我覺得它是故意的。
　　　　　　　　　I think it's doing it on purpose.

Quick
Test 03

這些句子用英語怎麼說？

規定時間 1 min

313 電腦突然不動了時

我電腦當機了。

ⓐ My computer fainted.

ⓑ My computer is dead.

ⓒ My computer froze up.

314 電腦的速度非常慢時

我的電腦太慢了。

ⓐ My computer has a lack.

ⓑ The computer is hanging on a rack.

ⓒ My computer is lagging.

315 電腦突然變得很奇怪的原因

我電腦中毒了。

ⓐ My computer ate a virus.

ⓑ My computer has a virus.

ⓒ My computer swallowed a virus.

316 用掃毒軟體清掃電腦病毒時

我得掃毒了。

ⓐ I need to pick up the virus.

ⓑ I need to debug my computer.

ⓒ I need to find a germ.

317 電腦被駭客侵入時

我被駭客攻擊了。

ⓐ I've been hacked.

ⓑ I've been hackered.

ⓒ I've been hacking.

318 為了不讓駭客侵入

定期更換密碼。

ⓐ Reset your password regularly.

ⓑ Recheck the secret code in time.

ⓒ Reshuffle the numbers on time.

Answer **313** ⓒ（電腦像被凍住了一樣）不動了 ▶ freeze up (freeze-froze-frozen) **314** ⓒ 走得極慢，落在後面 ▶ lag **315** ⓑ 中毒 ▶ have a virus **316** ⓑ（在電腦程式中）掃毒 ▶ debug（bug指「病毒」）**317** ⓐ 被駭客攻擊 ▶ be hacked **318** ⓐ 重新設置 ▶ reset ：定期 ▶ regularly

現在可以自信地說出來了嗎？ 規定時間

313

😎 約翰，怎麼了？現在凌晨1點了。
John, what's up? It's 1 a.m.

🤠 幫幫我。我電腦當機了。
Help me, man.

314

😮 哦不！我的電腦太慢了。
Oh, no!

😊 要是你有急事，就用我的電腦。
If you're in a hurry, use mine.

315

😮 你電腦螢幕上的那些是什麼照片啊？
What are all those pictures on your monitor?

😎 別誤會！我電腦中毒了。
It's not what you think!

316

😊 我得掃毒了。你有防毒軟體嗎？
                                    Do you have a vaccine program?

😮 有。可是借給你沒問題嗎？
Yes, I do. But is it safe to lend it to you?

317

🤠 我被駭客攻擊了。我應該報警嗎？
                          Should I call the police?

😮 當然。聯絡網路犯罪調查科。
Yes, contact the Cyber Crime Unit.

318

😮 從現在開始你要定期更換密碼。
                                    from now on.

😎 這是亡羊補牢啊。
It's locking the stable door after the horse is stolen.

stable 牲口棚

Quick Test 04

這些句子用英語怎麼說？

規定時間 1 min

DAY 11 ▼ 談論電腦

---

319 使用搜尋引擎在網上查詢資訊時

我上網查了。

ⓐ I researched it.

ⓑ I touched it.

ⓒ I googled it.

---

320 流覽各種網站時

我在用電腦。

ⓐ I'm an Internet surfer.

ⓑ I surfed the Internet.

ⓒ The Internet was shopped.

---

321 網路連線速度很慢時

網速太慢了。

ⓐ The Internet connection is slow.

ⓑ The Internet speed is great.

ⓒ The Internet line is zigzagging.

---

322 談論我寫的文章的點擊數時

點擊量很高。

ⓐ I'm getting lots of hits.

ⓑ There are so many numbers.

ⓒ The visitors are amazing.

---

323 我寫的文章留言很多時

我收到很多留言。

ⓐ I'm getting lots of mega papers.

ⓑ I'm getting lots of mini letters.

ⓒ I'm getting lots of comments.

---

324 對因為看到了惡意留言而傷心的人

別理那些惡意評論。

ⓐ Just adore the bad comments.

ⓑ Just ignore the hate comments.

ⓒ Just ignore the black comments.

Answer **319** ⓒ 網路檢索 ▶ google（由來：公司名稱（Google）） **320** ⓑ 上網 ▶ surf the Internet **321** ⓐ 連接，連結 ▶ connection **322** ⓐ 點擊量 ▶ hit **323** ⓒ 留言 ▶ comment **324** ⓑ 惡意留言 ▶ hate comment

現在可以自信地說出來了嗎？　規定時間 1 min

319

你怎麼這麼瞭解我的過去？

How do you know so much about my past?

我在網路上查了。

320

你今天一天都在做什麼？

What did you do all day?

用電腦。眼睛好痛。

My eyes are sore.

321

你查了嗎？怎麼花這麼久的時間？

Have you looked it up? What's taking you so long?

不好意思。網速太慢了。

Sorry!

322

你的部落格怎麼樣了？

How's your blog coming along?

非常好！點擊量很高。

Great!

323

看。我有很多留言。

Look.

哇。都有好幾百則了。

Wow, there must be several hundred.

324

怎麼能留這種言呢？

How can people write comments like these?

嘿，嘿，冷靜點。別理那些惡意評論。

There, there. Calm down.

Answer **319** I googled it. 我上網查了。　**320** I surfed the Internet. 我在用電腦。　**321** The Internet connection is slow. 網速太慢了。　**322** I'm getting lots of hits. 點擊量很高。　**323** I'm getting lots of comments. 我有很多留言。　**324** Just ignore the hate comments. 別理那些惡意評論。

Quick Test 05 這些句子用英語怎麼說？

DAY 11 ▼ 談論電腦

---

325 想要玩一下朋友玩的那個遊戲時

讓我玩一次。

ⓐ I want it all.

ⓑ Let me have a go.

ⓒ Allow me to show you.

---

326 請人把音量一下子開到很大聲時

把聲音調大聲。

ⓐ Level up the volume.

ⓑ Crank up the volume.

ⓒ Call up the volume.

---

327 因為要使用遊戲道具，所以需要付錢時

那是付費道具。

ⓐ That's a paid item.

ⓑ That's a golden item.

ⓒ That's a card item.

---

328 畫面清晰色彩飽滿

這螢幕是高畫質的。

ⓐ The screen has a high resolution.

ⓑ The screen has a high speculation.

ⓒ The screen has a high density.

---

329 要輸入密碼登錄時

輸入你的密碼。

ⓐ Press the secret source.

ⓑ Push your base number.

ⓒ Punch in your password.

---

330 過了遊戲的一關時

我過了一關！

ⓐ I wiped the level!

ⓑ I smashed the level!

ⓒ I cleared the level!

Answer **325** ⓑ 玩一次／試一次……▶ have a go **326** ⓑ 更使勁地擰（機器）▶ crank up **327** ⓐ 付錢的 ▶ paid **328** ⓐ（畫面）清晰度 ▶ resolution **329** ⓒ（敲擊電腦鍵盤等）輸入……▶ punch in **330** ⓒ 通過，跳過（一關）▶ clear

325

😀 哇！這個遊戲太好玩了。

Wow! I love this game.

😎 讓我玩一次。你都玩了一個小時了。

＿＿＿＿＿＿＿＿＿＿ You've been at it for an hour now.

326

🎩 我聽不清楚。把聲音調大聲。

I can't hear. ＿＿＿＿＿＿＿

😀 我覺得這樣比較好。我的精神更能集中。

I like it like this. I can concentrate better.

327

😎 用那把魔法劍把怪物殺死！

Use that magic sword to kill the monster!

😎 那是付費道具。你要買給我嗎？

＿＿＿＿＿＿＿＿＿ Will you buy it for me?

328

😀 這張圖太棒了！

Cool graphics!

😎 而且這螢幕是高畫質的。

＿＿＿＿＿＿＿＿＿＿＿＿, also.

329

😎 來，輸入你的密碼。

Come on. ＿＿＿＿＿＿＿＿

😎 哎呀，又忘了。我把密碼設得太複雜了。

Darn, I forgot it again. I made it too difficult.

330

😀 太好了！我終於過了一關！

Yes! ＿＿＿＿＿＿＿＿ finally!

😎 你真棒！嘿，現在該我玩了吧？

Good for you! Hey, can I take over from now on?

take over 接班，交接

Answer **325** Let me have a go. 讓我玩一次。 **326** Crank up the volume. 把聲音調大聲。 **327** That's a paid item. 那是付費道具。 **328** The screen has a high resolution. 這螢幕是高畫質的。 **329** Punch in your password. 輸入你的密碼。 **330** I cleared the level 我過了一關！

Day 11 Review | 在忘記以前複習一遍，怎麼樣？ | 規定時間 5 min

聽著MP3跟讀 🎧	看著中文說英語 👄
為了避免因沒儲存而導致文件不見的狼狽 **Did you save your file?**	你儲存文件了嗎？
不小心刪除了文件時 **I accidentally deleted the file.**	我不小心把文件刪除了。
為了以防萬一，備份文件時 **Did you backup this file?**	備份文件了嗎？
使用滑鼠移動文件時 **Drag and drop the file here.**	把文件拖到這裡。
請人列印自己的文件時 **Can you print this out for me?**	能幫我列印一下嗎？
將隨身碟連到電腦上時 **Plug in the USB flash drive.**	把隨身碟插上。
影印機壞了時 **The copy machine is out of order.**	影印機壞了。
影印機卡紙時 **The paper is jammed.**	卡紙了。
電腦突然不動了時 **My computer froze up.**	我電腦當機了。
電腦的速度非常慢時 **My computer is lagging.**	我的電腦太慢了。

DAY 11

▼ 談論電腦

📖 看著中文說英文時，用書籤擋住這個部分。

聽著MP3跟讀 🎧	看著中文說英語 👄
電腦突然變得很奇怪的原因 **My computer has a virus.**	我電腦中毒了。
電腦被駭客侵入時 **I've been hacked.**	我被駭客攻擊了。
使用搜尋引擎在網上查詢資訊時 **I googled it.**	我上網查了。
流覽各種網站時 **I surfed the Internet.**	我在用電腦。
網路連線速度很慢時 **The Internet connection is slow.**	網速太慢了。
我寫的文章留言很多時 **I'm getting lots of comments.**	我收到很多留言。
想要玩一下朋友玩的那個遊戲時 **Let me have a go.**	讓我玩一次。
畫面清晰色彩飽滿 **The screen has a high resolution.**	這螢幕是高畫質的。
要輸入密碼登錄時 **Punch in your password.**	輸入你的密碼。
過了遊戲的一關時 **I cleared the level!**	我過了一關！

已經學會的句型
330個/600個

📖 看著中文說英文時，用書籤擋住這個部分。

DAY 12

學習及休閒

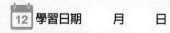 學習日期　　月　　日

 學習時間

聽例句

考試臨時抱佛腳時、和朋友一起看電影時，或是在KTV唱歌時，
你會用英語說有關學習或者玩的句子嗎？來檢測一下吧。

Quick Test 01

這些句子用英語怎麼說？

規定時間 1 min

DAY 12 ▼ 學習及休閒

---

331 因為想要出去玩而蹺課時

我蹺課了。

ⓐ I ran down the class.

ⓑ The class was beaten by me.

ⓒ I skipped class.

---

332 考試前抱佛腳時

我為了考試正在抱佛腳。

ⓐ I'm shocking my test.

ⓑ I'm cramming for my test.

ⓒ I'm thunderbolting my test.

---

333 考試時，抄別人的答案時

我考試的時候作弊了。

ⓐ I cunningly solved the test.

ⓑ I cheated on my test.

ⓒ I endured my test.

---

334 聽短期速成班課程時

我在上速成班。

ⓐ I'm taking a crash course.

ⓑ I'm teaching fast learning.

ⓒ I'm listening to the quick class.

---

335 通過中考、高考等考試時

她考上了。

ⓐ She jumped the school test.

ⓑ She passed the entrance test.

ⓒ She stepped into the college exam.

---

336 讀書到很晚的時候

他正在開夜車。

ⓐ He studies in the darkness.

ⓑ He's a night owl.

ⓒ He's burning the midnight oil.

Answer **331** ⓒ 蹺課 ▶ skip class **332** ⓑ 為了……而抱佛腳 ▶ cram for **333** ⓑ 考試的時候作弊 ▶ cheat on one's test **334** ⓐ 速成班 crash/ intensive course **335** ⓑ 入學考試 ▶ entrance test：通過考試 ▶ pass **336** ⓒ （學習或者工作）到很晚 ▶ burn the midnight oil

---

331

😊 你不是應該在學校嗎？

Aren't you supposed to be at school?

😎 我蹺課了。對了，我們現在去哪裡？

＿＿＿＿＿＿＿＿ By the way, where are we going?

332

😟 現在這個時候你在幹什麼？

What are you doing at this hour?

😴 我為了考試正在抱佛腳呢，媽媽。我好睏。

＿＿＿＿＿＿＿＿, mom. I'm so sleepy.

333

😠 你們老師為什麼要見我？

Why does your teacher want to see me?

😎 我考試的時候作弊了。

＿＿＿＿＿＿＿＿

334

🎩 你看起來很累啊。

You look very tired.

💇 我正在上跳傘速成班呢。

＿＿＿＿＿＿＿＿ on skydiving.

335

😊 為什麼有香檳？

What's this champagne for?

😊 為了你妹妹買的。她考上了。

It's for your sister. ＿＿＿＿＿＿＿＿

336

😊 賴瑞到現在還沒從圖書館回來嗎？

Larry still hasn't come back from the library?

😎 他正在開夜車呢。他想要得到獎學金。

＿＿＿＿＿＿＿＿ He wants to win the scholarship.

Quick Test 02

這些句子用英語怎麼說？

規定時間 1 min

DAY 12 ▼ 學習及休閒

---

337 有時間就看書的人

我是個書蟲。

ⓐ I'm mad about book-keeping.

ⓑ I'm a book animal.

ⓒ I'm a bookworm.

---

338 很有意思，吸引人一直看下去的書

這是一本引人入勝的書。

ⓐ This book is a page-maker.

ⓑ This book is a page-mover.

ⓒ This book is a page-turner.

---

339 書頁都皺了的書

書頁都被弄皺了。

ⓐ The pages are increased.

ⓑ The pages are creased.

ⓒ The pages are crushed.

---

340 粗略地讀一本書時

我大概翻了一下。

ⓐ I'll just leaf through it.

ⓑ I can magnify the book.

ⓒ I'll read the pages briefly.

---

341 在圖書館借書，詢問已經借出去的書的還書日期時

書什麼時候能還回來？

ⓐ When is it due back?

ⓑ Can you tell me its limits?

ⓒ When is the return ticket?

---

342 無法按時還書時

逾期罰款是多少？

ⓐ How much is the fuel fee?

ⓑ How much is the late fee?

ⓒ How much is the red card fee?

Answer **337** ⓒ 書蟲 ▶ bookworm **338** ⓒ（讓人讀得津津有味）很快就看完的書 ▶ page turner **339** ⓑ 皺了 ▶ crease **340** ⓐ 大概瀏覽（書等）▶ leaf through：就像隨風擺動的樹葉（leaf）一樣，很快地翻動書頁，瀏覽通過（through）的感覺 **341** ⓐ 規定返還的 ▶ due back **342** ⓑ 逾期罰款 ▶ late fee

337

😊 你的愛好是什麼？摔角？
What is your hobby? Wrestling?

🙂 你可能不相信，我是個書蟲。
You won't believe this, but

338

😊 你一天就看完了那本推理小說？
You read that mystery novel overnight?

😄 這是一本引人入勝的書。我借給你吧。

I'll lend it to you.

339

🎩 你看看這本書，書頁都被弄皺了。
Look at this book.

🙂 不好意思，先生。我幫您換一本。
Sorry, sir. I'll get you another one.

340

🎩 你怎麼能在一小時之內把這本書看完呢？
How can you read it in an hour?

🙂 沒問題的。我只大概翻了一下。
It's okay.

341

😎 我想借這本書。書什麼時候能還回來？
I'd like to borrow this book.

🙂 一週以後。
In a week.

342

🎩 這本書我晚還了。逾期罰款是多少？
I'm late in returning this book.

🙂 天哪，逾期了一年多。
Oh! It's been due for over a year!

Answer **337** I'm a bookworm. 我是個書蟲。 **338** This book is a page-turner. 這是一本引人入勝的書。 **339** The pages are creased. 書頁都被弄皺了。 **340** I'll just leaf through it. 我只大概翻了一下。 **341** When is it due back? 書什麼時候能還回來？ **342** How much is the late fee? 逾期罰款是多少？

Quick Test 03

這些句子用英語怎麼說？

規定時間 1 min

DAY 12 ▼ 學習及休閒

---

343 提議去看電影時

我們去看電影，怎麼樣？

ⓐ Would you mind making a movie?

ⓑ How about a movie?

ⓒ Listen to a movie with me?

---

344 是特定題材電影的愛好者時

我最喜歡看動作片了。

ⓐ I'm a must-have fan of action movies.

ⓑ I'm a see-it-now fan of action movies.

ⓒ I'm a die-hard fan of action movies.

---

345 告訴對方電影的長度時

那是一部3個小時的電影。

ⓐ That movie is 3 hours long.

ⓑ The sprinting time is 3 hours.

ⓒ The movie has 3 hours left.

---

346 是前一部電影的續集時

這部電影是《Once》的續集。

ⓐ This movie is secondary to "Once."

ⓑ This movie is a brother of "Once."

ⓒ This movie is a sequel to "Once."

---

347 預訂電影票時

我訂了兩張《Iron Dog》的票。

ⓐ Two tickets to "Iron Dog" are here.

ⓑ I booked two tickets to "Iron Dog."

ⓒ "Iron Dog" tickets are two now.

---

348 看了電影，感覺不太好時

很普通。

ⓐ It was so-so.

ⓑ It was a boo-boo.

ⓒ It was a no-no.

Answer **343** ⓑ（提出建議）……怎麼樣？▶ How about...? **344** ⓒ 狂熱的愛好者 ▶ die-hard fan, huge fan **345** ⓐ cf）電影的長度 ▶ running time **346** ⓒ ……的續篇 ▶ sequel to **347** ⓑ 預約（票、座位等）▶ book, reserve **348** ⓐ 很一般，很普通 ▶ so-so cf）特別棒！▶ It was awesome!

179

現在可以自信地說出來了嗎？ 規定時間 1 min

343

😊 我們去看電影，怎麼樣？

😊 不要，我太累了。還是回家看電視上的電影吧。

No, I'm tired. I'll just go home and watch a movie on TV.

344

😊 可是你都已經看了四遍《Die Hard》了。

But you've already seen "Die Hard" four times!

😊 我有什麼辦法呢。我最喜歡看動作片了。

I can't help it.

345

😊 那是一部3小時的電影。別看了。

Let's not watch it.

😊 可是我很喜歡看恐怖電影！而且今天還是我的生日。

But I love horror movies! And it's my birthday today.

346

😊 這部電影是《Once》的續集。

😊 哦，真的嗎？我很喜歡第一部！

Oh, really? I loved the first one!

347

😊 我訂了兩張《Iron Dog》的票。

😊 哦，太好了。我正想看動畫電影。

Oh, good. I felt like watching an animated movie.

348

😊 電影好看嗎？

Did you enjoy the movie?

😊 很一般。我不推薦。

I wouldn't recommend it.

Answer **343** How about a movie? 我們去看電影，怎麼樣？ **344** I'm a die-hard fan of action movies. 我最喜歡看動作片了。 **345** That movie is 3 hours long. 那是一部三小時的電影。 **346** This movie is a sequel to "Once." 這部電影是《Once》的續集。 **347** I booked two tickets to "Iron Dog." 我訂了兩張《Iron Dog》的票。 **348** It was so-so. 很普通。

Quick
Test 04

這些句子用英語怎麼說？

規定時間 1 min

DAY 12 ▼ 學習及休閒

---

349 說自己唱歌唱得不好時

我五音不全。

ⓐ I'm tone deaf.

ⓑ I'm melody dumb.

ⓒ I'm song stupid.

---

350 說這是自己最喜歡唱的歌時

這是我最喜歡的歌。

ⓐ My number 18 is this song.

ⓑ It's my 18th song.

ⓒ This is my favorite song.

---

351 聽起來很熟悉的歌曲

那首歌很耳熟。

ⓐ That song sounds familiar.

ⓑ I heard that melody just now.

ⓒ It's music to my ears.

---

352 練歌房的麥克風回音太厲害時

麥克風回音太大了。

ⓐ It's a bathroom for the mike.

ⓑ The mike has too much echo.

ⓒ There's a wind in the mike.

---

353 唱歌唱得嗓子啞了時

我嗓子啞了。

ⓐ I have an insect in my throat.

ⓑ I have a cramp in my throat.

ⓒ I have a frog in my throat.

---

354 說自己唱不上去高音時

我唱不上去。

ⓐ I can't ring the high notes.

ⓑ I can't hit the high notes.

ⓒ I can't blow the high notes.

Answer **349** ⓐ 耳朵聽不出音（tone）高的，五音不全的 ▶ tone deaf **350** ⓒ 最喜歡的 ▶ favorite **351** ⓐ 聽起來很熟悉 ▶ sound familiar **352** ⓑ 回音 ▶ echo **353** ⓒ 用嗓子裡有一隻青蛙比喻嗓子啞了 **354** ⓑ 夠到 ▶ hit：高音 ▶ high note, high-pitched tone

Quick Practice 現在可以自信地說出來了嗎？ 規定時間 1 min

349

😅 雖然我知道這只是我們第二次約會，但是去唱卡拉OK怎麼樣？

I know it's only our second date, but how about karaoke?

😀 不好意思。我五音不全。

Sorry.

350

🎩 好，來！哈，哈！這是我最喜歡的歌。

Okay, here we go! Ha, ha!

😊 又是這首歌啊？我都聽了幾百遍了。

Not that song again! I've heard it hundreds of times.

351

😀 那首歌很耳熟。我想不起來歌名是什麼了。

I can't remember the title.

😃 我也是，我最討厭這種感覺了！

Me, neither. I hate it when this happens!

352

😀 麥克風回音太大了。

😏 別找藉口了。快唱吧。

Don't make excuses. Just sing.

353

😊 我唱不了了。我嗓子啞了。

I can't sing.

🎩 好，那我去幫你拿點熱水來。

I see. I'll get you some warm water, then.

354

😊 來，我們一起唱副歌部分。

Come on, let's sing the chorus together!

😃 哦，不行，我唱不上去。

Oh, I can't.

Quick
Test 05
這些句子用英語怎麼說？

規定時間 1 min

---

355 發現想要坐的遊樂設施時

我想坐那個！

ⓐ There goes my ride!

ⓑ I want to ride that one!

ⓒ My ride is ready for me!

356 坐驚險又刺激的遊樂設施後的感想

那個遊樂設施真刺激！

ⓐ The ride was really exacting!

ⓑ The ride was really thrilling!

ⓒ The ride was really enervating!

---

357 有可以不限次數乘坐遊樂設施的通關票時

我有通關票。

ⓐ I have a freedom.

ⓑ I have a coupon.

ⓒ I have a daily pass.

358 走了一天，腳很痛時

我的腳痛死了。

ⓐ My feet are jamming me!

ⓑ My feet are biting me!

ⓒ My feet are killing me!

---

359 對想不排隊直接入場的人

喂，排隊！

ⓐ Hey, get in line!

ⓑ Hey, make the cut!

ⓒ Hey, stay in the line!

360 對想要不聲不響插隊的人

喂，別插隊！

ⓐ Hey, stop poking me!

ⓑ Hey, you're mean!

ⓒ Hey, don't cut in!

Answer **355** ⓑ 乘坐（遊樂設施）▶ ride　**356** ⓑ 遊樂設施 ▶ ride；刺激的 ▶ thrilling　**357** ⓒ 通關票 ▶ daily pass *cf*）入場券 ▶ admission-only ticket　**358** ⓒ〔直譯〕我的腳要把我殺了。　**359** ⓐ 排隊 ▶ get in line　**360** ⓒ 插隊 ▶ cut in (line)

Quick Practice

現在可以自信地說出來了嗎？ 規定時間 1 min

355

😄 我想坐那個！快走吧。
_____ Let's hurry.

😮 哦，天哪，看那長長的隊伍。
Oh, my. Look at the line.

356

🤓 怎麼樣？
How was it?

😊 那個遊樂設施真刺激！我還想再坐一次。
_____ I want to go on it again.

357

😊 我有通關票。你呢？
_____ How about you?

😄 我就看你坐就可以了。
I'll just watch you on the ride.

358

😣 我的腳痛死了。我們找個地方坐一下吧。
_____ Let's sit somewhere.

🎩 好主意。我們找個陰涼的地方。
Good idea. Let's find some shade.

359

🎩 喂，排隊！
_____

😊 啊，我沒意識到。
Oh, I didn't know.

360

😊 喂，別插隊！
_____

😄 不好意思，我英語不好。
Sorry, I don't speak English.

Day 12 Review — 在忘記以前複習一遍，怎麼樣？

規定時間 5 min

聽著MP3跟讀	看著中文說英語
因為想要出去玩而蹺課時 **I skipped class.**	我蹺課了。
考試以前抱佛腳時 **I'm cramming for my test.**	我為了考試正在抱佛腳呢。
考試時，抄別人的答案時 **I cheated on my test.**	我考試的時候作弊了。
通過中考、高考等考試時 **She passed the entrance test.**	她考上了。
有時間就看書的人 **I'm a bookworm.**	我是個書蟲。
很有意思，吸引人一直看下去的書 **This book is a page-turner.**	這是一本引人入勝的書。
粗略地讀一本書時 **I'll just leaf through it.**	我就大概翻了一下。
在圖書館借書，詢問已經借出去的書的還書日期時 **When is it due back?**	書什麼時候能還回來？
提議去看電影時 **How about a movie?**	我們去看電影，怎麼樣？
告訴對方電影的長度時 **That movie is 3 hours long.**	那是一部3個小時的電影。

DAY 12 ▼ 學習及休閒

📖 看著中文說英文時，用書籤擋住這個部分。

是前一部電影的續集時 **This movie is a sequel to "Once."**	這部電影是《Once》的續集。
看了電影，感覺不太好時 **It was so-so.**	很普通。
說自己唱歌唱得不好時 **I'm tone deaf.**	我五音不全。
說這是自己最喜歡唱的歌時 **This is my favorite song.**	這是我最喜歡的歌。
聽起來很熟悉的歌曲 **That song sounds familiar.**	那首歌很耳熟。
唱歌唱得嗓子啞了時 **I have a frog in my throat.**	我嗓子啞了。
坐驚險又刺激的遊樂設施後的感想 **The ride was really thrilling!**	那個遊樂設施真刺激！
有可以不限次數乘坐遊樂設施的通票時 **I have a daily pass.**	我有通關票。
走了一天，腳很疼時 **My feet are killing me!**	我的腳痛死了。
對想要不聲不響插隊的人 **Hey, don't cut in!**	喂，別插隊！

已經學會的句型
360個/600個

看著中文說英文時，用書籤擋住這個部分。

從起床到睡覺

聽例句

因為別人打呼的聲音睡不好覺的時候、牙齦出血的時候，或是馬桶壞了的時候，
你會用英語說這些日常生活中需要的句子嗎？來檢測一下吧。

Quick Test 01 這些句子用英語怎麼說？ 規定時間 1 min

DAY 13 ▼ 從起床到睡覺

361 到了起床時間，叫別人起床時

天亮了。起床了！

ⓐ Up and morning!

ⓑ Rise and shine!

ⓒ Sunshine and morning!

362 睡覺很晚才起床時

我睡過頭了。

ⓐ I overslept!

ⓑ I turned in my sleep!

ⓒ I fell asleep late!

363 忘了定鬧鐘時

我忘了定鬧鐘了。

ⓐ I didn't mark my alarm clock.

ⓑ I didn't push my alarm clock.

ⓒ I didn't set my alarm clock.

364 雖然起床了，但是還沒有完全清醒時

我還沒睡醒。

ⓐ I'm still half-dreaming.

ⓑ I'm still half-closed.

ⓒ I'm still half-asleep.

365 起床以後互相問候的話

睡得好嗎？

ⓐ Did you sleep well?

ⓑ Did you sleep fine?

ⓒ Did you sleep deep?

366 對方眼角上掛著眼屎時

你眼睛上還有眼屎。

ⓐ You have drops in your eyes.

ⓑ You have sleep in your eyes.

ⓒ You have dreams in your eyes.

Answer **361** ⓑ 太陽升起來了（shine）該起床（rise）了的意思 **362** ⓐ 睡過頭 ▶ oversleep **363** ⓒ 定鬧鐘 ▶ set one's alarm clock **364** ⓒ 還沒睡醒，似夢非夢的狀態 ▶ half-asleep **365** ⓐ **366** ⓑ 眼屎 ▶ sleep

361

😊 天亮了。起床了！

😴 嗯……我再睡5分鐘。
Mmm... Just five more minutes.

362

🤓 我睡過頭了。怎麼不叫我？
Why didn't you wake me up?

😊 不好意思，你剛才睡得特別香。你遲到了？
Sorry, you were so sound asleep. Are you late?

363

😊 嘿！我的生日派對已經結束了。你怎麼這麼晚來？
Hey! My birthday party is already over. What kept you?

🤓 不好意思。我忘了定鬧鐘了。
Sorry.

364

😊 我要做作業，你能幫幫我嗎？
Can you help me with my homework?

😊 當然可以。不過我先告訴你……我還沒睡醒。
Sure, but bear in mind...

365

🤵 睡得好嗎？

🤓 不好，我的狗睡覺的時候一直嗚嗚叫。
No, my dog whined in his sleep.

366

😴 怎麼了？我臉上有番茄醬嗎？
What? Do I have ketchup on my face?

😊 不是，你眼睛上還帶著眼屎。
No.

whine （動物）嗚嗚叫

Answer **361** Rise and shine! 天亮了。起床了！ **362** I overslept! 我睡過頭了。 **363** I didn't set my alarm clock. 我忘了定鬧鐘了。 **364** I'm still half-asleep. 我還沒睡醒。 **365** Did you sleep well? 睡得好嗎？ **366** You have sleep in your eyes. 你眼睛上還帶著眼屎。

Test 02 這些句子用英語怎麼說？ 規定時間 1 min

367 跟要去睡覺的人道晚安時

晚安。

ⓐ Have your dream.
ⓑ Sleep tight.
ⓒ Go to sleepy world.

368 一覺睡到天明時

我睡得特別香。

ⓐ I slept like a basket.
ⓑ I slept like a dog.
ⓒ I slept like a log.

369 睜著眼睛到天明時

我完全沒睡著。

ⓐ I didn't sleep a wink.
ⓑ I didn't sleep a blink.
ⓒ I didn't sleep a pinch.

370 睡覺時總是翻身

我睡得一點也不安穩。

ⓐ I had trouble sleeping.
ⓑ I fell off my sleep.
ⓒ The night was white for me.

371 睡覺打呼的人

他有時會打呼。

ⓐ He snores from time in time.
ⓑ He snores to time from time.
ⓒ He snores from time to time.

372 睡覺時說夢話的人

你說夢話了。

ⓐ You drop in your sleep.
ⓑ You rattle in your sleep.
ⓒ You talk in your sleep.

Answer **367** ⓑ 一般對孩子說 **368** ⓒ 意思是就像木頭（log）一樣，睡得非常踏實 **369** ⓐ 完全沒睡著
▶ not sleep a wink **370** ⓐ cf）失眠 ▶ insomnia **371** ⓒ 有時會 ▶ from time to time；打呼 ▶ snore
372 ⓒ 說夢話 ▶ talk in one's sleep

367

😊 晚安，我的女兒。

_____, my girl.

😀 爸爸，晚安。做個好夢。

You too, Dad. Sweet dreams.

368

😎 哇，我整晚都睡得特別香。

Wow, _____
all night.

😀 天哪！你睡了12個小時。

Oh, my! You slept for 12 hours.

369

😊 你有聽說竊盜案的事了嗎？

Did you hear about the
burglary?

😀 聽說了！昨天晚上我完全沒睡著。

Yeah! _____
last night.

burglary 盜竊，入室盜竊

370

😎 昨天晚上我睡得一點也不安穩。

_____
last night.

😊 什麼，吃了我給你的安眠藥也沒睡安穩？

What, even though I gave you
that sleeping pill?

sleeping pill 安眠藥

371

😎 他的睡眠習慣怎麼樣？

What kind of sleeping habits
does he have?

😀 他不磨牙。但是他有時會打呼。

He doesn't grind his teeth. But
_____

372

😊 你說夢話。所以我幫你錄音了。

_____ So
I recorded you.

😎 真的嗎？我們聽聽吧！

Really? Let's listen to it
together!

Answer **367** Sleep tight 晚安。 **368** I slept like a log 我睡得特別香。 **369** I didn't sleep a wink 我完全沒睡著。 **370** I had trouble sleeping 我睡得一點也不安穩。 **371** he snores from time to time. 他有時會打呼。 **372** You talk in your sleep. 你說夢話了。

Quick Test 03

這些句子用英語怎麼說？

規定時間 1 min

---

373 確認對方是否洗漱好了或者洗完澡了時

洗完了嗎？

ⓐ Have you brushed your face?

ⓑ Have you rubbed your body?

ⓒ Have you washed?

---

374 洗完臉以後，臉上還留著香皂泡沫時

把臉上的香皂洗掉。

ⓐ Slide the soap off your face.

ⓑ Melt the soap out of your face.

ⓒ Rinse the soap off your face.

---

375 要對方馬上刷牙時

吃完飯應該馬上刷牙。

ⓐ Brush your teeth right after you've eaten.

ⓑ Brush your teeth right before you've eaten.

ⓒ Brush you teeth right until you've eaten.

---

376 確認對方是不是用過牙線了時

用牙線了嗎？

ⓐ Did you tie your tooth?

ⓑ Did you use the strings?

ⓒ Did you floss?

---

377 刷牙時，牙齦出血了

牙齦出血了。

ⓐ My teeth bases are bleeding.

ⓑ My gums are bleeding.

ⓒ My gummy tooth is bleeding.

---

378 發現耳屎很多時

我耳屎特別多！

ⓐ I have so much ear dust!

ⓑ I have so much earwax!

ⓒ I have so many ear droppings!

Answer **373** ⓒ 問是不是洗完了，使用現在完成時進行提問　**374** ⓒ 沖洗掉…… ▶ rinse...off　**375** ⓐ ……
後馬上 ▶ right after, immediately after　**376** ⓒ 用牙線 ▶ floss　**377** ⓑ 牙齦 ▶ gum　**378** ⓑ 耳屎 ▶ earwax

DAY 13

▼ 從起床到睡覺

現在可以自信地說出來了嗎？ 規定時間 1 min

373

😎 洗完了嗎？

😊 沒有，還沒有。你先洗吧。我等等洗。
No, not yet. You go ahead. I can wait.

374

👦 把臉上的香皂洗掉。

😊 我洗了！媽媽，我已經20歲了。
I already did! Mom, I'm 20 years old.

375

😊 我等等再刷牙不行嗎？
Can't I brush my teeth a little bit later?

🧑 不行。吃完飯應該馬上刷牙。
No.

376

👦 用牙線了嗎？

👧 一定要用嗎？
Is it really necessary?

377

😀 天哪。我的牙齦出血了。
Oh, dear.

🤠 又出血了？好，我帶你去牙科醫院吧。
Again? Right. I'm taking you to the dentist.

378

😎 哇，我耳屎特別多！
Wow,

🧑 你不用給我看。
You don't have to show it to me.

Answer **373** Have you washed? 洗完了嗎？ **374** Rinse the soap off your face. 把臉上的香皂洗洗。 **375** Brush your teeth right after you've eaten. 吃完飯應該馬上刷牙。 **376** Did you floss? 用牙線了嗎？ **377** My gums are bleeding. 我的牙齦出血了。 **378** I have so much earwax! 我耳屎特別多。

Quick Test 04

這些句子用英語怎麼說？

規定時間 1 min

---

379 在浴缸裡接好了熱水時

洗澡水準備好了。

ⓐ The bath is ready.

ⓑ The bath water is timed.

ⓒ The bath tub is revealed.

---

380 水不夠熱時

洗澡水太冷了。

ⓐ The bath water is rapid.

ⓑ The bath water is tepid.

ⓒ The bath water is poured.

---

381 洗澡時搓澡

我要搓澡。

ⓐ I'm going to exfoliate.

ⓑ I'm going to take off.

ⓒ I'm going to rub my body.

---

382 對洗頭髮的時候不認真沖洗洗髮精泡沫的人

把洗髮精沖乾淨。

ⓐ Shampoo your hair properly.

ⓑ Rinse your hair thoroughly.

ⓒ Gargle your hair alternately.

---

383 建議洗頭髮後用吹風機吹乾頭髮時

用吹風機吹乾頭髮。

ⓐ Blow up your hair.

ⓑ Blow away your hair.

ⓒ Blow dry your hair.

---

384 洗完澡出來以後覺得很舒服時

真清爽。

ⓐ I feel refreshed.

ⓑ I feel watered down.

ⓒ I feel calm.

DAY 13

▼ 從起床到睡覺

Answer **379** ⓐ 洗澡水 ▶ bath (water) **380** ⓑ （溫度）不夠熱 ▶ tepid, lukewarm **381** ⓐ 搓澡 ▶ exfoliate **382** ⓑ 好好地 ▶ thoroughly, properly **383** ⓒ 用吹風機吹乾頭髮 ▶ blow dry **384** ⓐ 清爽的，痛快的 ▶ refreshed

379

😊 洗澡水準備好了，親愛的。

_____ , dear.

😀 謝謝，老婆。等一下，我的橡皮鴨在哪裡？

Thank you, darling. Wait, where's my rubber duck?

380

🎩 什麼呀？洗澡水太冷了。

What?

😊 你上次不是說水太熱了嗎？

You said it was too hot last time!

381

😊 浴缸用完了吧？現在該我用了吧。

Are you done with the bathtub? It's my turn now.

😊 我還得再待一下。我要搓澡。

I'm going to be in here for a while.

382

😊 把洗髮精沖乾淨，提莫西。

_____ , Timothy.

😊 哎呀，洗髮精跑進眼睛裡了，媽媽，快來幫我。

Ouch, I have soap in my eyes, mommy. Help me.

383

😊 我要擦乾頭髮還需要幾條毛巾。

I need more towels to dry my hair.

😊 直接用吹風機吹乾頭髮。

Just

384

🎩 呼！真清爽。我想來瓶啤酒。

Phew!
I feel like a beer.

😊 自己出去買。

You go out and buy it yourself.

Answer **379** The bath is ready 洗澡水準備好了。 **380** The bath water is tepid. 洗澡水太冷了。 **381** I'm going to exfoliate. 我要搓澡。 **382** Rinse your hair thoroughly. 把洗髮精沖乾淨。 **383** Blow dry your hair. 用吹風機吹乾頭髮。 **384** I feel refreshed. 真清爽！

Quick Test 05

這些句子用英語怎麼說？

規定時間 1 min

385 隱晦地說要去廁所時

我去方便一下。

ⓐ I want to see a toilet.
ⓑ The toilet is there.
ⓒ Nature calls.

386 有人一直敲廁所的門時

有人！

ⓐ There's a human!
ⓑ It's occupied!
ⓒ There's a body!

DAY 13

▼ 從起床到睡覺

387 馬桶堵住了時

馬桶堵住了。

ⓐ The toilet won't sink down.
ⓑ The toilet won't open up.
ⓒ The toilet won't flush.

388 馬桶堵住了，水溢出來時

馬桶水溢出來了。

ⓐ The toilet is overflowing.
ⓑ The toilet is a river.
ⓒ The toilet is a maximum.

389 下水道堵住了，水不往下流時

得修下水道了。

ⓐ We need to fix the horn.
ⓑ We need to fix the basin.
ⓒ We need to fix the drain.

390 沒關水龍頭，水一直流時

關一下水龍頭。

ⓐ Turn off the valve.
ⓑ Turn off the faucet.
ⓒ Turn off the hose.

Answer **385** ⓒ 用「自然的召喚」指稱大小便等生理現象 **386** ⓑ （房間等）在使用中 ▶ occupied **387** ⓒ 馬桶 ▶ toilet ：（馬桶的）水沖下去 ▶ flush **388** ⓐ （水等）溢出來 ▶ overflow **389** ⓒ 下水道，排水管 ▶ drain **390** ⓑ 水龍頭 ▶ faucet

---

385

😊 怎麼在這裡停車了？車壞了嗎？
Why are we stopping here? Did the car break down?

🤓 不是。我去方便一下。
Nope.

386

😊 裡面有人嗎？
Is anybody in here?

🎩 有人！

387

🤓 等一下，別去那間。馬桶堵住了。
Wait, don't go in that booth.

🎩 哦！謝謝。
Oh! Thank you.

388

😮 天哪！這是什麼味道？
Oh, my! What's this smell?

😊 沒什麼。馬桶水溢出來了。
It's nothing.

389

🎩 又來了！老婆，得修下水道了。
Not again! Dear,

😊 哦，好。不過這次叫水電工吧。
Oh, okay. But let's call the plumber this time.

390

😮 洗完了就關緊水龍頭。
_____ when you're done.

😊 我還沒洗完呢。還有你到外面等我吧！
I'm not done yet. And why don't you wait outside!

Answer **385** Nature calls. 我去方便一下。 **386** It's occupied! 有人！ **387** The toilet won't flush. 馬桶堵住了。 **388** The toilet is overflowing. 馬桶水溢出來了。 **389** We need to fix the drain. 得修下水道了。 **390** Turn off the faucet. 關緊水龍頭。

Day 13
Review

在忘記以前複習一遍，怎麼樣？

規定時間 **5 min**

聽著MP3跟讀 👂	看著中文說英語 👄
睡覺很晚才起床時 **I overslept!**	我睡過頭了。
忘了定鬧鐘時 **I didn't set my alarm clock.**	我忘了定鬧鐘了。
雖然起床了，但是還沒有完全清醒時 **I'm still half-asleep.**	我還沒睡醒。
對方眼角上掛著眼屎時 **You have sleep in your eyes.**	你眼睛上還有眼屎。
跟要去睡覺的人道晚安時 **Sleep tight.**	晚安。
睜著眼睛到天明時 **I didn't sleep a wink.**	我完全沒睡著。
睡覺時總是翻身 **I had trouble sleeping.**	我睡得一點也不安穩。
睡覺打呼的人 **He snores from time to time.**	他有時會打呼。
確認對方是否洗漱好了或者洗完澡了時 **Have you washed?**	洗完了嗎？
確認對方是不是用過牙線了時 **Did you floss?**	用牙線了嗎？

DAY 13

▼ 從起床到睡覺

📖 看著中文說英文時，用書籤擋住這個部分。

刷牙時，牙齦出血了 **My gums are bleeding.**	牙齦出血了。
發現耳屎很多時 **I have so much earwax!**	我耳屎特別多！
在浴缸裡接好了熱水時 **The bath is ready.**	洗澡水準備好了。
對洗頭髮的時候不認真沖洗洗髮精泡沫的人 **Rinse your hair thoroughly.**	把洗髮精沖乾淨。
建議洗頭髮後用吹風機吹幹頭髮時 **Blow dry your hair.**	用吹風機吹乾頭髮。
洗完澡出來以後覺得很痛快時 **I feel refreshed.**	真清爽。
隱晦地說要去廁所時 **Nature calls.**	我去方便一下。
有人一直敲廁所的門時 **It's occupied!**	有人！
馬桶堵住了時 **The toilet won't flush.**	馬桶堵住了。
沒關水龍頭，水一直流時 **Turn off the faucet.**	關緊水龍頭。

已經學會的句型
390個/600個

📖 看著中文說英文時，用書籤擋住這個部分。

打掃衛生及洗衣服

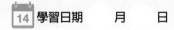

聽例句

打掃亂得一團糟的房間時、洗衣服、晾衣服時、做飯時，或是吃飯時，
你會用英語說這些有關家務勞動的句子嗎？來檢測一下吧。

Test 01 這些句子用英語怎麼說？ 規定時間 1 min

---

391 家裡特別亂時

家裡亂死了。

ⓐ The house is a trash mountain.

ⓑ The house is a rabbit hole.

ⓒ The house is a total mess.

---

392 確認是否使用了吸塵器時

你有用吸塵器了嗎？

ⓐ Did you vacuum?

ⓑ Did you clean up?

ⓒ Did you sweep it?

---

393 不用拖布，而是趴在地上擦地時

我用抹布擦。

ⓐ I'll wipe it with a wet creek.

ⓑ I'll wipe it with a wet broom.

ⓒ I'll wipe it with a wet rag.

---

394 提著垃圾袋遞給對方，讓他去倒垃圾時

把垃圾丟了。

ⓐ Throw the trash.

ⓑ Take out the trash.

ⓒ Trade the trash.

---

395 告訴對方應該將垃圾分類後丟掉時

丟垃圾的時候應該分類。

ⓐ Separate the trash.

ⓑ Put down the garbage.

ⓒ Grind the waste.

---

396 確認是否是可回收垃圾時

這個可回收嗎？

ⓐ Is this recoverable?

ⓑ Is this recyclable?

ⓒ Is this replaceable?

DAY 14 ▼ 打掃衛生及洗衣服

Answer **391** ⓒ（髒且）亂的狀態 ▶ mess **392** ⓐ 用吸塵器 ▶ vacuum *cf*）吸塵器 ▶ vacuum cleaner **393** ⓒ（用抹布等）擦 ▶ wipe ：（用做抹布等的）破布 ▶ rag **394** ⓑ 拿出去扔了 ▶ take out：垃圾 ▶ trash **395** ⓐ 分開 ▶ separate **396** ⓑ 可回收的 ▶ recyclable

391

👦 什麼啊？家裡亂死了。

What?

😊 不好意思，明天我就收拾好。

Sorry, I'll clean it all up by tomorrow.

392

👩 你有用吸塵器吸了嗎？

😊 嗯，怎麼了？有什麼地方我沒吸到嗎？

Yes, why? Did I miss something?

393

😊 我用吸塵器吸了，廚房的地還是很髒。

I vacuumed, but the kitchen floor is still so dirty.

👩 是嗎？別擔心。我用抹布擦。

Really? Don't worry.

394

👧 你是要出去抽煙吧？順便把垃圾倒了。

Are you going out to smoke? _____ while you're at it.

🎩 我戒煙了。

I quit smoking.

395

👩 不對，不對，不是那樣的。倒垃圾的時候應該分類。

No, no. Not like that. _____

😊 不好意思。我是第一次處理垃圾。

Sorry. I'm new at this.

396

🤓 請問，這個可回收嗎？

Excuse me, _____

🎩 你的啤酒罐嗎？當然可以！

Your beer can? Of course!

Answer **391** The house is a total mess. 家裡亂死了。 **392** Did you vacuum? 你有用吸塵器吸了嗎？
393 I'll wipe it with a wet rag. 我用抹布擦。 **394** Take out the trash 把垃圾丟了。 **395** Separate the trash. 倒垃圾的時候應該分類。 **396** is this recyclable? 這個可回收嗎？

Test 02 這些句子用英語怎麼說？

規定時間 1 min

---

397 用洗衣機洗衣服時

我們來洗衣服吧。

ⓐ Let's do the laundry.

ⓑ Let's go to the laundry.

ⓒ Let's have the laundry.

---

398 衣服洗了以後變小了時

縮水了！

ⓐ It tore!

ⓑ It went down!

ⓒ It shrank!

---

399 衣服上有洗不掉的污漬時

這塊污漬要怎麼洗掉呢？

ⓐ How do I get this dot out?

ⓑ How do I get this stain out?

ⓒ How do I get this puncture out?

---

400 衣服都晾乾了時

把衣服收起來吧。

ⓐ Let's take up the laundry.

ⓑ Let's take over the laundry.

ⓒ Let's take down the laundry.

---

401 讓對方把乾衣服疊起來時

疊一疊衣服吧。

ⓐ Fold the laundry.

ⓑ Twirl the laundry.

ⓒ Grab the laundry.

---

402 主動要熨衣服時

衣服我來熨。

ⓐ Leave the ironing.

ⓑ I'll do the ironing.

ⓒ Throw me the iron.

Answer **397** ⓐ 洗衣服 ▶ do the laundry（laundry 要洗的衣服）*cf*）洗衣機 ▶ washing machine **398** ⓒ 變小 ▶ shrink（shrink-shrank-shrunk）**399** ⓑ 有污漬了 ▶ get this stain out（stain 污漬）**400** ⓒ 收（晾乾了的衣服）▶ take down *cf*）晾（衣服）▶ hang out **401** ⓐ 疊（衣服）▶ fold **402** ⓑ 熨衣服 ▶ do the ironing（ironing 熨衣服）

DAY 14 ▼ 打掃衛生及洗衣服

397

我們來洗衣服吧。

這可不是個好主意。馬上就要下雨了。
That's a bad idea. It's going to rain soon.

398

啊！縮水了！
Oh, no!

可能是洗衣服的水太熱了。
The water must've been too hot!

399

這塊污漬要怎麼洗掉呢？

哎呦，可能洗不掉了。
Oops, I don't think it will come out.

400

把衣服收起來吧。

好像還沒乾吧。
I don't think it's dry yet.

401

你要去哪裡？疊一疊衣服吧。
Where are you going?

等一下。我得休息一下。
Hold on. I need a break.

402

衣服我來熨。

不行，你要是再把衣服燒掉了怎麼辦。
No, you might burn the clothes again.

Quick Test 03

這些句子用英語怎麼說？

規定時間 1 min

---

403 剛做好菜，嚐味道的時候

味道剛剛好。

ⓐ It's well-seasoned.

ⓑ It's well-cooked.

ⓒ It's well-done.

---

404 放涼吃才好吃的菜

這個最好放涼吃。

ⓐ This is best served broiled.

ⓑ This is best served chilled.

ⓒ This is best served frozen.

---

405 為了做菜打開瓦斯爐時

把瓦斯爐打開。

ⓐ Turn on the gas stove.

ⓑ Fire the gas range.

ⓒ Turn away the gas stove.

---

406 用微波爐加熱食物時

用微波爐加熱一下吧。

ⓐ Smoke it in the microwave.

ⓑ Fire it in the microwave.

ⓒ Heat it in the microwave.

---

407 食物煮了太長時間時

都燒焦了。

ⓐ I've burned it.

ⓑ It has become toast.

ⓒ The food is tanned.

---

408 比起在飯店吃，家裡的飯菜更好吃時

我想吃家裡做的飯菜。

ⓐ I want the food on the house.

ⓑ I want a home-cooked meal.

ⓒ I want a cook in the home.

DAY 14 ▼ 打掃衛生及洗衣服

Answer **403** ⓐ 調味 ▸ season *cf*）調味料 ▸ seasoning **404** ⓑ〔直譯〕這個菜放涼（chilled）上菜（serve）最好。 **405** ⓐ 開（瓦斯爐）▸ turn on, light：瓦斯爐 ▸ gas stove **406** ⓒ 熱（菜）▸ heat：微波爐 ▸ microwave **407** ⓐ 燒焦 ▸ burn (burn-burned-burned) **408** ⓑ 家裡做的飯菜 ▸ home-cooked meal

---

403

😀 幫我嚐嚐味道怎麼樣，好嗎？
Can you taste this for me?

😊 嗯。味道剛剛好。
Mmm.

404

😊 這道菜是不是太冷了？
Isn't this dish too cold?

😊 不會。這個最好放涼吃。
No.

405

😊 把瓦斯爐打開。

🎩 哦，你終於準備好材料了。
Oh, you're finally ready to cook!

406

👩 瓦斯爐壞了。
The gas stove isn't working.

😊 那用微波爐加熱一下吧。
                                    then.

407

😀 這是什麼味道？千層麵怎麼了？
What's this smell? What happened to the lasagna?

😊 對不起，燒焦了。
Sorry.

408

😊 老公，在外面吃飯的時候，我覺得好幸福。
Darling, I'm so happy when we eat out.

🎩 啊，我想吃家裡做的飯菜。
Argh,

Answer **403** It's well-seasoned. 味道剛剛好。 **404** This is best served chilled. 這個最好放涼吃。 **405** Turn on the gas stove. 把瓦斯爐打開。 **406** Heat it in the microwave. 用微波爐加熱一下吧。 **407** I've burned it. 都燒焦了。 **408** I want a home-cooked meal. 我想吃家裡做的飯菜。

Quick Test 04

這些句子用英語怎麼說？

規定時間 1 min

409 在飯桌上擺餐具時

我來擺桌子。

ⓐ I'll stage the table.

ⓑ I'll provide the table.

ⓒ I'll set the table.

410 把飯菜擺在桌子上之前，擦桌子

用抹布把桌子擦一擦。

ⓐ Wipe the table with a tea towel.

ⓑ Wipe the table with a dishcloth.

ⓒ Wipe the table with a dish napkin.

411 對嘴裡嚼著食物還說話的人

吃飯時候不要講話。

ⓐ Don't talk with your mouth full.

ⓑ Pause chewing while eating.

ⓒ Don't gossip with your face full.

412 對剩飯的人

不能剩飯。

ⓐ Empty your food.

ⓑ Gulp your food.

ⓒ Finish your food.

413 吃飽了後不再繼續吃時

我吃飽了。

ⓐ I can't eat.

ⓑ I'm finished.

ⓒ The food doesn't fit in.

414 當對方只吃肉或者飯時

蔬菜也得吃。

ⓐ Eat all colors.

ⓑ Eat your greens.

ⓒ Eat as much as you can.

DAY 14 ▼ 打掃衛生及洗衣服

Answer **409** ⓒ 擺桌子 ▶ set the table **410** ⓑ 擦 ▶ wipe；抹布 ▶ dishcloth **411** ⓐ〔直譯〕嘴裡都是食物的時候不要說話。 **412** ⓒ（沒有剩下）都吃完了 ▶ finish cf）剩下的飯菜 ▶ leftovers **413** ⓑ **414** ⓑ 蔬菜 ▶ greens

Quick Practice 現在可以自信地說出來了嗎？ 規定時間 1 min

409

😊 我來擺桌子。

😎 說什麼呢！今天是你的生日，你什麼都不用做。
No, you don't! It's your birthday today. Just relax.

410

😊 用抹布把桌子擦一擦。

😊 什麼，用這個？真噁心！
What, with this? Yuck!

411

😊 吃飯時候不要講話。

😊 哦！對不起。你的湯裡掉進了什麼嗎？
Oops! Sorry. Did I get something in your soup?

412

😊 不能剩飯。

😎 但是我現在都要吐了！
But I'm about to throw up!

413

😊 我吃飽了。可以先走嗎？
May I be excused?

😊 等一下，那飯後甜點呢？
Wait, what about dessert?

414

😊 蔬菜也得吃。為了你自己的健康。
It's for your health.

😊 那爸爸為什麼還抽煙呢？
If that's the case, why do you smoke, Dad?

Answer **409** I'll set the table. 我來擺桌子。 **410** Wipe the table with a dishcloth. 用抹布把桌子擦一擦。 **411** Don't talk with your mouth full. 吃飯時候不要講話。 **412** Finish your food. 不能剩飯。 **413** I'm finished. 我吃飽了。 **414** Eat your greens. 蔬菜也得吃。

Quick Test 05

這些句子用英語怎麼說？

規定時間 1 min

---

415 發現是誰放了屁時

他放屁了。

ⓐ He opened wind.

ⓑ He squeezed wind.

ⓒ He broke wind.

---

416 突然開始連續打嗝時

我一直打嗝。

ⓐ I have the hiccups.

ⓑ I have the bulge.

ⓒ I have the frogs.

---

417 鼻子很癢，總是打噴嚏時

我一直打噴嚏。

ⓐ My nose is running.

ⓑ I can't stop sneezing.

ⓒ The sneezing is growing.

---

418 對沒有禮貌地當眾打嗝的人

別再打嗝了。

ⓐ Stop dangling.

ⓑ Stop popping.

ⓒ Stop burping.

---

419 看到肩膀上白色的頭皮屑時

他有頭皮屑。

ⓐ He's got the flu.

ⓑ He's got lice.

ⓒ He's got dandruff.

---

420 喉嚨裡有痰時

我喉嚨裡有痰。

ⓐ I have phlegm in my throat.

ⓑ I have asthma in my throat.

ⓒ I have some salmon in my throat.

DAY 14 ▼ 打掃衛生及洗衣服

Answer **415** ⓒ 用吹開風（break wind）來形容放屁，非常有意思的表達方式 *cf*）放屁 ▶ fart, pass gas
416 ⓐ 連續打嗝 ▶ hiccup **417** ⓑ 打噴嚏 ▶ sneeze **418** ⓒ 打嗝 ▶ burp **419** ⓒ 頭皮屑 ▶ dandruff **420** ⓐ
痰 ▶ phlegm

現在可以自信地說出來了嗎？ 規定時間

415

😊 他放屁了。

😊 什麼？現在？在電梯裡？
What, now? Inside this elevator?

416

🎩 我可能是太緊張了。我一直打嗝。
I must be nervous.

⛄ 來，喝點熱水吧。
Here. Try drinking this warm water.

417

😆 哈啾！天哪，我一直打噴嚏。
Ah-choo! Man,

😊 哦！你被傳染了嗎？
Oh, dear! Is it contagious?

contagious 被傳染的

418

😊 別再打嗝了。

😊 我有什麼辦法。我喝了碳酸飲料。
I can't help it. I'm drinking soda.

419

😊 哦，天哪！他有頭皮屑。
Oh, wow!

😊 別嘲笑他。我也有。
Don't make fun of him. I have it, too.

420

🎩 我喉嚨裡有痰。

😊 別在這裡吐。那邊有廁所。
Don't spit it out yet. There's a restroom over there.

spit out 吐痰

Answer **415** He broke wind. 他放屁了。 **416** I have the hiccups. 我一直打嗝。 **417** I can't stop sneezing. 我一直打噴嚏。 **418** Stop burping. 別再打嗝了。 **419** He's got dandruff. 他有頭皮屑。 **420** I have phlegm in my throat. 我喉嚨裡有痰。

14_6.mp3

聽著MP3跟讀	看著中文說英語
家裡特別亂時 **The house is a total mess.**	家裡亂死了。
確認是否使用了吸塵器時 **Did you vacuum?**	你有用吸塵器了嗎？
提著垃圾袋遞給對方，要他去倒垃圾時 **Take out the trash.**	把垃圾丟了。
告訴對方應該將垃圾分類後丟掉時 **Separate the trash.**	倒垃圾的時候應該分類。
用洗衣機洗衣服時 **Let's do the laundry.**	我們來洗衣服吧。
衣服上有洗不掉的污漬時 **How do I get this stain out?**	這塊污漬要怎麼洗掉呢？
衣服都晾乾了時 **Let's take down the laundry.**	把衣服收起來吧。
請對方把乾衣服疊起來時 **Fold the laundry.**	疊一疊衣服吧。
剛做好菜，嚐味道的時候 **It's well-seasoned.**	味道剛剛好。
放涼吃才好吃的菜 **This is best served chilled.**	這個最好放涼吃。

DAY 14 ▼ 打掃衛生及洗衣服

📖 看著中文說英文時，用書籤擋住這個部分。

213

為了做菜打開瓦斯爐時 **Turn on the gas stove.**	把瓦斯爐打開。
用微波爐加熱食物時 **Heat it in the microwave.**	用微波爐加熱一下吧。
再飯桌上擺餐具時 **I'll set the table.**	我來擺桌子。
對嘴裡嚼著食物還說話的人 **Don't talk with your mouth full.**	吃飯時候不要講話。
對剩飯的人 **Finish your food.**	不能剩飯。
當對方只吃肉或者飯時 **Eat your greens.**	蔬菜也得吃。
發現是誰放了屁時 **He broke wind.**	他放屁了。
突然開始連續打隔時 **I have the hiccups.**	我一直打嗝。
鼻子很癢，總是打噴嚏時 **I can't stop sneezing.**	我一直打噴嚏。
對沒有禮貌地當眾打隔的人 **Stop burping.**	別再打嗝了。

已經學會的句型
420個/600個

看著中文說英文時，用書籤擋住這個部分。

DAY **15**

談論家人・家庭

學習時間

聽例句

介紹父母兄弟等時、告訴別人自己懷孕了時，或是介紹自己生活的地方時，
你會用英語說這些有關家人和自己家的句子嗎？來檢測一下吧。

Quick Test 01

這些句子用英語怎麼說？

規定時間 1 min

---

421 回答對方自己家裡有幾口人時

我家有四口人。

ⓐ All of the numbers are four.

ⓑ We are totally four.

ⓒ There are four of us.

---

422 不和家人生活在一起，自己一個人住時

我自己一個人住。

ⓐ I live by myself.

ⓑ I live with me.

ⓒ I live a lonely life.

---

423 作為一家之長賺錢養家時

我養家。

ⓐ I'm the steak winner.

ⓑ I support my family.

ⓒ My money eats my family.

---

424 家人或者親戚去世時

我奶奶去世了。

ⓐ My grandmother turned a corner.

ⓑ My grandmother passed away.

ⓒ My grandmother climbed away.

---

425 自己家的狗就像家庭裡的成員之一，介紹它時

我有一隻伴侶犬。

ⓐ I have a companion dog.

ⓑ I have a guard dog.

ⓒ I have a watch dog.

---

426 想要結婚生子時

我想要成家立業。

ⓐ I want to start a family.

ⓑ I want to take a family.

ⓒ I want to open a family.

DAY 15

▼ 談論家人・家庭

Answer **421** ⓒ **422** ⓐ （沒有其他人）自己一個人 ▶ by myself cf) 一人家庭 ▶ one-person household
423 ⓑ 供養 ▶ support **424** ⓑ 去世 ▶ pass away （為了回避die而使用）cf) 自然死亡 ▶ natural death
425 ⓐ 伴侶犬 ▶ companion dog （companion伴侶，志同道合的朋友） **426** ⓐ 組建家庭 ▶ start a family

421

😃 你家有幾口人？

How many members are there in your family?

😊 我家有四口人。

422

👧 你和父母住在一起嗎？

Do you live with your parents?

😎 不是，我自己一個人住。

No,

423

😃 你丈夫賺錢賺得多嗎？

Does your husband earn a lot of money?

👩 我養家。

424

😃 我不能參加派對了。我奶奶去世了。

I can't come to your party.

👧 天哪！什麼時候舉行葬禮？

Oh, dear! When is the funeral?

425

😃 你有孩子嗎？

Do you have any kids?

😎 沒有，不過我有一隻伴侶犬。

No, but

426

👩 你的新年願望是什麼？

What is your New Year's wish?

😊 說實話，我想要成家立業。

Actually,

Answer **421** There are four of us. 我家有四口人。 **422** I live by myself. 我自己一個人住。 **423** support my family. 我養家。 **424** My grandmother passed away. 我奶奶去世了。 **425** I have a companion dog. 我有一隻伴侶犬。 **426** I want to start a family. 我想要成家立業。

Quick Test 02　這些句子用英語怎麼說？

規定時間 1 min

427 說自己沒有兄弟姐妹時

我是獨生女。

ⓐ I'm an only daughter.

ⓑ I'm a single daughter.

ⓒ I'm a solo daughter.

428 說自己是大兒子時

我是老大。

ⓐ The top son is me.

ⓑ I'm the biggest son.

ⓒ I'm the eldest son.

429 說自己有幾個兄弟，自己是第幾個孩子時

我家有兩個孩子，我是老么。

ⓐ I'm the smallest from two.

ⓑ I'm the youngest of two.

ⓒ I'm the weakest among the two.

430 說自己和兄弟相差幾歲時

我們差兩歲。

ⓐ We're spaced 2 years apart.

ⓑ We're spaced 2 years away.

ⓒ We're spaced 2 years within.

431 是長得一模一樣的同卵雙生雙胞胎時

我們是同卵雙生的雙胞胎。

ⓐ We're close twins.

ⓑ We're like twins.

ⓒ We're identical twins.

432 兄弟感情很好時

我們兄弟感情很好。

ⓐ I get along well with my nieces.

ⓑ I get along well with my siblings.

ⓒ I get along well with my bandits.

DAY 15

▼ 談論家人・家庭

427

你有幾個兄弟姐妹？

How many brothers and sisters do you have?

我是獨生女。看得出來嗎？

Does it show?

428

為什麼你的父母要和我們一起生活？

Why do your parents have to live with us？

這不是很明顯嗎？我是老大。

Isn't it obvious？

429

我家有兩個孩子，我是老么。

真的？我還以為你是獨生女呢。

Really? I thought you were an only child.

430

那是我哥哥。我們差兩歲。

That's my older brother.

真的？我還以為是你爸爸呢。

Really? I thought he was your Dad.

431

我們是同卵雙生的雙胞胎。

你不說我也能看出來。

No need to tell me that.

432

替我介紹一下你的家庭吧。

Tell me about your family.

好，我們兄弟感情很好，還有……

Well,

, and...

Answer **427** I'm an only daughter. 我是獨生女。 **428** I'm the eldest son. 我是老大。 **429** I'm the youngest of two. 我家有兩個孩子，我是老么。 **430** We're spaced 2 years apart. 我們差兩歲。 **431** We're identical twins. 我們是同卵雙生的雙胞胎。 **432** I get along well with my siblings 我們兄弟感情很好。

433 告訴別人自己妻子懷孕了時

我老婆懷孕了。

ⓐ My wife is giving birth.
ⓑ My wife is expecting.
ⓒ My wife is calling.

434 因為懷孕害喜非常痛苦時

我孕吐很嚴重。

ⓐ I have terrible mouth sickness.
ⓑ I have terrible morning sickness.
ⓒ I have terrible baby sickness.

435 懷孕以後，肚子慢慢大起來時

肚子越來越大了。

ⓐ My waist is getting bigger.
ⓑ My baby space is getting bigger.
ⓒ My belly is getting bigger.

436 感覺到胎動時

我感覺到孩子踢腿了。

ⓐ I can feel the baby pushing.
ⓑ I can feel the baby kicking.
ⓒ I can feel the baby pressing.

437 告訴對方預產期時

我下個月的預產期。

ⓐ The baby is due next month.
ⓑ The baby is on next month.
ⓒ The baby is going next month.

438 沒有剖腹產生下孩子時

我是自然產的。

ⓐ I had a natural birth.
ⓑ I had a good-natured baby.
ⓒ The birth was controlled.

DAY 15
▼ 談論家人・家庭

Answer **433** ⓑ 等著（expect）出生的意思 *cf*）懷孕的 ▶ pregnant　**434** ⓑ 害喜 ▶ morning sickness （由來：懷孕初期常見的上午出現孕吐的現象）　**435** ⓒ 肚子 ▶ belly *cf*）開始陣痛 ▶ go into labor　**436** ⓑ **437** ⓐ 預產期的 ▶ due *cf*）生孩子 ▶ childbirth　**438** ⓐ 自然產 ▶ natural birth *cf*）剖腹產 ▶ C-section

221

現在可以自信地說出來了嗎？ 規定時間 1 min

433
你為什麼要請我喝啤酒？
Why are you buying me beer?

我老婆懷孕了。我要當爸爸了
_____ I'm going to be a dad!

434
最近我孕吐很嚴重。
_____ lately.

天哪，堅持一下。
Oh, dear. Hang in there.

435
看我。我的肚子越來越大了。
Look at me.

你看起來很可愛，親愛的。
You look lovely, dear.

436
哦！我感覺到孩子踢腿了。
Oh!

哇！讓我也摸摸！
Wow! Let me feel, too!

437
我下個月預產期。
_____

是嗎！你需要什麼就告訴我。
I see! Tell me if you need any help.

438
你是剖腹產嗎？
Did you have a C-section?

不是。我是自然產的。
No. _____

C-section 剖腹產

Answer **433** My wife is expecting. 我老婆懷孕了。 **434** I have terrible morning sickness 我孕吐很嚴重。 **435** My belly is getting bigger. 我的肚子越來越大了。 **436** I can feel the baby kicking. 我感覺到孩子踢腿了。 **437** The baby is due next month. 我下個月預產期。 **438** I had a natural birth. 我是自然產的。

Quick Test 04

這些句子用英語怎麼說？

規定時間 1 min

---

439 同時說出自己是否結婚和有幾名子女時

我結婚了，有兩個孩子。

ⓐ I'm married for two children.

ⓑ I'm married as I have two children.

ⓒ I'm married with two children.

---

440 孩子長得很像爸爸時

他和爸爸像一個模子刻出來一樣。

ⓐ He's a carbon copy of his dad.

ⓑ He's a baked cake of his dad.

ⓒ He's a printed copy of his dad.

---

441 特別愛孩子的時候

我兒子是我的心頭肉。

ⓐ I can put my son in my eye.

ⓑ My son is the apple of my eye.

ⓒ My son is the apple in my eye.

---

442 遺傳了身體特徵或者性格時

這是家族遺傳的。

ⓐ It runs in the family.

ⓑ It walks in the family.

ⓒ It sits in the family.

---

443 非常嚴格地教育孩子時

我對孩子很嚴格。

ⓐ My children are rude.

ⓑ I'm strict with my children.

ⓒ I have plans for my children.

---

444 正在撫養的孩子不是自己親生的時

我有個領養的兒子。

ⓐ I have an adapted son.

ⓑ I have an adept son.

ⓒ I have an adopted son.

DAY 15

▼ 談論家人・家庭

Answer **439** ⓒ **440** ⓐ 與……長得完全一樣 ▶ a carbon copy of（本來carbon copy是「複本」的意思）
441 ⓑ ……是最愛的人 ▶ the apple of one's eye **442** ⓐ 家族遺傳 ▶ run in the family **443** ⓑ 對……很嚴格 ▶ be strict with **444** ⓒ 領養的 ▶ adopted cf）適應的 ▶ adapted，熟練的 ▶ adept

現在可以自信地說出來了嗎？ 規定時間 1 min

439

😎 請您自我介紹一下，麥克唐納先生。

Tell me about yourself, Mr. MacDonald.

🎩 好。我結婚了，有兩個孩子。

Sure.

440

😊 看他！他和爸爸像一個模子刻出來一樣。

Look at him!

😉 哦，他太可愛了！

Oh, he's so cute!

441

😎 我兒子是我的心頭肉。

🎩 能看出來。你一定很幸福。

I can tell. You must be happy.

442

👩 你和你姐姐都是左撇子嗎？

Your sister and you are both left-handed?

😎 這是我們家遺傳的。

443

😊 詹姆士非常有禮貌，班森夫人。

James is very well-mannered, Mrs. Benson.

😎 哦，太好了。這是因為我對孩子很嚴格。

Oh, good. It's because

444

👩 我有個領養的兒子。請你保守這個秘密。

But please keep this a secret.

🎩 當然。我的口風很緊的。

Of course. My lips are sealed.

well-mannered 有禮貌的

Answer **439** I'm married with two children. 我結婚了，有兩個孩子。 **440** He's a carbon copy of his dad. 他和爸爸像一個模子刻出來一樣。 **441** My son is the apple of my eye. 我兒子是我的心頭肉。 **442** It runs in the family. 這是我們家遺傳的。 **443** I'm strict with my children. 我對孩子很嚴格。 **444** I have an adopted son. 我有個領養的兒子。

445 告訴對方自己住在什麼樣的房子裡時

我住在公寓大樓裡。

ⓐ I live in a parted building.

ⓑ I live in an apartment.

ⓒ I live apart.

446 住在遠離城市中心比較清靜的地方

我住在農村。

ⓐ I live in a green house.

ⓑ I live in a country house.

ⓒ I live in a tree house.

447 住在首爾近郊時

我住在首爾近郊。

ⓐ I live in the suburbs of Seoul.

ⓑ I live in the district of Seoul.

ⓒ I live in the high streets of Seoul.

448 告訴對方自己的家在幾層時

我住在10樓。

ⓐ I live on the tenth floor.

ⓑ I live in the tenth floor.

ⓒ I live over the tenth floor.

449 覺得自己家的房租比較合理時

每月的房租蠻合理的。

ⓐ The monthly fee is manageable.

ⓑ The monthly deposit is balanced.

ⓒ The monthly rent is reasonable.

450 搬家到這裡時間還不長時

我剛搬到這裡。

ⓐ I just moved in.

ⓑ I just made a move.

ⓒ I just came by.

DAY 15

▼ 談論家人・家庭

Answer **445** ⓑ 住在……▶ live in ：公寓大樓 ▶ apartment **446** ⓑ 農村的房子 ▶ country house *cf*) 房前屋後可以種植植物的地 ▶ kitchen/ vegetable garden **447** ⓐ ……的近郊，郊區 ▶ suburbs of **448** ⓐ 在10樓 ▶ on the tenth floor **449** ⓒ 月租金 ▶ monthly rent ：（價格）合理的 ▶ reasonable **450** ⓐ 搬來 ▶ move in *cf*) 搬走 ▶ move out

445

😊 我住在公寓大樓裡。

😊 有地下停車場嗎？
Does it have underground parking?

446

🎩 我住在農村。

😊 太幸福了！我討厭死城市生活了。
Lucky you! I'm fed up with the city life.

447

😊 我住在首爾近郊。

🎩 這樣啊。那你怎麼通勤呢？
I see. Then how do you commute to work?

448

😊 不好意思，我是不是認識你？
Excuse me, don't I know you?

😊 當然啦。我住在10樓。
Of course.

449

😊 你覺得住在這裡怎麼樣？
How do you like living here?

😊 嗯，每月的房租蠻合理的。我只在乎這個。
Well,
That's all I care about.

450

😊 嘿！你為什麼跟著我？
Hey! Why are you following me?

🎩 沒，沒有啊。我是你的新鄰居。我剛搬到這裡。
Oh, no. I'm your new neighbor.

Answer **445** I live in an apartment. 我住在公寓樓裡。 **446** I live in a country house. 我住在農村。 **447** I live in the suburbs of Seoul. 我住在首爾近郊。 **448** I live on the tenth floor. 我住在10樓。 **449** the monthly rent is reasonable. 每月的房租蠻合理的。 **450** I just moved in. 我剛搬到這裡。

聽著MP3跟讀	看著中文說英語

Day 15
Review

在忘記以前複習一遍，怎麼樣？

規定時間 5 min

聽著MP3跟讀	看著中文說英語
回答對方自己家裡有幾口人時 **There are four of us.**	我家有四口人。
不和家人生活在一起，自己一個人住時 **I live by myself.**	我自己一個人住。
家人或者親戚去世時 **My grandmother passed away.**	我奶奶去世了。
自己家的狗就像家庭裡的成員之一，介紹它時 **I have a companion dog.**	我有一隻伴侶犬。
說自己沒有兄弟姐妹時 **I'm an only daughter.**	我是獨生女。
說自己是大兒子時 **I'm the eldest son.**	我是老大。
說自己有幾個兄弟，自己是第幾個孩子時 **I'm the youngest of two.**	我家有兩個孩子，我是老么。
說自己和兄弟相差幾歲時 **We're spaced 2 years apart.**	我們差兩歲。
告訴別人自己妻子懷孕了時 **My wife is expecting.**	我老婆懷孕了。
因為懷孕害喜非常痛苦時 **I have terrible morning sickness.**	我孕吐很嚴重。

DAY 15 ▼ 談論家人‧家庭

📖 看著中文說英文時，用書籤擋住這個部分。

懷孕以後，肚子慢慢大起來時 **My belly is getting bigger.**	我的肚子越來越大了。
告訴對方預產期時 **The baby is due next month.**	我下個月的預產期。
同時說出自己是否結婚和有幾名子女時 **I'm married with two children.**	我結婚了，有兩個孩子。
孩子長得很像爸爸時 **He's a carbon copy of his dad.**	他和爸爸像一個模子刻出來的似的。
特別愛孩子的時候 **My son is the apple of my eye.**	我兒子是我的心頭肉。
遺傳了身體特徵或者性格時 **It runs in the family.**	這是我們遺傳的。
告訴對方自己住在什麼樣的房子裡時 **I live in an apartment.**	我住在公寓樓裡。
告訴對方自己家在幾層時 **I live on the tenth floor.**	我住在10樓。
覺得自己家的房租比較合適時 **The monthly rent is reasonable.**	每月的房租蠻合理的。
搬家到這裡時間還不長時 **I just moved in.**	我剛搬到這裡。

已經學會的句型
450個/600個

📖 看著中文說英文時，用書籤擋住這個部分。

NOTE

Lightening!

Learn to Boost Your
English Skills
Everyday Expression **600**

Day 16

Day 20

DAY 16

搭車上下班

學習日期　　月　　日

 學習時間

聽例句

說自己上下班的時間時、幫車子加油時，或是發生交通事故時，
你會用英語說有關上下班和汽車的句子嗎？來檢測一下吧。

Quick Test 01 這些句子用英語怎麼說？ 規定時間 1 min

---

451 說自己平時出門上班的時間時

我早上8點去上班。

ⓐ I leave for work at 8 a.m.

ⓑ I start at work at 8 a.m.

ⓒ I open the door at 8 a.m.

452 每天準時下班時

我準時下班。

ⓐ My leaving hour is a knife.

ⓑ I leave work exactly on time.

ⓒ I leave for the exit like a bee.

---

453 上下班時使用的交通工具

比起公車，我更喜歡坐地鐵。

ⓐ I prefer the subway to the bus.

ⓑ I prefer the bus to the subway.

ⓒ I prefer the bus to the underground.

454 從家到公司所需的時間

上下班要花50分鐘。

ⓐ It takes 50 minutes to go-and-return.

ⓑ It takes 50 minutes to connect to work.

ⓒ It takes 50 minutes to commute.

---

455 從家到公司走路所需的時間

走路30分鐘。

ⓐ It's a 30-minute walk.

ⓑ It's a 30-minute journey.

ⓒ It's a 30-minute road.

456 多人搭車去上班時

我搭車上班。

ⓐ I pull a car to work.

ⓑ I carpool to work.

ⓒ I'm coupling to work.

DAY 16 ▸ 搭車上下班

Answer **451** ⓐ 去上班 ▸ leave for work **452** ⓑ 下班 ▸ leave work ；準時 ▸ exactly on time **453** ⓐ 比起A來，更喜歡B ▸ prefer B to A **454** ⓒ 通勤 ▸ commute **455** ⓐ【類似句型】▸ It takes 30 minutes on foot. **456** ⓑ 共乘 ▸ carpool

Quick Practice　現在可以自信地說出來了嗎？　規定時間

451
😎 我早上8點去上班。

😀 你家離公司很近吧。我7點就出門。
You must live near work. It's 7 o'clock for me.

452
😀 我每天準時下班。

every day.

😀 你這樣真的明智嗎？
Do you think that's wise?

453
😎 比起公車，我更喜歡坐地鐵。

😀 我兩個都不喜歡。所以我每天開車上班。
I prefer neither. That's why I drive to work.

454
😀 上下班要花50分鐘。

😀 還算不錯啊。我真羨慕你。
That's not so bad. I envy you.

455
😎 走路去要多長時間？
How long does it take on foot?

😎 嗯。走路30分鐘。
Umm.

456
😎 我搭車上班。

😀 真是好主意！我也能一起共乘嗎？
What a great idea! Can I join, too?

16_2.mp3

這些句子用英語怎麼說？

規定時間 1 min

---

457 跟著導航開車時

跟著導航走。

ⓐ Follow the GPC.
ⓑ Follow the JPS.
ⓒ Follow the GPS.

---

458 塞車的時候

塞車塞得很嚴重。

ⓐ It's number plate to number plate.
ⓑ It's headlight to tail light.
ⓒ It's bumper to bumper.

---

459 就算繞點路，也能更快到達時

繞路走吧。

ⓐ Let's take a tour.
ⓑ Let's take a toll.
ⓒ Let's take a detour.

---

460 從國道進入高速公路時

我們要上高速公路了。

ⓐ We're pulling over on the highway.
ⓑ We're entering the highway.
ⓒ We're grinding the highway.

---

461 請對方繫好安全帶時

繫上安全帶。

ⓐ Fasten your seatbelt.
ⓑ Tie your seatbelt.
ⓒ Wrap your seatbelt.

---

462 調整汽車座椅的位置和角度時

調一下座椅。

ⓐ Adjust your seat.
ⓑ Shake your seat.
ⓒ Practice your seat.

DAY 16

▼ 搭車上下班

Answer **457** ⓒ 導航 ▶ GPS (global positioning system) **458** ⓒ（汽車）一輛接著一輛，塞車 ▶ bumper to bumper **459** ⓒ 繞路 ▶ detour **460** ⓑ 上高速公路 ▶ enter the highway **461** ⓐ 繫（安全帶）▶ fasten, put on：安全帶 ▶ seatbelt **462** ⓐ 調整（座椅靠背等）▶ adjust

235

457

這是哪裡啊？跟著導航走就行了。

Where are we? Just

你不相信我嗎？

Don't you trust me?

458

老婆，我會晚點到。今天塞車塞得很嚴重。

Honey, I'll be late.
                    today.

很累吧！開車小心點。

You poor thing! Drive home safely.

459

繞路走吧。那邊應該塞得不是這麼厲害。

                    There'll be less traffic.

我聽你的，親愛的。

I'll leave it up to you, honey.

460

我們要上高速公路了。你們在哪裡呢？

How about you?

我們迷路了。

We're lost.

461

我看到巡邏車了。快繫上安全帶。

I see a patrol car!
                    quickly.

爸爸，我的安全帶壞了。

Dad, mine's broken.

462

嘿，你車的駕駛座好窄啊。

Hey, your driver's seat is cramped.

調一下座椅。你得手動調整。

                    You have to do it manually.

cramped 狹窄的 manually 手動的，用手的

Answer **457** follow the GPS. 跟著導航走。 **458** It's bumper to bumper 塞車塞得很厲害。 **459** Let's take a detour. 繞路走吧。 **460** We're entering the highway. 我們要上高速公路了。 **461** Fasten your seatbelt 繫上安全帶。 **462** Adjust your seat. 調一下座椅。

Quick
Test 03

這些句子用英語怎麼說？

規定時間 1 min

---

463 請對方開一下後車箱時

開一下後車箱。

ⓐ Peel the trunk.
ⓑ Pop the trunk.
ⓒ Swipe the trunk.

---

464 因為在禁止停車的區域停了車

我被開罰單了。

ⓐ I got a parking ticket.
ⓑ I got a parking paper.
ⓒ I got a parking memo.

---

465 要下車辦一點事，告訴在車裡等的人

別熄火，等我一下。

ⓐ Keep the switch running.
ⓑ Keep the engine burning.
ⓒ Keep the engine running.

---

466 後照鏡破了，看不到後面的情況時

後照鏡破了。

ⓐ The back mirror is broken.
ⓑ The white mirror is broken.
ⓒ The rear view mirror is broken.

DAY 16

▼ 搭車上下班

---

467 在飯店等處請停車場工作人員幫忙停車時

請幫我停車。

ⓐ I'd like to use valet parking.
ⓑ I'd like to use free parking.
ⓒ I'd like to be a valet.

---

468 停的車被拖走了時

我的車被拖走了。

ⓐ My car has been pulled over.
ⓑ My car has been dragged.
ⓒ My car has been towed.

Answer **463** ⓑ（就像碰一聲彈開一樣）打開蓋子 ▶ pop **464** ⓐ 違章停車罰單 ▶ parking ticket *cf*）罰金 ▶ fine **465** ⓒ〔直譯〕讓發動機繼續工作。 **466** ⓒ 後照鏡 ▶ rear view mirror **467** ⓐ（停車場工作人員代替客人停車）代客泊車服務 ▶ valet parking **468** ⓒ 拖 ▶ tow

463

開一下後車箱。

你又帶啤酒來了？太好了！
You brought more beer? Great!

464

你怎麼這麼晚？
Why are you late?

我被開罰單了。我併排停車了。
I was double-parked.

465

別熄火，等我一下。我馬上就回來。
I'll be back soon.

不行，那樣的話會污染環境。
No, that's bad for the environment.

466

真倒楣！照後鏡破了。
Darn!

哦，天哪！兩邊的側鏡也都破了。
Oh, no! Both of the side mirrors are too.

467

請幫我停車。小心點啊。
Please be careful.

一定一定，夫人。
Of course, ma'am.

468

我的車被拖走了。

不是吧，好像是被偷走了。
No, I think it's been stolen!

Answer **463** Pop the trunk. 開一下後車箱。 **464** I got a parking ticket. 我被開罰單了。 **465** Keep the engine running. 別熄火，等我一下。 **466** The rear view mirror is broken. 後照鏡碎了。 **467** I'd like to use valet parking. 請幫我停車。 **468** My car has been towed. 我的車被拖走了。

Test 04　這些句子用英語怎麼說？　規定時間 1 min

---

469 在加油站把油加滿時

幫我把油加滿。

ⓐ Fill her up.

ⓑ Maximize the oil.

ⓒ Insert the petrol tank.

---

470 只想加一定數額的汽油時

幫我加50美元的油。

ⓐ Just 50 dollars worth of gas.

ⓑ Just 50 dollars on the gas tank.

ⓒ Just 50 dollars of petrol left.

---

471 比起其他車來，油耗比較低時

我的車油耗很低。

ⓐ My car has great power.

ⓑ My car has great fuel.

ⓒ My car has great mileage.

---

472 汽車輪胎漏氣時

爆胎了。

ⓐ My car is a punk.

ⓑ I have a flat tire.

ⓒ The tire has damaged my car.

---

473 發現引擎漏油時

引擎漏油了。

ⓐ The engine oil is building up.

ⓑ The engine oil is cracked.

ⓒ The engine oil is leaking.

---

474 到維修站裝了行車記錄器時

我裝了行車記錄器。

ⓐ I had the black box watched.

ⓑ I had a black box installed.

ⓒ I had my black box fixed.

DAY 16 ▶ 搭車上下班

Answer **469** ⓐ （汽車加油）加滿了 ▶ fill...up：因為將船、汽車等看做女性，因此使用 her **470** ⓐ （加在汽車裡的）汽油，油 ▶ gas, gasoline **471** ⓒ 續駛里程，油耗 ▶ mileage **472** ⓑ 沒氣了的輪胎 ▶ flat tire（flat 扁扁的，沒有氣的） **473** ⓒ （液體·氣體）漏 ▶ leak **474** ⓑ （讓別人）安裝…… ▶ have...installed

469

你好！幫我把油加滿，謝謝。
Excuse me! _____,
please.

先生，這裡是自助加油站。
Sir, this is a self-service gas
station.

470

幫我加50美元的油，謝謝。
_____,
please.

先生，消費滿100美元，優惠5%。
Sir, you get 5% off if you spend
100 dollars.

471

我的車耗油量很低。

可是看起來不是那麼堅固。
But it doesn't look very sturdy.

sturdy 結實，堅固的

472

怎麼辦？爆胎了。
What should I do?

別慌。把車慢慢停下。
Don't panic. Let's pull over
slowly.

pull over 停車

473

哎呀。引擎漏油了。
Oh, man.

快把煙弄滅！
Put out your cigarette now!

put out 滅（火）

474

我裝了行車記錄器。

太好了！現在我覺得安全了。
Great! I feel safe now.

Answer **469** Fill her up 幫我把油加滿。 **470** Just 50 dollars worth of gas 幫我加50美元的油。 **471** My car has great mileage. 我的車耗油量很低。 **472** I have a flat tire. 爆胎了。 **473** The engine oil is leaking. 引擎漏油了。 **474** I had a black box installed. 我裝了行車記錄器。

Quick Test 05

這些句子用英語怎麼說？

規定時間 1 min

475 只是輕輕撞了前面車的保險桿，發生這樣輕微的事故時

這只是小事故。

ⓐ It was a fender-mender.

ⓑ It was a fender-bender.

ⓒ It was a fender-cracker.

476 兩輛車對面相撞

兩輛車面對面相撞了。

ⓐ It was a head-in collision.

ⓑ It was a head-off collision.

ⓒ It was a head-on collision.

477 由交通事故引發爭吵或鬥毆事件時

我和人起了爭執。

ⓐ I got into a scuffle.

ⓑ I got into a punching bag.

ⓒ I got into a mouth-to-fist.

478 通過後視鏡看不到的地方

那是視線死角。

ⓐ It was in a fourth wall.

ⓑ It was in my blind spot.

ⓒ It was in my closed angle.

DAY 16 ▼ 搭車上下班

479 稱自己沒有酒駕時

我沒有酒駕。

ⓐ I didn't drink and drive.

ⓑ I'm not drunk.

ⓒ My car doesn't have alcohol.

480 稱自己沒有超速時

我沒超速。

ⓐ I was pushing the speed limit.

ⓑ I wasn't gambling the speed limit.

ⓒ I was under the speed limit.

Answer **475** ⓑ（汽車的）輕微事故 ▶ fender-bender：意思是只是汽車的擋泥板（fender）彎了（bend）這樣的小事故。 **476** ⓒ 正面碰撞 ▶ head-on：衝撞 ▶ collision **477** ⓐ 爭執，爭吵 ▶ scuffle **478** ⓑ 視線死角 ▶ blind spot **479** ⓐ 酒駕 ▶ drink and drive **480** ⓒ 沒超過規定時速 ▶ under the speed limit

475

是很嚴重的事故嗎？
Was it a serious car accident?

不是。這只是小事故。
No.

476

兩輛車面對面相撞了。

有人受傷嗎？
Was anyone injured?

477

這是在交通事故中撞到淤青的嗎？
Did the car accident cause that bruise?

不是。我和對方司機起了爭執。
No.
with the other driver.

478

你怎麼沒看到其他車開過來？
Why didn't you see the other car coming?

那是視線死角。我也沒辦法。
I couldn't help it.

479

我沒有酒駕。

過來，吹一下。
Come on, blow into this.

480

我沒超速。

我知道。是因為你的尾燈。尾燈壞了。
I know. It's your tail light. It's broken.

tail light 尾燈

Answer **475** It was a fender-bender. 這只是小事故。 **476** It was a head-on collision. 兩輛車面對面相撞了。 **477** I got into a scuffle 我發生了爭執。 **478** It was in my blind spot. 那是視線死角。 **479** I didn't drink and drive. 我沒有酒駕。 **480** I was under the speed limit. 我沒超速。

Day 16 Review

在忘記以前複習一遍，怎麼樣？

規定時間 5 min

聽著MP3跟讀	看著中文說英語
說自己平時出門上班的時間時 **I leave for work at 8 a.m.**	我早上8點去上班。
每天準時下班時 **I leave work exactly on time.**	我準時下班。
上下班時使用的交通工具 **I prefer the subway to the bus.**	比起公車，我更喜歡坐地鐵。
從家到公司所需的時間 **It takes 50 minutes to commute.**	上下班要花50分鐘。
跟著導航開車時 **Follow the GPS.**	跟著導航走。
塞車的時候 **It's bumper to bumper.**	塞車塞得很嚴重。
就算繞點路，也能更快到達時 **Let's take a detour.**	繞路走吧。
讓對方繫好安全帶時 **Fasten your seatbelt.**	繫上安全帶。
讓對方開一下後車箱時 **Pop the trunk.**	開一下後車箱。
因為在禁止停車的區域停了車 **I got a parking ticket.**	我被開罰單了。

DAY 16 ▼ 搭車上下班

📖 看著中文說英文時，用書籤擋住這個部分。

要下車辦一點事，告訴等在車裡的人 **Keep the engine running.**	別熄火，等我一下。
停著的車被拖走了時 **My car has been towed.**	我的車被拖走了。
在加油站把油加滿時 **Fill her up.**	幫我把油加滿。
只想加一定數額的汽油時 **Just 50 dollars worth of gas.**	幫我加50美元的油。
汽車輪胎漏氣時 **I have a flat tire.**	爆胎了。
到維修站裝了行車記錄器時 **I had a black box installed.**	我裝了行車記錄器。
只是輕輕撞了前面車的保險桿，發生這樣輕微的事故時 **It was a fender-bender.**	這只是小事故。
兩輛車對面相撞 **It was a head-on collision.**	兩輛車面對面相撞了。
稱自己沒有酒駕時 **I didn't drink and drive.**	我沒有酒駕。
稱自己沒有超速時 **I was under the speed limit.**	我沒超速。

已經學會的句型
480個/600個

📖 看著中文說英文時，用書籤擋住這個部分。

賺錢及存錢

🕐 學習時間

聽例句

信用卡刷爆了的時候、零用錢都用完了的時候，或是買基金賠了錢的時候，
你會用英語說這些有關錢的句子嗎？來檢測一下吧。

Quick Test 01

這些句子用英語怎麼說？

規定時間 1 min

---

481 夫妻兩人都有收入時

我們是雙薪家庭。

ⓐ We're a money-making couple.

ⓑ We're a double-income couple.

ⓒ We're a earn-together couple.

---

482 賺到的錢很多時

他很能賺錢。

ⓐ He makes a lot of money.

ⓑ He creates a lot of money.

ⓒ He builds a lot of money.

---

483 因為生意成功賺了很多錢時

她腰纏萬貫。

ⓐ She's rolling on a money carpet.

ⓑ She's rolling inside a golden rug.

ⓒ She's rolling in money.

---

484 因為股票、投資等突然賺了大錢時

他突然賺了一大筆錢。

ⓐ He hit the jackpot.

ⓑ He hit the giant pot.

ⓒ He hit the biggest pumpkin.

---

485 因為做生意失敗，虧得沒有錢了時

我窮得叮噹響了。

ⓐ I'm an empty man.

ⓑ I have no credit.

ⓒ I'm flat broke.

---

486 說自己賺錢不多時

我手頭不太寬裕。

ⓐ I'm not doing well walletwise.

ⓑ I'm not doing well pocketwise.

ⓒ I'm not doing well moneywise.

DAY 17

▼ 賺錢及存錢

Answer **481** ⓑ 雙薪家庭 ▶ double/dual-income couple *cf*）全職主婦 ▶ homemaker **482** ⓐ 賺錢 ▶ make money **483** ⓒ 錢多得到處滾的意思 **484** ⓐ 突然賺了一大筆錢 ▶ hit the jackpot **485** ⓒ 完全沒有錢了，破產狀態的 ▶ flat broke：〔直譯〕我已經變得扁扁的了。 **486** ⓒ 有關錢的：moneywise

481

你和你丈夫都工作嗎？

Do you and your husband both work?

嗯。我們是雙薪家庭。

Yes.

482

我介紹你和麥克相親吧。他很能賺錢。

Let me set you up with Mike.

不要，琳達。我希望找到真愛。

No, Linda. I want true love.

set A up with B 介紹A和B相親

483

你侄女琳達過得好嗎？

How's your cousin Linda doing?

哎呀！她腰纏萬貫。她的公司上市了。

Oh, man!
Her company went public.

go public （公司）上市

484

我聽說約翰在炒股票？

I heard John is investing in stocks?

他賺了一大筆錢。

485

我窮得叮噹響了。琳達，能借給我點錢嗎？

Linda, can you lend me some money?

真可憐。你要借多少？

I'm sorry to hear that. How much do you need?

486

約翰，你要給我的新公司投資點嗎？

John, will you invest in my start-up company?

不好意思。我手頭不太寬裕。

Sorry,

start-up 新公司（特別指網路公司）

Answer **481** We're a double-income couple. 我們是雙薪家庭。 **482** He makes a lot of money. 他很能賺錢。 **483** She's rolling in money. 她腰纏萬貫。 **484** He hit the jackpot. 他賺了一大筆錢。 **485** I'm flat broke. 我窮得叮噹響了。 **486** I'm not doing well moneywise. 我手頭不太寬裕。

Test 02 這些句子用英語怎麼說？ 規定時間 **1 min**

487 很節省的人

她很節儉。

ⓐ She's thrifty.

ⓑ She's money-strong.

ⓒ She's a small bank.

488 花錢像流水的人

她花錢像流水。

ⓐ She spends money like dirt.

ⓑ She spends money like water.

ⓒ She burns money everywhere.

489 特別吝嗇、不花錢的人

他太摳了。

ⓐ He's too salty.

ⓑ He's such a tiny spender.

ⓒ He's a penny pincher.

490 家庭收入情況不好，需要盡最大的努力節省時

我們要勒緊褲帶了。

ⓐ We need to grab our money.

ⓑ We need to tighten our belts.

ⓒ We need to hasten the delivery.

491 零用錢都用完了時

零用錢都花完了。

ⓐ I'm out of pocket money.

ⓑ My pocket money is zero.

ⓒ There's no extra money left.

492 把撲滿裡的錢都拿出來時

把我的小豬撲滿打破了。

ⓐ I cut down my pork can.

ⓑ I tore up my pig box.

ⓒ I broke open my piggy bank.

DAY 17 ▼ 賺錢及存錢

Answer **487** ⓐ 節儉的 ▶ thrifty *cf*）樸素的 ▶ frugal **488** ⓑ = She throws money around. **489** ⓒ （一分錢都捨不得花的）吝嗇鬼，小氣鬼 ▶ penny pincher **490** ⓑ 勒緊褲帶 ▶ tighten one's belt **491** ⓐ ……見底了，都用完了 ▶ out of：零花錢 ▶ pocket money **492** ⓒ 砸開 ▶ break open：小豬撲滿 ▶ piggy bank

487

😊 她是什麼樣的人呢？
What kind of person is she?

👧 她很節儉。她有十個戶頭呢。
_____ She has ten savings accounts.

488

😊 和莫妮卡結婚並不是一個明智的選擇。她花錢像流水。
It's not a wise idea to marry Monica.

🎩 你應該早點告訴我。
You should have told me earlier.

489

😊 他太摳了。

👩 我同意。他從來不請人吃飯。
I agree. He never buys you lunch.

490

😊 我被公司炒魷魚了，你還沒找到工作。
I got fired from work and you're still out of work.

😊 我知道。我們要勒緊褲帶了。
I know.

491

😊 爸爸，零用錢都花完了。
Dad,

🎩 我可不能給你上次那麼多了。
I can't give you as much as last time.

492

😊 這些硬幣都是哪裡來的？
Where did you get all these coins?

👩 我把我的小豬撲滿打破了。我零用錢不夠用。
_____ I didn't get enough pocket money.

Answer **487** She's thrifty. 她很節儉。 **488** She spends money like water. 她花錢像流水。 **489** He's a penny pincher. 他太摳了。 **490** We need to tighten our belts. 我們要勒緊褲帶了。 **491** I'm out of pocket money. 零用錢都花完了。 **492** I broke open my piggy bank. 我把我的小豬存錢罐打破了。

Test 03 這些句子用英語怎麼說？ 規定時間 1 min

---

493 在銀行開了帳戶時

我開了帳戶。

ⓐ I opened up an account.

ⓑ I opened up a bank window.

ⓒ I opened up a money package.

---

494 從銀行領了錢時

我領錢了。

ⓐ I pulled out my savings.

ⓑ I've taken in money.

ⓒ I've made a withdrawal.

---

495 在銀行存了錢時

我存錢了。

ⓐ I've made a deposit.

ⓑ I've made a payment.

ⓒ I've made a down payment.

---

496 新開了一個整存款帳戶時

我開了存款帳戶。

ⓐ I started up a mortgage fund.

ⓑ I opened an installment savings account.

ⓒ I signed an insurance contract.

---

497 用網路銀行轉帳時

我已經轉帳了。

ⓐ I transferred the money.

ⓑ I dislocated the money.

ⓒ I transformed the money.

---

498 向銀行貸了款時

我貸款了。

ⓐ I took out a rent.

ⓑ I took out a bank card.

ⓒ I took out a loan.

DAY 17

▼ 賺錢及存錢

Answer **493** ⓐ 開存摺，開帳戶 ▸ open up an account　**494** ⓒ 取款 ▸ make a withdrawal　**495** ⓐ 存錢 ▸ make a deposit　**496** ⓑ 存款帳戶 ▸ installment savings account　**497** ⓐ 轉帳 ▸ transfer　**498** ⓒ 貸款 ▸ take out a loan

251

現在可以自信地說出來了嗎？ 規定時間 1 min

493

😎 我開了帳戶。

😊 太好了！啊，對了。你買壽險了嗎？
Good for you! Oh, yeah. What about life insurance?

life insurance 壽險

494

😠 親愛的，我們的銀行帳戶怎麼空了呢？
Darling, why is our bank account empty?

😊 我領錢了。

495

😊 剛才我存錢了。

_____ just now.

😊 做得好。對了，你可以把密碼告訴我嗎？
Well done. Now, can you tell me the password?

496

😠 最近我開了存款帳戶。

_____ recently.

😊 這樣啊。什麼時候到期？
I see. When will it mature?

mature （存款、保險等）到期

497

😊 一個小時以前我已經轉帳給你了。

_____ to you an hour ago.

😊 ？ .
What? I haven't received it yet.

498

🎩 我要開一家商店，所以我貸款了。
I'm setting up my own shop. So _____

😊 貸了多少？
How much is the loan?

Answer **493** I opened up an account. 我開了帳戶。 **494** I've made a withdrawal. 我領錢了。
495 I've made a deposit. 我存錢了。 **496** I opened an installment savings account. 我開了存款帳戶。 **497** I transferred the money. 我已經轉帳了。 **498** I took out a loan. 我貸款了。

252

Quick Test 04

這些句子用英語怎麼說？

規定時間 1 min

499 要求把錢換成一定單位一張的紙幣時

幫我換成5美元一張的。

ⓐ Cut this into 5-dollar bills.

ⓑ Write this into 5-dollar bills.

ⓒ Break this into 5-dollar bills.

500 要求把紙幣換成硬幣時

幫我把這100美元紙幣換成硬幣。

ⓐ Can you undo this hundred-dollar paper?

ⓑ Can you break this hundred-dollar bill?

ⓒ Can you crack this hundred-dollar note?

501 現金不夠，找ATM時

我得找自動提款機。

ⓐ I need to use the BTM.

ⓑ I need to use the ATM.

ⓒ I need to use the cash drawer.

502 在銀行櫃檯視窗領取現金時

我要領點錢。

ⓐ I'd like to take off some money.

ⓑ I'd like to withdraw some money.

ⓒ I'd like to pull out some money.

503 帳戶裡沒想要領的那麼多錢時

餘額不足了。

ⓐ I'm overpaid.

ⓑ I'm overdrawn.

ⓒ I'm overcharged.

504 將金融產品換成現金時

換成現金吧。

ⓐ Let's turn it around.

ⓑ Let's return the money.

ⓒ Let's cash in.

DAY 17

▼ 賺錢及存錢

Answer **499** ⓒ 換（錢）▶ break **500** ⓑ 紙幣 ▶ bill, note **501** ⓑ 自動提款機 ▶ ATM(automated teller machine), cash machine **502** ⓑ （從帳戶中）領錢 ▶ withdraw **503** ⓑ 取款數額超過（帳戶中的存款）▶ overdrawn **504** ⓒ （保單等到期以前）換成現金 ▶ cash in

253

499

😊 幫我換成5美元一張的。

😊 不好意思，我也需要5美元的。
Sorry, I need them myself.

500

😊 幫我把這100美元紙幣換成硬幣。

😊 不好意思，我一點現金都沒有。
Sorry, I don't have any cash on me.

501

🎩 我現金不夠了。我要用自動提款機。.
I need more cash.

😊 不用，不用，這樣的話，我來付錢吧。
No, no. If that's the case, I'll pay.

502

😊 你好，我要領點錢。
Excuse me.

😊 好，先生。請稍等一下。
Yes, sir. Just a moment, please.

503

😊 所以你從銀行領錢了嗎？
So, did you get the money from the bank?

😊 沒取。餘額不足了。我的一萬美元到哪裡去了？
I couldn't.
What happened to my ten thousand dollars?

504

🎩 看我們贏的這些籌碼！現在換成現金吧。
Look at the poker chips we won!   now.

😊 為什麼要那麼著急？
What's the hurry?

Answer **499** Break this into 5-dollar bills. 幫我換成5美元一張的。 **500** Can you break this hundred-dollar bill? 幫我把這100美元紙幣換成硬幣。 **501** I need to use the ATM. 我要用自動提款機。 **502** I'd like to withdraw some money. 我要領點錢。 **503** I'm overdrawn. 餘額不足了。 **504** Let's cash in. 換成現金吧。

Quick Test 05

這些句子用英語怎麼說？

規定時間 1 min

---

505 使用信用卡超過了卡的額度時

我的卡刷爆了。

ⓐ There's been an override.

ⓑ My credit card maxed out.

ⓒ My credit card is out of limits.

---

506 信用卡到期不能用了時

我的信用卡到期了。

ⓐ My credit card has crumbled.

ⓑ My credit card has expired.

ⓒ The date of my credit card is gone.

---

507 把我國的錢換成其他國家的錢時

我得把錢換成人民幣。

ⓐ I need to change my money into yuan.

ⓑ I need to trade my money into yuan.

ⓒ I need to switch my money into yuan.

（譯者注：這裡需要改成其他國家的貨幣，因為原書是以韓國人為物件的）

---

508 把錢存在銀行裡也沒有多少利息時

銀行利率很低。

ⓐ The money barrier is too low.

ⓑ There are a few interested banks.

ⓒ The bank interest rate is low.

---

509 投資基金，損失很大時

我買基金把錢都虧了。

ⓐ I blew my money on funds.

ⓑ I whistled my money on funds.

ⓒ I crashed my money on funds.

---

510 匯率時高時低不穩定時

匯率像是蹺蹺板。

ⓐ The exchange rates are ticking.

ⓑ The exchange rates are bursting.

ⓒ The exchange rates are volatile.

DAY 17

▼ 賺錢及存錢

Answer **505** ⓑ 到達了最高限度 ▶ max out **506** ⓑ 到期了 ▶ expire **507** ⓐ 把A換成B ▶ change A into B **508** ⓒ 利率 ▶ interest rate **509** ⓐ 虧了錢 ▶ blow money **510** ⓒ 匯率 ▶ exchange rate：變化無常的 ▶ volatile

505

😎 哎呦，我的卡刷爆了。

Oops.

👦 那你想要我怎麼辦？

So what do you expect me to do about it?

506

😊 怎麼辦？我的信用卡到期了。

Oh, no.

👧 你怎麼又來了？

You're doing it again, aren't you?

507

🤓 我付不了飯錢。我得把錢換成人民幣。

I can't pay for the food.

👩 別擔心。這裡也收韓幣。

Don't worry. They accept Korean won here, too.

508

😊 我不要把錢存在銀行裡了。

I'm not going to put my money in the bank.

😎 真聰明。最近銀行利率很低。

Good thinking. nowadays.

509

😊 我買基金把錢都虧了。

👩 那我們怎麼結婚？

Then how are we going to get married?

510

👧 爸爸，怎麼不寄一些錢給我？

Daddy, why aren't you sending me money?

😎 最近匯率像是在坐蹺蹺板。再等一天，好嗎？

It's because right now. Wait just one more day, okay?

Answer **505** My credit card maxed out. 我的卡刷爆了。 **506** My credit card has expired. 我的信用卡到期了。 **507** I need to change my money into yuan. 我得把錢換成人民幣。 **508** The bank interest rate is low 銀行利率很低。 **509** I blew my money on funds. 我買基金把錢都虧了。 **510** The exchange rates are volatile. 匯率像是在坐蹺蹺板。

Day 17 Review	在忘記以前複習一遍，怎麼樣？ 規定時間 5 min
聽著MP3跟讀	看著中文說英語

聽著MP3跟讀	看著中文說英語
夫妻兩人都有收入時 **We're a double-income couple.**	我們是雙薪家庭。
賺到的錢很多時 **He makes a lot of money.**	他很能賺錢。
因為股票、投資等突然賺了大錢時 **He hit the jackpot.**	他賺了一大筆錢。
因為做生意失敗，虧得沒有錢了時 **I'm flat broke.**	我窮得叮噹響了。
很節省的人 **She's thrifty.**	她很節儉。
花錢像流水的人 **She spends money like water.**	她花錢像流水。
特別吝嗇、不花錢的人 **He's a penny pincher.**	他太摳了。
零用錢都用完了時 **I'm out of pocket money.**	零用錢都花完了。
在銀行開了帳戶時 **I opened up an account.**	我開了帳戶。
從銀行領了錢時 **I've made a withdrawal.**	我領錢了。

DAY 17

▼ 賺錢及存錢

📖 看著中文說英文時，用書籤擋住這個部分。

| --- | --- |
在銀行存了錢時 **I've made a deposit.**	我存錢了。
用網路銀行轉帳時 **I transferred the money.**	我已經轉帳了。
要求把錢換成一定單位一張的紙幣時 **Break this into 5-dollar bills.**	幫我換成5美元一張的。
要求把紙幣換成硬幣時 **Can you break this hundred-dollar bill?**	幫我把這100美元紙幣換成硬幣。
現金不夠，找ATM時 **I need to use the ATM.**	我得找自動提款機。
將金融產品換成現金時 **Let's cash in.**	換成現金吧。
使用信用卡超過了卡的額度時 **My credit card maxed out.**	我的卡刷爆了。
把我國的錢換成其他國家錢時 **I need to change my money into yuan.**	我得把錢換成人民幣。
把錢存在銀行裡也沒有多少利息時 **The bank interest rate is low.**	銀行利率很低。
投資基金，損失很大時 **I blew my money on funds.**	我買基金把錢都虧了。

已經學會的句型
510個/600個

📖 看著中文說英文時，用書籤擋住這個部分。

DAY **18**

運動及減肥

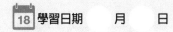

聽例句

因為長胖了要減肥的時候，或是鼻塞打噴嚏的時候，
你會用英語說有關運動、減肥、感冒的句子嗎？來檢測一下吧。

Quick Test 01

這些句子用英語怎麼說？

規定時間 1 min

511 每天都運動時

我每天運動。

ⓐ I work out every day.

ⓑ I work inside every day.

ⓒ I work around every day.

512 開始新運動時

我開始練瑜伽了。

ⓐ I've made up yoga.

ⓑ I've taken up yoga.

ⓒ I've interrupted yoga.

513 因為沒有運動，身體不好時

我缺乏運動。

ⓐ I lack stamina.

ⓑ I exercise sufficiently.

ⓒ I don't get enough exercise.

514 大幅度擺臂快步走時

我每天快步走。

ⓐ I go mega walking every day.

ⓑ I go ultra walking every day.

ⓒ I go power walking every day.

515 為了減肥，要多消耗卡路里時

我得消耗卡路里。

ⓐ I need to burn calories.

ⓑ I need to heat up calories.

ⓒ I need to destroy calories.

516 非常享受鍛煉身體及心靈的冥想時

我經常冥想。

ⓐ I wonder a lot.

ⓑ I meditate a lot.

ⓒ I close my eyes a lot.

DAY 18 ▼ 運動及減肥

Answer **511** ⓐ 運動 ▶ work out, exercise **512** ⓑ（作為興趣愛好）學習……，開始 ▶ take up **513** ⓒ 足夠的運動 ▶ enough exercise **514** ⓒ（作為運動）快步走 ▶ power walk **515** ⓐ 消耗／燃燒卡路里 ▶ burn calories **516** ⓑ 冥想 ▶ meditate

511

你的二頭肌太帥了！
Your biceps are awesome!

謝謝。我每天運動。
Thanks.

bicep 二頭肌

512

你做什麼運動？
What do you do for exercise?

最近我開始練瑜伽了。
　　　　　　　　　　recently.

513

看看你的大肚子。
Look at that pot belly.

我知道。我缺乏運動。
I know.

514

你保持健康的秘訣是什麼？
What is your secret to staying
in shape?

很簡單。我每天快步走。
It's simple.

515

比基尼季就要到了。我得快點消耗卡路里。
The bikini season is coming.
　　　　　　　　　　quickly.

每天跑10英里怎麼樣？
How about running ten miles
every day?

516

你怎麼總是這麼從容呢？
How come you're so calm all
the time?

我經常冥想。

Answer **511** I work out every day. 我每天運動。 **512** I've taken up yoga. 我開始練瑜伽了。
513 I don't get enough exercise. 我缺乏運動。 **514** I go power walking every day. 我每天快步走。
515 I need to burn calories. 我得快點消耗卡路里。 **516** I meditate a lot. 我經常冥想。

Quick Test 02

這些句子用英語怎麼說？

規定時間 1 min

---

517 最近體重增加了時

我胖了。

- ⓐ I've ate up some flesh.
- ⓑ I've put on some weight.
- ⓒ I've sucked up some body fat.

518 透過努力，體重變輕了時

我瘦了5公斤。

- ⓐ I've cut off 5 kilograms.
- ⓑ I've melted 5 kilograms.
- ⓒ I've lost 5 kilograms.

---

519 重度肥胖時

他是重度肥胖。

- ⓐ He has a fat body.
- ⓑ He's extremely obese.
- ⓒ He's mega big.

520 最近正在減肥時

我正在減肥。

- ⓐ I'm on a diet.
- ⓑ I'm in a diet.
- ⓒ I'm under a diet.

---

521 為了減肥，一直不吃晚飯時

我一直不吃晚飯。

- ⓐ I've been over dinner.
- ⓑ I've been shrinking dinner.
- ⓒ I've been skipping dinner.

522 快速減掉的體重又長回來了時

復胖了。（這是溜溜球效應。）

- ⓐ It's the yo-yo effect.
- ⓑ It's the yo-yo trend.
- ⓒ It's the yo-yo fashion.

DAY 18 ▶ 運動及減肥

Answer **517** ⓑ 長胖 ▶ put on/gain weight **518** ⓒ （體重）輕了 ▶ lose, slim down **519** ⓑ 極度地 ▶ extremely；肥胖的 ▶ obese **520** ⓐ 正在減肥 ▶ on a diet **521** ⓒ 不吃晚飯 ▶ skip dinner **522** ⓐ 這裡「現象」一詞不用 phenomenon 而用 effect 表達。

517

😮 最近我胖了。

recently.

😊 沒有。一點也不胖。
No, you haven't at all.

518

🤓 哇！你怎麼變了？
Wow! What happened to you?

😀 我看起來怎麼樣？我瘦了5公斤。
How do I look?

519

🎩 傑克要做抽脂了。
Jack is getting liposuction.

👩 這樣啊。也是，他是重度肥胖。
I see. Well,

liposuction 抽脂

520

😀 來！想吃什麼就點什麼。
All right! Order anything you want.

😀 不用了，謝謝。我正在減肥。我喝水就好了。
No, thanks.
I'll just have some water.

521

😊 哇！你瘦了好多！秘訣是什麼？
Wow! You've lost a lot of weight! What's your secret?

😀 其實我一直不吃晚飯。
Actually,

522

🎩 我以為你瘦了呢？怎麼回事？
I thought you lost weight?
What happened?

😀 復胖了。

Answer **517** I've put on some weight. 我胖了。 **518** I've lost 5 kilograms. 我瘦了5公斤。 **519** He's extremely obese. 他是重度肥胖。 **520** I'm on a diet. 我正在減肥。 **521** I've been skipping dinner. 我一直不吃晚飯。 **522** It's the yo-yo effect. 復胖了。

Quick Test 03

這些句子用英語怎麼說？

規定時間 1 min

---

523 不論怎麼休息都還是覺得累時

我總是覺得累。

ⓐ I feel swollen all the time.

ⓑ I feel cozy all the time.

ⓒ I feel tired all the time.

---

524 一直注意運動，身體狀態很好時

我狀態特別好。

ⓐ I'm in great shape.

ⓑ I'm a great case.

ⓒ I'm very good to my body.

---

525 身體非常不好，需要去醫院看看時

我身體不好。

ⓐ I'm in poor health.

ⓑ I'm in a bad body.

ⓒ My body type is a minus.

---

526 透過運動和飲食保養身體的人

我非常注意身體健康。

ⓐ I'm the health-fad type.

ⓑ I'm the health-knowing type.

ⓒ I'm the health-conscious type.

---

527 一直覺得心情沉重憂鬱時

最近很憂鬱。

ⓐ I feel black nowadays.

ⓑ I feel melancholy nowadays.

ⓒ I feel like a cloud nowadays.

---

528 覺得頭很重，打不起精神時

我的頭昏沉沉的。

ⓐ My head feels fuzzy.

ⓑ My head feels numb.

ⓒ My head feels worn.

DAY 18

▼ 運動及減肥

Answer **523** ⓒ 疲勞，累 ▶ tired：總是，經常 ▶ all the time cf）疲勞 ▶ fatigue **524** ⓐ（身體）狀態／狀況非常好 ▶ in great shape **525** ⓐ 身體不好 ▶ in poor health **526** ⓒ 注意身體 ▶ health-conscious（conscious特別注意的） **527** ⓑ（長期且不知道具體原因的）憂鬱 ▶ melancholy **528** ⓐ 糊塗的，含糊不清的 ▶ fuzzy

523

😋 什麼？你又喝咖啡了？

What? You're drinking coffee again?

😊 我也沒辦法。我總是覺得累。

I can't help it. It's because

524

😎 今天的馬拉松你有信心嗎？

Are you confident about today's marathon?

🎩 當然。我狀態特別好。

Of course.

525

😊 你要去哪裡？

Where are you headed?

😀 去醫院。我身體不好。

To the hospital.

526

😊 您有定期運動嗎？

Do you exercise regularly?

😊 嗯。我非常注意身體健康。

Yes.

527

🎩 最近很憂鬱。

😊 這種狀態持續多久了？

How long have you been feeling this way?

528

😊 我們休息一下吧。我的頭昏沉沉的。

Let's take a break.

😊 好。去透透氣，怎麼樣？

I see. How about getting some fresh air?

Answer **523** I feel tired all the time. 我總是覺得累。 **524** I'm in great shape. 我狀態特別好。 **525** I'm in poor health. 我身體不好。 **526** I'm the health-conscious type. 我非常注意身體健康。 **527** I feel melancholy nowadays. 最近很憂鬱。 **528** My head feels fuzzy. 我的頭昏沉沉的。

Quick Test 04

這些句子用英語怎麼說？

規定時間 1 min

---

529 流鼻涕的時候

我流鼻涕了。

ⓐ My nose is overflowing.

ⓑ My nose is slowing down.

ⓒ My nose is running.

---

530 感冒之後，覺得鼻塞時

我鼻塞。

ⓐ I have a sleepy nose.

ⓑ I have a stopped nose.

ⓒ I have a stuffy nose.

---

531 得了感冒，喉嚨痛時

我喉嚨痛。

ⓐ I have a sore throat.

ⓑ I have a blocked throat.

ⓒ I have a twitching throat.

---

532 一直咳嗽時

我一直咳嗽。

ⓐ I can't stop bluffing.

ⓑ I can't stop coughing.

ⓒ I can't stop puffing.

---

533 一直打噴嚏時

我一直打噴嚏。

ⓐ I keep sneezing.

ⓑ I'm sneezing off and on.

ⓒ I keep spitting a lot.

---

534 身體發冷，發抖時

我一直打冷顫。

ⓐ I'm waving like crazy.

ⓑ I'm shivering like crazy.

ⓒ I'm like a crazy leaf.

Answer **529** ⓒ 流（鼻涕）▶ run **530** ⓒ 堵住，發悶 ▶ stuffy **531** ⓐ （嗓子）疼，刺痛 ▶ sore：喉嚨 ▶ throat **532** ⓑ 咳嗽 ▶ cough **533** ⓐ 總是／一直…… ▶ keep -ing：打噴嚏 ▶ sneeze **534** ⓑ 打冷顫 ▶ shiver：（像瘋了一樣）非常嚴重 ▶ like crazy

529

天哪！我流鼻涕了。
Oh dear!

拿去，用我的手帕吧。
Here, use my handkerchief.

530

我鼻塞。

那就再用力一點擤鼻子。
Then blow harder.

531

我不能說太多話了。我喉嚨痛。
I can't talk much.

我幫你煮一杯熱檸檬茶吧。
I'll make you some hot lemon tea.

532

我一直咳嗽。

哎呀。電影馬上就要開始了。
Oops. The movie is about to start.

533

我一直打噴嚏。

你對貓過敏嗎？我有養貓。
Are you allergic to cats? I have a cat.

534

我一直打冷顫。我可能感冒了。
Maybe I'm coming down with a cold.

我們現在就去醫院看看吧。
Let's take you to a doctor right now.

Answer **529** My nose is running. 我流鼻涕了。 **530** I have a stuffy nose. 我鼻塞。 **531** I have a sore throat. 我喉嚨痛。 **532** I can't stop coughing. 我一直咳嗽。 **533** I keep sneezing. 我一直打噴嚏。 **534** I'm shivering like crazy. 我一直打冷顫。

Quick Test 05

這些句子用英語怎麼說？

規定時間 1 min

---

535 好像要感冒了時

我好像要感冒了。

ⓐ I have a cold sip.

ⓑ I have a bit of a cold.

ⓒ It's a cold time for me.

---

536 得了流行性感冒時

我得了流感。

ⓐ I have the ice.

ⓑ I have the flu.

ⓒ I have a tick.

---

537 傷風感冒，全身酸痛時

我全身痛。

ⓐ I'm aching all over.

ⓑ My whole body is gone.

ⓒ Pain is all over the place.

---

538 馬上要感冒時，全身發冷

我全身發冷。

ⓐ I have the freeze.

ⓑ I have Siberia.

ⓒ I have the chills.

---

539 感覺到馬上就要感冒了時

我可能感冒了。

ⓐ Maybe I'm coming over with a cold.

ⓑ Maybe I'm coming down with a cold.

ⓒ Maybe I'm coming out with a cold.

---

540 感冒很嚴重，躺在床上起不來時

我病倒了。

ⓐ I'm laid up in bed.

ⓑ I'm locked up in bed.

ⓒ I'm trapped in bed.

DAY 18

▼ 運動及減肥

Answer **535** ⓑ 感冒的徵兆 ▶ a bit of a cold **536** ⓑ 流行性感冒 ▶ flu **537** ⓐ （一直）酸疼，感到疼痛 ▶ ache：到處 ▶ all over **538** ⓒ 發冷 ▶ chills **539** ⓑ 得感冒 ▶ come down with a cold **540** ⓐ （因為生病・受傷等）躺在床上 ▶ be laid up

現在可以自信地說出來了嗎？ 規定時間

535

😊 我好像要感冒了。

🎩 這樣的話，我幫你煮雞肉湯吧。
In that case, let me make you some chicken soup.

536

😊 別過來。我得了流感。
Don't come near me.

😊 好。
Okay!

537

😎 哎呦！我全身痛。
Oh, man!

😊 泡個熱水澡怎麼樣？
How about taking a long, hot bath?

538

😊 我全身發冷。我好像要感冒了。
I have a bit of a cold, you see.

😊 是嗎？那快到裡面來。
Really? Then, let's hurry and get inside.

539

😊 哎呀。我可能感冒了。
Oh, no.

😊 你應該早點睡覺。
You should go to bed early.

540

😊 什麼？你說你不能來參加樂隊排練了？
What! You can't come to band practice?

😎 嗯。我病倒了。
Yes.

Day 18 *Review*	**在忘記以前複習一遍，怎麼樣？**	規定時間 5 min

聽著MP3跟讀	看著中文說英語
每天都運動時 **I work out every day.**	我每天運動。
開始新運動時 **I've taken up yoga.**	我開始練瑜伽了。
因為沒有運動，身體不好時 **I don't get enough exercise.**	我缺乏運動。
大幅度擺臂快步走時 **I go power walking every day.**	我每天快步走。
最近體重增加了時 **I've put on some weight.**	我胖了。
通過努力，體重變輕了時 **I've lost 5 kilograms.**	我瘦了5公斤。
最近正在減肥時 **I'm on a diet.**	我正在減肥。
為了減肥，一直不吃晚飯時 **I've been skipping dinner.**	我一直不吃晚飯。
不論怎麼休息都還是覺得累時 **I feel tired all the time.**	我總是覺得累。
一直注意鍛煉身體，身體狀態很好時 **I'm in great shape.**	我狀態特別好。

DAY 18 ▼ 運動及減肥

看著中文說英文時，用書籤擋住這個部分。

聽著MP3跟讀 👂	看著中文說英語 👄
身體非常不好，需要去醫院看看時 **I'm in poor health.**	我身體不好。
一直覺得心情沉重憂鬱時 **I feel melancholy nowadays.**	最近很憂鬱。
流鼻涕的時候 **My nose is running.**	我流鼻涕了。
感冒之後，覺得鼻塞時 **I have a stuffy nose.**	我鼻塞。
得了感冒，喉嚨痛時 **I have a sore throat.**	我喉嚨痛。
一直咳嗽時 **I can't stop coughing.**	我一直咳嗽。
好像要感冒了時 **I have a bit of a cold.**	我好像要感冒了。
傷風感冒，全身酸痛時 **I'm aching all over.**	我全身疼。
馬上要感冒時，全身發冷 **I have the chills.**	我全身發冷。
感覺到馬上就要感冒了時 **Maybe I'm coming down with a cold.**	我可能感冒了。

已經學會的句型
540個/600個

📖 看著中文說英文時，用書籤擋住這個部分。

272

DAY 19

討論疾病疼痛

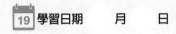

聽例句

發燒頭痛的時候、上吐下瀉的時候，或是手臂發麻酸痛的時候，
你會用英語表達這些有關疾病和疼痛的句子嗎？來檢測一下吧。

541 頭暈的時候

我頭暈。

ⓐ I feel like spinning.
ⓑ I feel busy.
ⓒ I feel dizzy.

542 額頭發熱，發燒的時候

我發燒了。

ⓐ I'm running a fever.
ⓑ My head is heated.
ⓒ The heat is over my head.

543 頭的一側痛時

我偏頭痛。

ⓐ I have a side-ache.
ⓑ I have a migraine.
ⓒ I have a seizure.

544 覺得頭很重，打不起精神的時候

我的頭隱隱作痛。

ⓐ I have a dull brain.
ⓑ I have a dull headache.
ⓒ I have a dual headache.

545 頭一陣陣地刺痛時

我的頭一陣陣地刺痛。

ⓐ I have a blooming headache.
ⓑ I have a jogging headache.
ⓒ I have a throbbing headache.

546 頭疼欲裂的時候

我的頭痛得要裂開了。

ⓐ Something's poking my brain.
ⓑ My head has been cut open.
ⓒ I have a splitting headache.

DAY 19　▼ 討論疾病疼痛

Answer **541** ⓒ 暈 ▶ dizzy　**542** ⓐ（醫學上的異常症候群）發熱 ▶ fever　**543** ⓑ 偏頭痛 ▶ migraine
544 ⓑ 鈍的，不鋒利的 ▶ dull　**545** ⓒ 刺痛 ▶ throbbing　**546** ⓒ 頭像要裂開了一樣 ▶ splitting

275

541

嘿！你怎麼注意力不集中呢？
Hey! Why can't you concentrate?

我頭暈。你剛才說什麼？
_____ What did you say just now?

542

我發燒了。
_____

我跟你說了別不帶傘淋雨走路。
I told you not to walk in the rain without an umbrella!

543

我偏頭痛。我去躺一下。
_____ I'm going to lie down for a bit.

好。我幫你拿藥去。
Sure. I'll get you some medicine.

544

我的頭隱隱作痛。怎麼辦呢？
_____ What should I do?

我們休息5分鐘吧。你不會感冒了吧？
Let's take five. You're not getting a cold, are you?

545

你要去哪裡？我們還沒結束呢。
Where are you going? We're not finished yet.

我要回家。我的頭一陣陣地刺痛。
I'm going home. _____

546

我的頭痛得要裂開了。
_____

這是宿醉的一個症狀。
It's all part of a hangover.

hangover 宿醉

Answer **541** I feel dizzy. 我頭暈。 **542** I'm running a fever. 我發燒了。 **543** I have a migraine. 我偏頭痛。 **544** I have a dull headache. 我的頭隱隱作痛。 **545** I have a throbbing headache. 我的頭一陣陣的刺痛。 **546** I have a splitting headache. 我的頭痛得要裂開了。

547 消化不良，肚子脹氣時

我肚子脹。

ⓐ I feel pumped up.

ⓑ I feel full.

ⓒ I feel bloated.

548 胃裡不舒服，想吐的時候

我覺得反胃。

ⓐ I feel stuffy.

ⓑ I feel nauseated.

ⓒ I feel packed.

549 一般情況下，說肚子痛時

我肚子痛。

ⓐ My stomach hurts.

ⓑ My belly is sour.

ⓒ I feel my stomach dying.

550 胃裡不舒服，反胃的時候

我想吐。

ⓐ I feel like throwing over.

ⓑ I feel like throwing up.

ⓒ I feel like throwing down.

551 一直拉肚子時

我拉了一個晚上的肚子。

ⓐ The night angel visited me.

ⓑ I had diarrhea all night.

ⓒ My stomach has fainted.

552 不經常上廁所的人

我便秘。

ⓐ I am motivated.

ⓑ I am adjusted.

ⓒ I am constipated.

DAY 19

▼ 討論疾病疼痛

Answer **547** ⓒ 肚子脹 ▶ bloated **548** ⓑ 噁心，作嘔 ▶ feel nauseated **549** ⓐ 疼 ▶ hurt **550** ⓑ 感覺要…… ▶ feel like -ing：嘔吐 ▶ throw up, vomit **551** ⓑ 拉肚子 ▶ diarrhea **552** ⓒ 便秘 ▶ constipated

現在可以自信地說出來了嗎？ 規定時間 1 min

547

我肚子脹。可能是吃得太多了。
_____ Maybe I ate too much.

拿去。喝一點這種茶。
Here. Drink some of this tea.

548

我覺得反胃。你有塑膠袋嗎？
_____ Have you got a plastic bag?

我都用完了。我真想快點下船。
I used them all. I can't wait to get off this ship.

549

媽媽！我肚子痛。
Mommy! _____

是哪裡？指給媽媽看。
Where exactly? Point to it with your finger for Mommy.

550

你怎麼一直去廁所呢？
Why do you keep going to the bathroom?

不好意思。因為我想吐。
Sorry. It's because _____

551

親愛的。我拉了一個晚上的肚子。
Darling, _____

我知道。我都聽見了。
I know. I heard you.

552

我便秘。怎麼辦呢？
_____ What should I do?

你應該多吃點梅乾。
You should try eating lots of prunes.

prune 梅乾

Answer **547** I feel bloated. 我肚子脹。 **548** I feel nauseated. 我感覺反胃。 **549** My stomach hurts. 我肚子痛。 **550** I feel like throwing up. 我想吐。 **551** I had diarrhea all night. 我拉了一個晚上的肚子。 **552** I am constipated. 我便秘。

Quick Test 03　這些句子用英語怎麼說？

規定時間 1 min

---

553 因為乾燥嘴唇裂開了時

我嘴唇裂了。

ⓐ I have chapped lips.

ⓑ I have sealed lips.

ⓒ I have puffed lips.

---

554 流鼻血時

我流鼻血了。

ⓐ I've got a nosebleed.

ⓑ There's blood inside my nose.

ⓒ My nose is watering blood.

---

555 在高空，耳朵的不適症狀

我耳朵嗡嗡響。

ⓐ My ears are slapped.

ⓑ My ears are muffled.

ⓒ My ears are shot down.

---

556 因為外部刺激或身體異常而耳鳴時

我耳鳴。

ⓐ My ears are a jingle bell.

ⓑ My ears are ringing.

ⓒ My ears are bulging.

---

557 耳朵痛時

我耳朵痛。

ⓐ I have an earache.

ⓑ I have an earbomb.

ⓒ I have an earbug.

---

558 因為特定的物質、食物，身體有異常反應時

我是過敏體質。

ⓐ I'm next to allergies.

ⓑ I'm assigned to allergies.

ⓒ I'm prone to allergies.

DAY 19　▼　討論疾病疼痛

Answer **553** ⓐ（皮膚或者嘴唇）裂開，乾裂 ▶ chapped　**554** ⓐ 鼻血 ▶ nosebleed　**555** ⓑ 消音 ▶ muffle　**556** ⓑ 響 ▶ ring　**557** ⓐ 耳朵痛 ▶ earache　**558** ⓒ 很容易……，有……的傾向 ▶ be prone to cf) 體質 ▶ constitution

---

553

😊 我嘴唇裂了。我一到冬天就這樣。
_____ **It happens to me every winter.**

😊 我只有潤唇膏。你要用嗎？
I only have lip gloss. Do you want to use it?

554

😊 我流鼻血了。你有紙巾嗎？
_____ **Do you have a tissue?**

😊 當然有。給你。
Sure. Here you go.

555

😊 我耳朵嗡嗡響。還頭暈。
_____ **I feel dizzy, too.**

😊 是因為你在坐電梯。快到了。
It's because of the elevator. It won't take long.

556

😊 我一直耳鳴。煩死了。
_____ **all the time. It's annoying!**

😊 醫生怎麼說？
What did the doctor say?

557

😊 我耳朵痛。我怎麼了，醫生？
_____ **What's wrong with me, doctor?**

😊 我看看。哦，天哪！
Let's have a look. Oh, dear!

558

😊 你說你不想吃我做的花生奶油三明治？
You won't eat my peanut butter sandwich?

😊 不好意思。我不能吃花生。我是過敏體質。
Sorry, I can't eat peanuts.

Answer **553** I have chapped lips. 我嘴唇裂了。　**554** I've got a nosebleed. 我流鼻血了。　**555** My ears are muffled. 我耳朵嗡嗡響。　**556** My ears are ringing. 我耳鳴。　**557** I have an earache. 我耳朵痛。　**558** I'm prone to allergies. 我是過敏體質。

---

559 腿或者手臂因血液不流通發麻時

我手臂麻了。

ⓐ There's a cat on my arm.

ⓑ My arm fell asleep.

ⓒ I can't feel my armpit.

---

560 背部肌肉痛時

我後背痛。

ⓐ My back is sore.

ⓑ My spine is crushed.

ⓒ My backside is upside down.

---

561 睡覺姿勢不良，脖子落枕的時候

我落枕了。

ⓐ I have a muscle in my neck.

ⓑ I have a cricket in my neck.

ⓒ I have a crick in my neck.

---

562 腿部肌肉突然發生痙攣時

我腿抽筋了。

ⓐ I have a mouse on my leg.

ⓑ I have a cramp in my leg.

ⓒ I have a rock on my leg.

---

563 撞瘀青了時

我臉上瘀青了。

ⓐ I have a dot on my face.

ⓑ I have a mole on my face.

ⓒ I have a bruise on my face.

---

564 扭傷了腰時

我腰上貼藥膏片了。

ⓐ I have put a pass on my back.

ⓑ I have put a pain relief patch on my back.

ⓒ I have put a muscle cleanser on my back.

DAY 19
▼ 討論疾病疼痛

Answer **559** ⓑ 手臂像睡著了一樣沒有感覺了的意思 **560** ⓐ（因為炎症或肌肉過度運動）疼痛 ▶ sore **561** ⓒ（脖子或者腰部）急性硬直，肌肉抽筋 ▶ crick **562** ⓑ（肌肉）抽筋 ▶ cramp *cf*）筋肉痙攣 ▶ muscle spasm **563** ⓒ 瘀青，挫傷 ▶ bruise **564** ⓑ 藥膏片 ▶ pain relief patch（「緩解疼痛的貼片」的意思）

559

簡，起床了。我手臂麻了。

Jane, wake up.

嗯……躺在你的手臂上睡覺真好。

Mmm... I love having your arm as my pillow.

560

哎呦！露營回來後我後背痛。

Ouch! _____ after our camping trip.

當然了。我們昨天是在地上睡覺的啊。

No wonder. We slept on the ground yesterday.

561

我落枕了。

別動。我去拿針灸來。

Don't move. I'll bring my acupuncture kit.

acupuncture 針灸

562

等一下。我腿抽筋了。

Wait!

好。我們休息一下吧。

Okay. Let's rest a bit.

563

我臉上瘀青了。有雞蛋嗎？

You got an egg?

天哪。我都煮了。

Oops. I boiled them all.

564

這是什麼味道啊？

What's that smell?

我腰上貼藥膏片了。我參加橄欖球訓練了。

_____ I had rugby practise.

Answer **559** My arm fell asleep. 我手臂麻了。 **560** My back is sore 我後背痛。 **561** I have a crick in my neck. 我落枕了。 **562** I have a cramp in my leg. 我腿抽筋了。 **563** I have a bruise on my face. 我臉上瘀青了。 **564** I have put a pain relief patch on my back. 我腰上貼藥膏片了。

Quick Test 05
這些句子用英語怎麼說？

規定時間 1 min

---

565 被紙割破了手時

我被紙割傷了。

ⓐ The paper hurt me.

ⓑ This paper cut me in half.

ⓒ I got a paper cut.

---

566 被粗糙的樹枝或碎了的玻璃渣紮了手時

我的手被刺到了。

ⓐ I've got a splinter in my finger.

ⓑ I've got a problem in my finger.

ⓒ I've got some glass in my finger.

---

567 被熱水燙傷時

我被燙傷了。

ⓐ I got scared.

ⓑ I got swept away.

ⓒ I got scalded.

---

568 心臟負荷過重，喘不過氣來時

我喘不過氣來了。

ⓐ I'm out of breath.

ⓑ I'm out of space.

ⓒ I'm out of mouth.

---

569 有香港腳的人

他有香港腳。

ⓐ He has athlete's foot.

ⓑ He has farmer's foot.

ⓒ He has monster's foot.

---

570 因為心理上的、精神上的刺激喪失意識時

她暈倒了。

ⓐ She closed out.

ⓑ She passed out.

ⓒ She clinked out.

DAY 19 ▼ 討論疾病疼痛

Answer **565** ⓒ 被紙割破的傷口 ▶ paper cut　**566** ⓐ（樹枝、金屬、玻璃等的）碎片 ▶ splinter　**567** ⓒ 被（液體）燙傷 ▶ get scalded　**568** ⓐ 喘不上氣 ▶ out of breath cf）喘氣 ▶ pant　**569** ⓐ 香港腳 ▶ athlete's foot（athlete 運動員）　**570** ⓑ 喪失意識，暈倒 ▶ pass out, faint

565

哎呦！我被紙割傷了。

Ouch!

天哪！傷得很嚴重呢！

Oh, dear! That looks nasty!

nasty 嚴重的，危險的

566

哎呀！我的手被刺到了。

Ouch!

】別擔心。我正好有鑷子。

Don't worry. I happen to have a pair of tweezers.

tweezers 鑷子

567

我需要冰塊，快！我被燙傷了。

I need ice, quickly!

拿去，用我杯子裡的冰塊吧。

Here, use this ice from my cup!

568

別跑了。我喘不過氣來了。

Let's stop running.

你真的要減肥了。

You really need to lose some weight.

569

我只是想告訴你⋯⋯他有香港腳。

Just to let you know...

你怎麼這麼瞭解班？

How do you know so much about Ben?

570

她暈倒了。

天哪，我得摘下面具來了。

Oops, I'll take off the mask.

Answer 565 I got a paper cut. 我被紙割傷了。 566 I've got a splinter in my finger. 我的手被刺到了。 567 I got scalded. 我被燙傷了。 568 I'm out of breath. 我喘不過來了。 569 He has athlete's foot. 他有香港腳。 570 She passed out. 她暈倒了。

Day 19
Review

在忘記以前複習一遍，怎麼樣？

規定時間 5 min

聽著MP3跟讀	看著中文說英語
頭暈的時候 **I feel dizzy.**	我頭暈。
額頭發熱，發燒的時候 **I'm running a fever.**	我發燒了。
覺得頭很重，打不起精神的時候 **I have a dull headache.**	我的頭隱隱作痛。
頭痛欲裂的時候 **I have a splitting headache.**	我的頭痛得要裂開了。
消化不良，肚子脹氣時 **I feel bloated.**	我肚子脹脹的。
胃裡不舒服，想吐的時候 **I feel nauseated.**	我覺得反胃。
一般情況下，說肚子痛時 **My stomach hurts.**	我肚子痛。
胃裡不舒服，反胃的時候 **I feel like throwing up.**	我想吐。
因為乾燥嘴唇裂開了時 **I have chapped lips.**	我嘴唇裂了。
流鼻血時 **I've got a nosebleed.**	我流鼻血了。

DAY 19 ▼ 討論疾病疼痛

📖 看著中文說英文時，用書籤擋住這個部分。

在高空，耳朵的不適症狀 **My ears are muffled.**	我耳朵嗡嗡響。
因為外部刺激或是身體異常而耳鳴時 **My ears are ringing.**	我耳鳴。
腿或者手臂因血液不流通發麻時 **My arm fell asleep.**	我手臂麻了。
背部肌肉痛時 **My back is sore.**	我後背痛。
睡覺姿勢不良，脖子落枕的時候 **I have a crick in my neck.**	我落枕了。
腿部肌肉突然發生痙攣時 **I have a cramp in my leg.**	我腿抽筋了。
被紙割破了手時 **I got a paper cut.**	我被紙割傷了。
被熱水燙傷時 **I got scalded.**	我被燙傷了。
心臟負荷過重，喘不過氣來時 **I'm out of breath.**	我喘不過氣來了。
有香港腳的人 **He has athlete's foot.**	他有香港腳。

已經學會的句型
570個/600個

看著中文說英文時，用書籤擋住這個部分。

DAY 20

說明傷痛及接受治療

20 學習日期　　　月　　　日

學習時間

聽例句

扭到腳的時候、治療蛀牙的時候，或是長針眼的時候，
你會用英語說明自己不舒服的地方並接受治療嗎？來檢測一下吧。

571 不小心扭傷了腳時

我腳扭傷了。

ⓐ I slammed my ankle.

ⓑ I sprained my ankle.

ⓒ I cuddled my ankle.

572 保護骨頭的韌帶拉傷了時

我韌帶拉傷了。

ⓐ I pulled a ligament.

ⓑ My muscle is torn.

ⓒ A pain has been felt in the joint.

573 骨頭斷了或是裂了時

我的腿骨折了。

ⓐ I fractured my leg.

ⓑ I lined up my leg.

ⓒ I bent my leg.

574 為了接好斷了的骨頭

我手臂打石膏了。

ⓐ I got a bandage on my arm.

ⓑ I got a gib on my arm.

ⓒ I got a cast on my arm.

575 摔了尾椎裂了時

我的尾椎裂了。

ⓐ I have a large crack in my tailbone.

ⓑ I have a hairline fracture in my tailbone.

ⓒ I have a pretty crack in my tailbone.

576 擔心傷口會留下疤痕時

真希望不會留疤。

ⓐ I hope it doesn't leave a scar.

ⓑ I hope it doesn't slap a scar.

ⓒ I hope it doesn't kiss a scar.

Answer **571** ⓑ 扭傷 ▸ sprain, twist **572** ⓐ 韌帶拉傷 ▸ pull a ligament **573** ⓐ 骨折 ▸ fracture **574** ⓒ 石膏 ▸ cast **575** ⓑ 骨頭上有細小的裂紋 ▸ hairline fracture **576** ⓐ 留疤 ▸ leave a scar

DAY 20 ▼ 說明傷痛及接受治療

571

你怎麼突然一拐一拐的了？

Why are you limping all of a sudden?

我腳扭傷了。我們走慢一點吧。

_____ Let's walk slowly.

limp 一拐一拐地走

572

我韌帶拉傷了。要2週才能恢復。

_____ It will take two weeks to heal.

啊，我知道了。我把我們的滑雪旅行延期吧。

Oh, I see. I'll postpone our ski trip.

heal 治癒

573

你今天怎麼沒來學校？

Why weren't you at school today?

我的腿骨折了。對了！作業是什麼？

_____ Oh, yeah! What's for homework?

574

我手臂打石膏了。你喜歡這個顏色嗎？

_____

Do you like the color?

什麼？你把石膏塗成粉紅色了？

What? You colored it pink!

575

別客氣，坐下吧。

Don't be shy and sit down.

我坐不了。我的尾椎裂了。

I can't. _____

576

看我的下巴，縫了10針。

Look at my chin. I got ten stitches.

希望不會留疤。

_____

stitch 縫針

Answer **571** I sprained my ankle. 我腳扭傷了。　**572** I pulled a ligament. 我韌帶拉傷了。　**573** I fractured my leg. 我的腿骨折了。　**574** I got a cast on my arm. 我手臂打石膏了。　**575** I have a hairline fracture in my tailbone. 我的尾椎裂了。　**576** I hope it doesn't leave a scar. 希望不會留疤。

這些句子用英語怎麼說？

規定時間 1 min

577 牙痛的時候

我覺得是蛀牙。

ⓐ I think it's a tooth cave.

ⓑ I think it's a cavity.

ⓒ I think it's a root insect.

578 為了牙齒健康

我得去洗牙了。

ⓐ My teeth need scaring.

ⓑ My teeth need scaling.

ⓒ My teeth need dentures.

579 不是牙痛而是牙齦痛時

我牙齦痛。

ⓐ My teeth skin hurt.

ⓑ My gums hurt.

ⓒ My tooth fairy is hurt.

580 在牙科醫院拔了牙時

我拔牙了。

ⓐ I had my tooth taken out.

ⓑ My tooth is pushed out.

ⓒ My dentist cracked my tooth.

581 在牙科醫院接受了根管治療時

我做了根管治療。

ⓐ I got a root canal.

ⓑ I got a tooth canal.

ⓒ I got a nerve canal.

582 發現新長出來的智齒時

我正在長智齒。

ⓐ My wisdom tooth is going up.

ⓑ My wisdom tooth has an opening.

ⓒ My wisdom tooth is coming in.

Answer **577** ⓑ 蛀牙 ▶ cavity, decayed tooth **578** ⓑ 洗牙 ▶ scaling *cf* 去牙石 ▶ remove tartar
579 ⓑ 牙齦 ▶ gum *cf* 牙齦病 ▶ gum disease **580** ⓐ〔直譯〕我找人拔了我的牙。（take out拔掉）
581 ⓐ 根管治療 ▶ root canal (therapy) **582** ⓒ 智齒 ▶ wisdom tooth

DAY 20 ▼ 說明傷痛及接受治療

577

😷 我痛得嚴重。好像是蛀牙。

It aches so much.

😀 我看看。把嘴張大。

Let me take a look. Open wide.

578

😀 嗯，你的牙齒有點黃。

Oh, your teeth are brownish.

😎 是吧？我覺得我得去洗牙了。

They are, aren't they? I think

579

😀 我牙齦痛。怎麼辦呢？

What should I do?

😀 我推薦這種牙膏。你試試吧。

I recommend this toothpaste. Try it.

580

😀 我終於拔了牙。

finally.

😷 可是我很喜歡你的虎牙啊！

But I loved your snaggletooth!

snaggletooth 虎牙

581

😀 你怎麼一直皺眉頭？哪裡不舒服？

Why do you keep wincing? Are you in pain?

😎 嗯。其實我做了根管治療。

Yeah. It's just that

wince （臉上的表情）皺著眉頭

582

😀 我正在長智齒呢。

😎 哎呦！一定很痛吧！

Oh, man! That must hurt a lot.

Answer **577** I think it's a cavity. 好像是蛀牙。 **577** My teeth need scaling. 我得去洗牙了。 **578** My gums hurt. 我牙齦痛。 **580** I had my tooth taken out. 我拔了牙。 **581** I got a root canal. 我做了根管治療。 **582** My wisdom tooth is coming in. 我正長智齒呢。

Quick
Test 03 　這些句子用英語怎麼說？

規定時間 1 min

---

583 視力越來越不好時
我視力越來越不好了。

ⓐ My foresight is getting worse.
ⓑ My eyesight is getting worse.
ⓒ My eye power is falling down.

584 兩隻眼睛的視力都很好時
我兩隻眼睛都是1.0。

ⓐ I have ten-ten vision.
ⓑ I have twenty-twenty vision.
ⓒ I have hundred-hundred vision.

---

585 對眼睛充血的人
你眼睛充血了。

ⓐ Your eyes are bloodshot.
ⓑ Your eyes are bloody.
ⓒ Your bloody eyes are popping.

586 沒有保護眼睛，眼睛看不清楚時
我看不清楚了。

ⓐ My eyes are blinking.
ⓑ My eyes are slim.
ⓒ My eyes are dim.

---

587 對眼睛腫了的人
你眼睛腫了。

ⓐ The eyes have eaten you up.
ⓑ You have an owl on your eyes.
ⓒ Your eyes are puffy.

588 告訴別人自己長針眼了時
我右邊眼睛長針眼了。

ⓐ I have a bean in my right eye.
ⓑ I have a sty in my right eye.
ⓒ I have a corn in my right eye.

Answer **583** ⓑ 視力 ▶ eyesight, vision：不好了 ▶ get worse *cf*) 近視 ▶ nearsightedness **584** ⓑ 視力非常好的，兩隻眼睛視力都是1.0 ▶ twenty-twenty vision **585** ⓐ 充血的 ▶ bloodshot **586** ⓒ （眼睛）看不清楚 ▶ dim **587** ⓒ （眼睛‧臉等）腫了的 ▶ puffy **588** ⓑ 針眼 ▶ sty

DAY 20

▼ 說明傷痛及接受治療

293

583

😊 我視力越來越不好了。

😊 你父母是不是都戴眼鏡？
Do both of your parents wear glasses?

584

😊 我兩隻眼睛都是1.0。

🎩 你真幸運！我不戴眼鏡什麼都看不見。
Lucky you! I can't see a thing without my glasses.

585

😊 你怎麼了？你眼睛充血了。
What's wrong?

😊 是嗎？啊，應該是因為我的新隱形眼鏡。
Really? Oh, it must be my new contact lenses.

586

😊 我看不清楚了。房間裡好像太暗了。
I think the room is too dark.

😊 你怎麼早不說呢？
Why didn't you say so in the first place?

587

😊 你眼睛腫了。他是不是……
Did he...?

😊 對，他甩了我。
Yeah, he dumped me.

588

😊 我右邊眼睛長針眼了。

😊 你現在才告訴我？我們一起吃完午飯以後？
You're telling me this now? After we had lunch?

---

589 因為肚子很脹，消化不良

我吃了胃藥。

ⓐ I took some indigestion medicine.

ⓑ I took some stomach medicine.

ⓒ I took some intestine medicine.

---

590 痛得受不了了時

我得吃止痛藥了。

ⓐ I need some painful medicine.

ⓑ I need some killer pains.

ⓒ I need some painkillers.

---

591 為了預防流感打預防針時

我打了流感預防針。

ⓐ I got a flu shot.

ⓑ I got a cool shot.

ⓒ I got a syringe.

---

592 拿著處方去藥店買藥時

能幫我拿點藥嗎？

ⓐ Could you fit this description?

ⓑ Could you fill this prescription?

ⓒ Could you fill in this questionnaire?

---

593 因為睡不著吃安眠藥時

我在吃安眠藥。

ⓐ I'm eating between meals.

ⓑ I'm taking sleeping pills.

ⓒ I'm taking precautions.

---

594 吃了藥擔心副作用時

我擔心有副作用。

ⓐ I'm worried about the special effects.

ⓑ I'm worried about the next effects.

ⓒ I'm worried about the side effects.

Answer **589** ⓐ 胃藥 ▸ indigestion medicine（indigestion 消化不良）；吃（藥）▸ take **590** ⓒ 止痛藥 ▸ painkiller, pain reliever **591** ⓐ 流感預防針 ▸ flu shot **592** ⓑ（按照處方）配藥 ▸ fill a prescription **593** ⓑ 安眠藥 ▸ sleeping pill **594** ⓒ 副作用 ▸ side effect

DAY 20 ▼ 說明傷痛及接受治療

現在可以自信地說出來了嗎？ 規定時間 1 min

589

😊 你的胃怎麼樣了？

How's your stomach?

😃 現在好了。我吃了胃藥。

It's okay now.

590

😷 我得吃止痛藥了。太痛了。

It hurts so much.

😮 可是你一個小時以前才吃了啊。

But you had one just an hour ago.

591

😊 我打了流感預防針。哇，真痛啊。

Wow, it hurt.

😃 多少錢？

How much did it cost you?

592

😊 能幫我拿點藥嗎？

😮 我看看。哦，這種藥現在沒有。

Let's see. Oh, we are out of this drug at the moment.

593

😊 我在吃安眠藥。我失戀以後每天吃。

It's been like this every day since my breakup.

😃 用運動代替安眠藥怎麼樣？

How about doing some exercise instead?

breakup 分手

594

😊 說實話，我擔心有副作用。

Honestly,

😃 別擔心。看著我，一點事都沒有。

Don't worry. Look at me. I'm just fine!

Answer **589** I took some indigestion medicine. 我吃了胃藥。 **590** I need some painkillers. 我得吃止痛藥了。 **591** I got a flu shot. 我打了流感預防針。 **592** Could you fill this prescription? 能幫我拿點藥嗎？ **593** I'm taking sleeping pills. 我在吃安眠藥。 **594** I'm worried about the side effects. 我擔心有副作用。

Quick
Test 05　這些句子用英語怎麼說？

規定時間 1 min

---

595 為了接受內視鏡檢查等需要禁食時

禁食24小時。

ⓐ I'm on a 24-hour watch list.

ⓑ The doctor ordered me out.

ⓒ I need to fast for a day.

---

596 去醫院體檢以後

我去體檢了。

ⓐ I had a medical pass.

ⓑ I had a medical health.

ⓒ I had a medical checkup.

---

597 做了X光檢查以後

我拍了X光片。

ⓐ I had an X-ray photographed.

ⓑ I got an X-ray made.

ⓒ I had an X-ray done.

---

598 體檢結果良好時

沒有什麼特別的問題。

ⓐ Everything is ready to go.

ⓑ There's nothing particularly wrong.

ⓒ Nothing was found.

---

599 根據體檢結果，需要注意血壓時

我血壓有一點高。

ⓐ My blood pressure is a bit high.

ⓑ My blood vessel is a bit high.

ⓒ My blood tolerance is a bit high.

---

600 建議不要有太大壓力時

壓力是萬病的根源。

ⓐ Stress is the master of all illnesses.

ⓑ Stress is the cause of all illnesses.

ⓒ Stress is the hole of all illnesses.

Answer **595** ⓒ 禁食，斷食 ▶ fast **596** ⓒ 體檢 ▶ medical checkup **597** ⓒ X光 ▶ X-ray **598** ⓑ 特別地 ▶ particularly **599** ⓐ 血壓 ▶ blood pressure *cf*) 血管 ▶ blood vessel **600** ⓑ 原因 ▶ cause：疾病 ▶ illness

DAY 20 ▼ 說明傷痛及接受治療

Quick Practice 現在可以自信地說出來了嗎？ 規定時間

595

醫生要我禁食24小時。

The doctor told me _____ _____

你行嗎？哈，我們打個賭吧。

Do you think you can do that?
Oh, let's make a bet!

596

今天我去體檢了。

_____ today.

結果什麼時候出來？我蠻擔心你的肝的。

When do you get your results?
I'm worried about your liver.

597

我終於拍了X光片。一點也不痛。

_____ finally.
It didn't hurt a bit.

我一直都跟你這麼說！

That's what I've been telling you all along!

598

結果剛出來了。沒有什麼特別的問題。

I got the results back just now.

是嗎？那你的心臟呢？

Is that so? Then how about your heart?

599

你為什麼要吃那個藥？

Why are you taking that pill?

我血壓有一點高。別告訴我老婆。

_____
Don't tell my wife.

600

壓力是萬病的根源。

對。所以我也得有點愛好，好緩解壓力。

Yeah. So I think I should get a hobby to get rid of my stress.

Answer **595** I need to fast for a day. 禁食24小時。 **596** I had a medical checkup. 我去體檢了。 **597** I had an X-ray done. 我拍了X光片。 **598** There's nothing particularly wrong. 沒有什麼特別的問題。 **599** My blood pressure is a bit high. 我血壓有一點高。 **600** Stress is the cause of all illnesses. 壓力是萬病的根源。

| **Day 20** Review | 在忘記以前複習一遍，怎麼樣？ | 規定時間 5 min |

聽著MP3跟讀	看著中文說英語
不小心扭傷了腳時 **I sprained my ankle.**	我腳扭傷了。
保護骨頭的韌帶拉傷了時 **I pulled a ligament.**	我韌帶拉傷了。
骨頭斷了或者裂了時 **I fractured my leg.**	我的腿骨折了。
為了接好斷了的骨頭 **I got a cast on my arm.**	我手臂打石膏了。
牙痛的時候 **I think it's a cavity.**	好像是蛀牙。
為了牙齒健康 **My teeth need scaling.**	我得去洗牙了。
在牙科醫院拔了牙時 **I had my tooth taken out.**	我拔了牙。
在牙科醫院接受了根管治療時 **I got a root canal.**	我做了根管治療。
視力越來越不好時 **My eyesight is getting worse.**	我視力越來越不好了。
對眼睛充血的人 **Your eyes are bloodshot.**	你眼睛充血了。

DAY 20 ▼ 說明傷痛及接受治療

看著中文說英文時，用書籤擋住這個部分。

對眼睛腫了的人 **Your eyes are puffy.**	你眼睛腫了。
告訴別人自己長針眼了時 **I have a sty in my right eye.**	我右邊眼睛長針眼了。
因為肚子很脹，消化不良 **I took some indigestion medicine.**	我吃了胃藥。
痛得受不了了時 **I need some painkillers.**	我得吃止痛藥了。
為了預防流感打預防針時 **I got a flu shot.**	我打了流感預防針。
因為睡不著吃安眠藥時 **I'm taking sleeping pills.**	我吃安眠藥。
為了接受內視鏡檢查等需要禁食時 **I need to fast for a day.**	禁食24小時。
去醫院體檢以後 **I had a medical checkup.**	我去體檢了。
體檢結果良好時 **There's nothing particularly wrong.**	沒有什麼特別的問題。
建議不要有太大壓力時 **Stress is the cause of all illnesses.**	壓力是萬病的根源。

已經學會的句型
600個/600個

📖 看著中文說英文時，用書籤擋住這個部分。

NOTE

NOTE

易人外語 系列 *E0030*

20天閃電翻轉「聽‧說」英語速成班！
生活表達600句
用「先做題後學習」的高效步驟，訓練完美語感，一擊必殺！

作　　者	金在憲
譯　　者	于妍
總 編 輯	黃璽宇
主　　編	吳靜宜、姜怡安
執行主輯	李念茨
執行編輯	吳佳芬
美術編輯	王桂芳、張嘉容

初　　版	2020年04月
出　　版	含章有限公司
電　　話	（02）2752-5618
傳　　真	（02）2752-5619

定　　價	新台幣380元
產品內容	1書

總 經 銷	昶景國際文化有限公司
地　　址	236 新北市土城區民族街11 號3 樓
電　　話	（02）2269-6367
傳　　真	（02）2269-0299
E-mail:	service@168books.com.tw

港澳地區總經銷	和平圖書有限公司
地　　址	香港柴灣嘉業街12 號百樂門大廈17 樓
電　　話	（852）2804-6687
傳　　真	（852）2804-6409

▶本書部分圖片由 Shutterstock圖庫、freepik圖庫提供。

영어회화 벼락치기 ② 일상생활 600
Cram Lightening Quick 2 - to Boost Your English Speaking Skills by Jae Heun Kim
Copyright © 2015 Jae Heun Kim
All rights reserved.
Original Korean edition published by Gilbut Eztok, Seoul, Korea
Traditional Chinese Translation Copyright @ 2020 by Hanzhang Co., Ltd.
This Traditional Chinese edition arranged with Gibut Eztok through Agency Liang

國家圖書館出版品預行編目資料

20天閃電翻轉「聽‧說」英語速成班！生活表達600
句 / 金在憲著. -- 初版. -- 臺北市：含章, 2020.04
　　面；　公分

ISBN 978-986-98757-3-8(平裝)

1. 英語　2. 句法

805.169　　　　　　　　　　　　　　109001712